PRAISE FOR C. MICHELE DORSEY

Praise for *Permanent Sunset*:

"... The ensuing mystery, chockablock with unanticipated plot twists, complex supporting characters, and terrific dialogue, makes for mighty good page-turning fun."
--*Publishers Weekly* starred review

"A divine locale and a quick-thinking sleuth make this a great bet for vacation reading."
--*Booklist*

"Murder strikes in paradise... Dorsey's plot has the requisite twists, turns, and everything else."
--*Kirkus Reviews*

"Sabrina is a complex character, damaged by her past experiences, but looking to start a new life in a richly described tropical paradise. A series to watch."
--*Booklist*

Praise for the *No Virgin Island*:

"C. Michele Dorsey's debut novel, *No Virgin Island*, takes Nantucket refugee Sabrina Salter to a gloriously rendered Caribbean island for an emotional journey, littered with echoes of a past she tried to leave behind. A fast-paced, engaging story with an endearing main character who can't help but be her own worst enemy."
--Hallie Ephron, *New York Times* bestselling author of *Careful What You Wish For*

"A vulnerable, tough woman makes a difference in troubled lives. Fast-paced, gripping, terrific."
--Carolyn Hart, *New York Times* bestselling author of *Don t Go Home*

"Charming, beguiling, and full of surprises. Sabrina Salter is terrific - smart, endearing and determined heroine who will be your new best friend."
--Hank Phillippi Ryan, Anthony, Macavity, and Mary Higgins Clark award-winning author of *Her Perfect Life*

"The key to C. Michele Dorsey's writing is her knack for blending light, breezy (but not insubstantial),
 fast-paced reading with a bit of grit and real drama."
--*Noir Journal*

"The cast of characters is appealing...The plot is intricate with quite a few red herrings. Who wouldn't want to visit St. John?"
--*Library Journal*

TROPICAL DEPRESSION

TROPICAL DEPRESSION

A SABRINA SALTER MYSTERY

C. Michele Dorsey (signature)

C. MICHELE DORSEY

Copyright © 2021 pending by C.Michele Dorsey

All rights reserved.

No part of this book may be reproduced in any form or by any electronic or mechanical means, including information storage and retrieval systems, without written permission from the author, except for the use of brief quotations in a book review.

This is a work of fiction. All of the names, characters, organizations, places and events portrayed in this novel are either products of the author's imagination or are used fictitiously. Any resemblance to real or actual events, locales, or persons, living or dead, is entirely coincidental.

Published in the United States by Blue Willow Press.

*For my grandmother, Madeline "Nanna" Falvey
and
my granddaughter, Madeline "Maddie" Grant*

*"A grandmother is both a sword and a shield."
Fredrik Backman, My Grandmother Asked Me to Tell You She's Sorry*

September 2, 2017

Hurricane Irma Warning

Latitude 18.7N
Longitude -42.6W

1448 miles from St. John

Chapter 1

It wasn't the welcome Sabrina had expected when she returned home to paradise after a three-week vacation in hell. She had barely closed the door to the Ten Villas van Henry had picked her up in before he hit her with the news.

"You're going to kill me and I can't blame you. Hey, where's Neil?" Henry asked. Sabrina watched as he craned his neck to check out the few remaining figures on the dock searching for Sabrina's erstwhile boyfriend.

"He's traveling back on his own. It's a little complicated," Sabrina said. Her split with Neil was going to be a hot topic for the hungry island rumor mill.

"Oh," Henry said. When he failed to ask follow up questions, she knew she was in trouble. Henry had an insatiable appetite for gossip.

"So, tell me why I'm going to kill you, Henry," Sabrina said. She shook the rain from her black curls. They had relaxed into soft waves while she was on vacation but now recoiled in the sultry September humidity. Sabrina had rushed from the ferry to the van yet still got drenched by the sheets of warm tropical rain. She hadn't minded she was so relieved to be home.

Henry explained that he had given one of their three

seasonal employees not just the key to their storage container, but his entire ring of keys when he sent him to fetch a can of primer.

"Why would you ever do that?" It was a shriek, not a question.

Sabrina closed her eyes picturing the bracelet-sized ring filled with the keys to each of the ten villas they managed and to their personal homes and vehicles. Worse, close friends had also entrusted them with keys to their homes. If word got out, Ten Villas' business reputation would be ruined. Henry and Sabrina had labored tirelessly to rise to the top of the highly competitive St. John village management market. A breach like this would send Ten Villas into an instant plunge, one their competitors would delight in. If there were break-ins and property loss, the trust she and Henry had worked feverishly to establish would never be restored.

Sabrina pictured her ring of keys, which she normally wore on her work belt. She had left it in her cottage hanging from a nail on a shelf in the bathroom behind stacks of rolls of paper towels and toilet paper for the villas. She prayed it was still there and vowed to find a better hiding place if they recovered the missing keys.

Sabrina opened her eyes, said nothing, and looked at Henry for an explanation.

"It's a long stupid story. Eric borrowed a car from Katie, the bartender from The Tap Room, to get to work. They're roommates, I guess. I asked Eric to pick up more primer from our container at The Last Chance Center during his lunch break. We couldn't work outside any longer since the heavy rain had set in. Eric never returned to work after lunch leaving me with our other two guys twiddling their thumbs getting paid to watch it rain. Then I get a frantic call from Katie asking where the hell is Eric and her car. I ask her how would I know and she starts ranting about how she'll lose her job if she doesn't show up."

Sabrina sighed. Henry's big heart was one of the reasons she loved him. He was the dearest friend she'd ever had, save Ruth, the woman who had raised her. Sabrina knew what he was going to say next.

"I get it. I know Katie a little. She's had her fill of bad luck. You drove her to work so she wouldn't lose her job and that's why you haven't had time to hunt down Eric and find our keys, right? Look, let's just split up and look for Eric and those keys. There will be plenty of time for me to kill you later. Worse case, we'll change all of the locks tomorrow and pray nothing happens between now and then."

While Sabrina was distraught over the missing keys, she was comforted by the familiarity she felt joining Henry on a rescue mission. The events during the past three weeks in New England had left her feeling isolated and disconnected. Henry was her link to a world where she belonged.

"You check out Bar None. He likes to hang out there. I'll head up to The Last Chance Center," Henry said.

Bar None was the bar on the beach in Cruz Bay owned and operated by Neil Perry, former L.A. lawyer and Sabrina's boyfriend until their disastrous vacation in New England. Sabrina appreciated Henry was trying to give her the easier assignment, but the last place on the planet she wanted to be was at the bar owned by Neil whom she had left stranded without a car on an island in Maine.

"I've been on vacation taking it easy. I'll head up to Last Chance. You hit Bar None," Sabrina said.

Henry dropped her off at his condo on Gifft Hill where she picked up the Ten Villas Jeep. He gave her the key to it from the spare key ring they had the foresight to keep.

The Last Chance Center, which was housed within five storage containers, was located a few miles down on the same road. Sabrina was a big fan of The Last Chance Center, St. John's primitive answer to recycling which was almost impossible to implement on a Caribbean island. Ten Villas was both a consumer and a supplier of The Last Chance Center. During the day, it was a busy place where island residents dropped off items they no longer needed or purchased supplies that had been donated for a fraction of cost. It was a great place to find a bargain or pick up the latest island gossip. The center operated from early morning until mid-afternoon and was staffed largely by retirees. Behind it were several rows of privately owned storage containers, including the one owned by Ten Villas.

Sabrina slid onto the driver's seat and checked the sky through the windshield while the wipers worked furiously to clear the sheets of driving rain. None of the usual glittering constellations were out to guide her. A canopy of heavy gray clouds enveloped St. John. But even the wild wind and downpour couldn't dampen Sabrina's relief that she was home.

Sabrina had to remind herself to "Think Left," after driving for three weeks in the states on the right side of the road. She struggled to see through the windshield. It was difficult to maneuver the sharp turns in the road and to discern where The Last Chance Center was. Since it wasn't open during the night, the center had no lights, and its primitive hand-painted sign wasn't illuminated.

Sabrina slowed down after she passed Gifft Hill School on the right. After going by several island residences, Sabrina caught sight of the shadowy rectangular structures.

She pulled into the driveway, nearly hitting a vehicle that was sitting in the middle of the small parking area. She clicked her bright lights on and recognized the vehicle. It was Katie's banged up red Suzuki, a former rental car. An array of bumper stickers reciting "Save Coral Bay," "StJ," and "Birdie Sanders" adorned the rear of the vehicle. Katie's car was a typical St. John island-beater. The island was as hard on vehicles as it was on people.

Sabrina grabbed a flashlight and the slicker she always kept in the back seat and got out of the Jeep. She had worn flip-flops home on the plane and was now standing in more than an inch of water. She walked around the Suzuki peering inside and observing the usual detritus found in island cars. Empty beer cans. Water bottles, including the standard gallon size used to wash off sand from the beach. A faded towel on the seat and a pair of sunglasses on the dashboard.

The Last Chance Center lost its island charm without the chatter and bustle it had when it was open for business. Sabrina wished she had suggested to Henry that they check it out together. The only sound was the relentless rainfall. She was engulfed by darkness, as if she had fallen into a black hole. This wasn't the Caribbean she had longed to return to with greens and blues so vibrant they almost hurt your eyes.

Sabrina considered leaving. She'd accomplished what she came for. Eric wasn't there. Katie's car was. There was no reason to look further. But since she'd come this far, Sabrina thought she ought to have a look around. Sabrina slid in her flip-flops as a new downpour began. The pelting rain felt warm on her face. She walked around the five containers rented and operated by The Last Chance Center, which were lined up together in a row. She pointed her flashlight up and down. All containers were locked. There were no keys on the ground. She walked over to the Ten Villas container and pulled on the padlock. Her shoulders dropped in relief. The unit was snug. Whatever precious contents she and Henry had stashed in it were safe, unless Eric had already removed them. Sabrina put the brakes on her fears. She shouldn't teeter into tangential concerns but stay focused was on finding Eric and the keys. Wherever he was, it wasn't here.

Sabrina heard a sound from her cell phone signaling a text message.

"Eric not at Bar None. Dinner my condo. On grill. Power out AGAIN. No gas for generator," Henry's message said.

Sabrina groaned. Power outages were common in the Virgin Islands but that didn't make them less annoying. She looked around her and confirmed there were no lights from the houses across the street. She cursed Eric for hiding behind the black wet mask of night and not sitting on a stool at Bar None drinking beer while listening to the hum of the generator Neil had spent a fortune on. People took cover in bars on St. John when it rained. Where was Eric, if not home and not in a bar? Sabrina's frustration erupted into anger. She decided to call Eric and let him know how furious she was. Even if he didn't pick up, she would leave him a voice message he wouldn't forget.

She located Eric's contact information and hit "call." She began formulating what she would say to him when she was surprised to hear a faint ringing from inside one of the containers. One of The Last Chance containers. Sabrina walked through the puddles and mud closer to the container and confirmed the ringing was coming from within it. She jiggled the padlock she had checked only a few minutes before. It was secure.

"Eric? Eric, are you in there?" Sabrina repeated her plea several times, while she tried to remember more about him. He was older than the other two workers she and Henry had hired to help do maintenance and repairs to their villas, which were closed during the height of hurricane season. Good-looking with an engaging smile. More confident. A bit of a factotum. None of the details about him mattered. Eric wasn't answering.

Sabrina wanted to go home. Maybe she'd pick up her dog first, so she would get a proper welcome home. She wanted a shower. A drink. To pee. What she didn't want was to hear the ringing inside the container in front of her and consider what it meant. She couldn't shake the heaviness in her chest, the sense that something was wrong. All Sabrina had wanted after her three-week siege of misery was to return to the simple existence she had created on the tiny island she called home. It wasn't going to happen.

Sabrina considered calling the police. Her employee was missing. His phone was ringing from inside a container, which was highly suspicious. Certainly, this was a matter for the authorities. But maybe not on St. John. Sabrina recalled her previous experiences with the island police, which made her skeptical, even afraid to invite them into her life again.

She checked her phone directory and found the phone number for The Last Chance Center manager and hit dial. She explained her concern to Jay Callahan, who agreed to meet her without hesitation.

Sabrina sat in her jeep with the door open and dangled her bare feet outside so the rain would wash away the mud. She imagined Neil telling her, "Don't be foolish, Salty, lock the doors." But since he wasn't there, she ignored his voice. Her eyes locked on the container where she had heard the phone ringing. Maybe Eric had dropped his phone there and that was why no one could find him. Maybe it was as simple as that.

Jay arrived within ten minutes.

"Sorry to drag you out in the middle of a monsoon," Sabrina said, leading him toward the container.

"Don't apologize. I'd have done the same. Let's take a look," Jay said. He opened the padlock and stepped out of the way so Sabrina could enter.

Sabrina hopped up and into what Jay explained was the furniture and home décor container. It was dark and hot inside. She could smell the faint odor of rotting, not unusual in a climate where the temperature enhanced mold and decay.

"There's no lighting in here, so we're stuck with our flash lights," Jay said. He'd brought a large Mag-lite.

Sabrina flicked hers on and began spanning the container. She recognized an armoire from her friend Mara's villa. Mara was purging all furnishings that reminded her of her wretched ex-husband. Next to it, Sabrina glanced at a three-cushioned beige couch. One of the cushions along the back of the sofa was blemished with a large crimson stain next to the deep gash in Eric's neck. Eric was sprawled with his head against the back of the couch as if he were watching a bad play by the Patriots in a Super Bowl game. His eyes were wide open staring above toward the ceiling or more likely the God who had let this happen to him.

"Oh, sweet Jesus," Jay said in a whisper that sounded more like a prayer.

Sabrina's stomach dry-heaved. She hadn't eaten since having breakfast at Logan airport early that morning. It was the only thing she had done right all day.

Chapter 2

Sabrina shivered in the backseat of the cruiser while trying to erase the memory of the dead man's open eyes staring at her. It wasn't the first dead body she'd seen since she moved to St. John, but it had been the most disturbing. It struck her as odd that the blood had bothered her less than the eyes. Eric's smoldering blue eyes no longer resembled Bradley Cooper's. In death, they had stared like a Pearly-eyed Thrasher, the feathered island nemesis.

Jay Callahan had been placed in a different cruiser. Sabrina was grateful to have drawn Detective Lucy Detree to be questioned by and not one of the cops she had encountered before who had no respect for the people they served. She and Lucy were not friends, but they had become cordial acquaintances after several investigations brought them together. But still, being confined to a cop car triggered Sabrina. Memories she struggled to suppress popped up like ads on her iPhone the minute she slid into the cruiser. For a woman who just wanted to be left alone, Sabrina spent a lot of time with cops.

"Do you know who this man is?" Detective Detree asked

Sabrina after she slid into the back seat next to her taking refuge from the rain.

"His name is Eric. I'm sorry. I can't remember his last name. He works for us at Ten Villas. I'd have to check his job application file to tell you much more," Sabrina said. The adrenalin rush she had first experienced when she saw Eric had dissipated and been replaced by exhaustion. She was no longer hungry, but her mouth was dry. She took a sip of water from the bottle they had given her when she was asked to sit inside the cruiser. Her hand shook as she lifted the bottle to her mouth.

"What else can you tell me about Eric without checking his file, which I'll want to see first thing tomorrow?" Lucy asked. She reached into the pocket of her police slicker and pulled out a small notebook and pen. She placed the damp pad on her long bent legs as if they were her desk. Even though Sabrina admired Lucy, she had hung around Neil long enough to know the less she said, the better.

"Not much. He hasn't worked for us for very long. I've been away for the last three weeks, so I'm afraid I can't be of much help," Sabrina said.

"So, you don't know if Eric had a beef with someone, maybe another one of your workers, or even Henry?" Lucy's tone was gentle, but Sabrina had seen her in action and knew not to underestimate her intelligence.

There was no reason for Sabrina to tell her that Henry didn't like Eric. When they had interviewed workers for their fall maintenance crew, Henry told her the forty-something candidate was cocky and could be trouble. "We're only hiring him to paint and clean, not deal with our customers," Sabrina had reminded him. Plus, Eric was older and hopefully more mature and reliable than the two younger candidates they were hiring. Showing up was the number one quality employers sought in their employees on St. John.

But it seemed Sabrina had been wrong, which was okay. It was her turn. Henry had made the last near catastrophic blunder in their short careers as villa rental managers. He'd pressured her into adding an eleventh villa to Ten Villas several months before that debuted with the murder of a bride who never got to walk down the aisle.

"Sorry, I just arrived on the 4:00 p.m. ferry. All I know is that Eric took our keys to open our container to grab some primer and never returned to work," Sabrina said. She rubbed her eyes.

"How long were you here before you called Jay?" Lucy asked. Sabrina didn't like the switch she detected in her tone.

"Minutes. Less than ten, probably not even five. Can I leave now?" Sabrina asked.

"And you saw no one, right? No, you can't leave yet." Lucy flipped to the next page in her notebook.

The cruiser was claustrophobic and steamy. Sabrina could smell the sweat of every poor soul who had ever been thrown into its backseat. Even the sound of the steady rain on the roof of the cruiser didn't soothe Sabrina who normally loved everything about rain from the way it sounded to the smell of it. She closed her eyes but the dancing blue lights from the other police vehicles seeped through her eyelids. She remembered another time she had been sitting in the back seat of a police cruiser in the frigid cold and how that had turned out. She needed to get out of the cruiser.

"I already told you the only person I saw was Jay who came after I called him. Am I in custody? Charged with something? Why can't I leave?" Sabrina knew she had to ask this question. The one Neil would have asked had he been there.

"Because you are a material witness to a murder investigation. Let me ask you just a few more questions, and then you can go. You'll have to come down to the station tomorrow to sign a statement and bring me that file. You know the deal," Lucy said. She grinned at Sabrina like they were old buddies.

Sabrina tried to smile back and nodded her assent. She was

thrilled to answer a few more questions if it meant getting out of a police cruiser and into a warm shower and her own bed.

"What was the reason behind hiring Eric? He seems older than the others. Was Henry attracted to him, maybe?" Lucy kept her eyes on her notebook while she fired the questions at Sabrina, only glancing up to catch her reaction.

"You can't be serious. We don't hire our crew for personal reasons. Eric is older. We value the stability our mature workers bring to the job," Sabrina said. She glared at Lucy. She had given her more credit than she deserved.

Lucy said nothing.

"Look, Eric knew how to do a little bit of everything. Painting, plumbing, concrete work, minor electrical. He was a horticultural wizard. He even knew the botanical names of plants. We were lucky to get him. I overheard him talk about the books he was reading. He liked jazz. Eric was an island renaissance man. The only thing he had going against him was a little bit of arrogance, but on St. John that's a survival skill." Sabrina slumped back against the seat.

"I thought you didn't know him," Lucy said. She had stopped writing and stared directly into Sabrina's tired eyes.

Sabrina bristled. "I learned that in a half-hour interview. Maybe I should apply to become a detective and show you guys how to interview people."

Lucy didn't answer her. She slid out of the cruiser putting the hood of her jacket over her head. Sabrina cursed herself. She would never get home if she didn't shut her mouth.

Sabrina noticed Henry pulling up the Ten Villas van ahead of the multiple emergency vehicles that were crowded in front of the Last Chance Center. She hoped that Lucy had contacted him to take her home. Lucy had explained the vehicles she and Jay had driven to the Last Chance Center would need to remain at the scene of the crime to be processed before they could be released. The words "scene of the crime" had driven home the reality that Eric had been murdered. The wound to his neck

Sabrina had seen could never have been mistaken for an accident.

Sabrina saw Henry exit the driver's door of the van and walk toward Lucy. They shook hands, always a good sign. Lucy nodded and then shook her head. She pointed to a third cruiser. Henry followed her to it and got in the back seat. Sabrina panicked. What was going on? There was no reason to put Henry in what appeared to be custody. He hadn't even been at the scene of the crime.

Lucy returned and opened the cruiser door to let her out.

"Okay, Sabrina. The Ten Villas van has arrived. Henry left it running. You can have the jeep back after we've checked it out. We're done with you for tonight, but you know the routine. Don't leave the island. We'll have a lot more questions for you tomorrow when you come down to the station with Eric's file. Someone will give you a call to tell you when," Lucy said, looking impervious to the rain in her police department issued raingear.

"Wait a minute. What about Henry? Why is he in that cruiser?" Sabrina asked.

Lucy sighed. She had unmistakable dignity and a sense of calm even as the heavens broke loose with another deluge.

"We have a few questions to ask Henry," Lucy said.

"About what? Why do you need to talk to him? Jay and I are the ones who found the body. Come on, Lucy. Be straight with me. What's going on?"

"The machete. You have to understand that's a cause for concern, Sabrina," Lucy said in a quiet voice. The kind Sabrina remembered Ruth using when she had tested her patience, gone over the "fine line" when she was a kid. It didn't happen often, but Sabrina had learned to pay as close attention to what she called little voices as those that bellowed and boomed.

"What machete?" Sabrina asked.

"The one on the couch next to the victim. It appears to be the murder weapon," Lucy said.

"I didn't notice anything other than the wound and Eric's eyes. They were open, you know."

"I know. That's hard to look at. But there was a machete under the couch beneath him that we believe is what was used to kill him. Sabrina, it's Henry's machete. It has his name on it."

Chapter 3

Even under a slicker, Sabrina's clothes got drenched for the third time as she dashed to the van. Her sopping hair dripped onto her face. She opened the door to a blast of warm. Henry had left the heat blowing on high. The blast of warm air on her face reminded Sabrina of how it felt entering the warmth of Ruth's diner after walking home from school in the winter. She squeezed the water from her hair with the still damp towel she used just hours before when Henry first picked her up.

She was about to shift into drive when she noticed one of Henry's sticky notes stuck to the rearview mirror. Henry loved leaving her messages stuck in various places he was sure she would notice. Mirrors were a favorite, but her computer screen, the coffee maker, and the refrigerator were others. Sabrina had to put the light on to read the message.

"Contact Neil ASAP! I knew that guy was trouble. Sorry I didn't get to find a spot for your grandmother."

Sabrina was perplexed by the note but wanted to get away from the police and Eric's body more than she wanted to take time to interpret it. Did he mean he knew Neil was trouble? If so, she totally agreed. But he was probably referring to Eric and he was right. She waved at Jay who was getting into a vehicle driven by his wife. She felt bad that he had to be exposed to the awful sight of Eric's body. She felt even guiltier for leaving Henry behind.

The rain had let up a little but was still steady. Sabrina realized she didn't know where she should go. Worse, she didn't know whom to call. She knew she and Henry needed help. She didn't know if Neil had returned to the island, although she thought Henry would have mentioned it if he had seen him when he went to look for Eric at Bar None. Most of her friends were off island visiting the states until hurricane season was over. The one friend who remained on island was an older woman who was nursing a dying husband. Sabrina couldn't burden her.

Even the Fork in the Road, a local shrine featuring a giant illuminated dinner fork that reminded people why they flocked to St. John, was unlit and offered no guidance as she drove by. She turned into Henry's condo complex because she didn't know where else to go and he had a generator. Hopefully, he'd found gas for it. Whatever Sabrina had to do, it would be easier if she had light.

Sure enough, his complex was brightly lit. Sabrina picked up the remote from the console and punched in the code. The elegant entrance opened, allowing her to pass through and park the van next to Henry's front door. In the glow from the overhead light, she saw something yellow inside the screen door under flapping in the wild wind.

Once inside, Sabrina stripped off her wet clothes and snuggled into the terry robe Henry kept for her in the guest room. She perched on the white leather sofa in the same spot she always occupied when visiting him. She knew she should eat something but had no appetite. She looked at Henry's note again and knew she had to text Neil. Lucy's revelation that Henry's machete was the murder weapon had shocked Sabrina. No wonder it sounded as if Henry were the prime suspect for Eric's murder. Sabrina knew however angry she was with Neil, it should not prevent her from doing what was right to protect Henry. Her message to Neil would be clear she was only reaching out to help Henry. While Sabrina considered Neil insensitive, she knew he wouldn't be vindictive to Henry because of their breakup.

"URGENT: Ten Villas employee throat slashed with Henry's machete. He needs your HELP." She added, "He didn't do it. Obviously." She pressed "send," praying Neil hadn't blocked her.

Sabrina curled up tucking her feet under the soft white angora throw Henry kept over the arm of the couch. She placed her phone on her lap where she would be sure to see a return message from Neil or hear Henry call her to let her know what was going on.

She mulled over the events that had occurred in the short time since she had been away from St. John. Though St. John was not conflict-free, it was normally fairly tranquil. People might argue about whether a new traffic rotary should be installed or whether someone was ignoring building regulations when erecting a new condo complex. But a savage murder went far beyond the typically civil clashes among islanders that rarely became violent. What had happened to her little island? The question exhausted Sabrina until she finally dozed off, disappointed she had not heard back from Neil.

Sabrina was startled by the sound of the front door opening and voices. She sat up straight, unsure if she should call out. At first, she didn't recognize the voice that awakened her, although it was familiar.

"Do you want me to leave?" It was David, Henry's ex-lover, who had moved to St. John months before. He was patiently hoping for Henry's forgiveness, which hadn't been granted so far. Henry had been willing to meet David for an occasional drink or dinner at a public bar or restaurant. But he had declined invitations to the home David had recently purchased from a widow who sold him her late husband's seaplane as a bargain package. Henry confided to Sabrina that it was easier to resist temptation if they kept to neutral territory

"No. You can stay," Henry said.

Before Sabrina could warn him she was in the living room, he entered and leapt in surprise.

"Jesus, sweetie, I thought you'd be fast asleep in the guest room by now after the day you've had," Henry said. He rushed and leaned over to give her a hug, then flopped next to her, peeling a wet yellow sticky note off the palm of his hand.

"Are you okay? What's going on with the police, Henry?" Sabrina asked.

"Let me play bartender while you two talk this through. You both could probably use a drink," David said. He stood just inside the door that separated the living room from a long hallway that led to the front door.

"Knock yourself out. Bar's in the kitchen," Henry said pointing to a door on the other side of the living room.

"Martini, no Vermouth, olives. Please," Sabrina said.

"Make it two," Henry said.

"Tell me they don't really think you killed Eric, Henry. You must have an alibi," Sabrina said.

"That's what Lucy kept asking. And I do. Sort of. I mean I spent some of the afternoon with the guys at work. And I ran to Starfish Market to pick up some ingredients for appetizers. I still had the slip in my wallet to show her, but there are holes in between. Part of the time, I was here alone. I didn't think I'd have to account for my time," Henry said.

"Do you have any idea who might have taken your machete?" Sabrina asked. Sabrina knew how meticulous Henry was about his tools. Actually, she had accused him of being obsessive.

"Well, I suppose it was Eric. But I can't prove it. I only know I had it in the morning when I was working at Villa Tideaway clearing away that god-awful Catch'n Keep vine. I can't believe someone would do what they did to Eric, let alone with my machete."

Henry's eyes filled. He tried to turn away from Sabrina before she noticed, but they had been friends for too long for her to be fooled. She wished she could tell him help was on the way, that Neil had texted her to say he was back on island, and not to worry. Sabrina decided to distract him before he thought to ask about Neil.

"Look, Henry, I know you've had a rough day and Eric's death is going to complicate our lives until they find out who did it. But if you don't mind, I'm curious about your message about my grandmother. Why are you sorry you couldn't find her a spot?"

"I was just trying to help your grandmother find accommodations before Caneel closed for the season and had struck out so far. Wasn't that what I was supposed to do?" Henry's eyes widened. Sabrina realized her efforts to assuage Henry's level of anxiety had backfired and that hers was about to escalate.

"Don't tell me she's on St. John, Henry. Please don't," Sabrina said.

Henry hid his face in the palms of his hands. "You don't know? Seriously? She told me she was here to 'see things through' and to 'continue the conversation.' She was waiting for your return from your vacation with 'your charming beau.'"

"She said that?" Sabrina groaned as she listened to the clatter from the kitchen. Where was that frigging martini?

"Yes. I figured you'd made a go of your relationship and that she was coming for a visit. That's why I invited her here for a cocktail. To be cordial and support your reconnection. I was a little surprised you didn't give me a heads up when we spoke, but I figured you and Neil just wanted a full week to yourselves," Henry said. He stood to take a martini from David who was spilling both of the drinks he was carrying at an alarming rate. Henry handed one to Sabrina and took the second one for himself.

Sabrina's last call to Henry had been short, simply asking if she could go off the grid for her last week away. She promised details about her trip when she returned.

"Reconnection? How can there be a 're' when there never was a connection? Remember, I never met the woman before," Sabrina said She gulped her drink as David placed a bowl of cashews in front of her and disappeared again.

"You mean you didn't know she was coming to St. John?"

David returned and sat on the far edge of the couch next to Henry. He placed a martini on the coffee table on a cocktail napkin, then lifted Henry's drink and placed another napkin under it. Sabrina was sure he was alarmed by the tone of her voice, but she couldn't control it.

"How would I know that? I wouldn't know anything about her if I hadn't had lunch with her personal assistant after Grace ejected Neil and me from her home. Are you sure it's her?" Sabrina asked.

Henry chewed on the olives at the bottom of his empty glass, then switched it with David's full one. David took the empty glass, getting Henry's hint, so she handed him hers as well.

"Well, I didn't ask for her DNA or her Massachusetts driver's license," Henry said, slouching back on the couch, then pushing himself up straight. "Wait a minute. I wanted to tell you something I overheard the cops talking about at the Last Chance Center. Did you know Eric was from your hometown, Allerton?"

Sabrina sat stunned. Her homecoming to St. John was supposed to be a return to normalcy.

"Really? How do they know that?"

"From his license, I suppose," Henry said.

"I'm sure he gave a local address on his application. I would have noticed an Allerton address."

David entered carrying a tray filled with Henry's signature deviled eggs and cantaloupe slices wrapped with prosciutto. They were Sabrina's favorites from Henry's lengthy repertoire of appetizers they occasionally offered Ten Villas' clients as amenities.

"You made these for my grandmother? Are you kidding me?" Sabrina said beginning to feel the effects of the alcohol.

"Eat them for revenge," David said, passing her another martini.

"Hey, did you hear from Neil?" Henry asked, looking around the room as if Neil were hiding behind a piece of furniture.

Sabrina plucked an olive from her drink and popped it into her mouth.

"No. What's with the sticky note on your hand?" she asked. She had seen Henry place it on the coffee table when David had served the first round of drinks. She picked it up.

"Did I have the wrong night, Henry?" Grace Armstrong had signed the note in bold black marker. Her grandmother really was on St. John.

September 3, 2017

Hurricane Irma Warning

Latitude 17.9N
Longitude -47.9W

1105 miles from St. John

Chapter 4

The last thing Sabrina remembered was saying goodnight to Henry and David after another round of martinis and grilled cheese sandwiches David threw together. She had been too exhausted to recount her adventures in New England, so she and Henry made a pact to delve into the details of her discovery of Eric's body and her travel woes the next day.

She tiptoed out of the guest room in the terry cloth robe. Her clothes were still damp, hanging in the bathroom, not even a choice. Besides, it was early. No one would see her driving home in the robe. Sabrina wondered if David had spent the night but figured the answer would be part of the debriefing she and Henry owed each other.

She slipped into the Ten Villas van. The ride to her cottage in Fish Bay was short, but long enough to remind her how much she loved the deep blue and rich turquoise waters in St. John even when muted by a tropical haze. The combination of bulky robe and heavy muggy air made her want to jump in and cool off. Sabrina had missed her nightly swims from Hawksnest to Gibney beaches with her chocolate lab, Girlfriend, while she was in New England.

Sabrina drove up the winding hills toward her cottage knowing she had come home to a shit storm. Eric's murder was so brutal, Sabrina had dreamed about blood and machetes all night. She had never seen so much blood even when her husband had suffered a gunshot wound to the abdomen that had killed him in Nantucket. But it was the memory of Eric's open eyes that Sabrina still saw when she was awake.

She was skeptical about whether Eric came from Allerton, Massachusetts her hometown. Hiring someone from the coastal town where you grew up seemed like a bizarre coincidence. The arrival of her grandmother from Beechwood, the town next to Allerton, was more than she could absorb. Sabrina couldn't accept that both Eric and her grandmother had landed on St. John as a fluke. Yet, islanders joked that there were more people on island from Massachusetts than were left back in the Commonwealth.

Sabrina braced herself for the sight of the ugly container that blocked the view of her cottage from the road. Neil had ordered it so she would have a barrier to hide from the rabid journalists who had stalked her when she had been a person of interest in the death of a villa guest. The empty drab rust brown container had doubled as her garage, an unsightly reminder that there was no hiding after Nantucket. Even though she had been acquitted, Sabrina's criminal history was instantly available to her enemies in the digital age.

Rounding the last corner onto the short dirt road that led to the cottage, Sabrina gasped. The container was gone and had been replaced by a partially constructed stonewall. She pulled the van up close to the wall made of native stonework with shells and an occasional wine bottle. She stepped out, grabbed her bags and walked toward an arched gate next to the right side of the wall.

The black wrought iron gate was ajar. Sabrina hesitated. Something was seriously wrong here. She called out the island greeting, "Inside," and moved tentatively onto the stone path like a visitor to her own home.

"What the hell?" Sabrina gaped at a swimming pool surrounded by stonework and immature plants in the area that had previously housed the container. Leaving her bags behind, she walked around the kidney shaped pool filled with water. She realized someone had made a terrible mistake and installed it on her property while she was away. She had no idea what to do. Returning it to its rightful owner didn't seem an option.

Sabrina dipped her toe into the water, which was warm and inviting. It was still too early for her to barge in and visit her neighbors, Lyla and Evan Banks. She'd left Girlfriend with the elderly couple, who adored spoiling the pup as if she were one of their grandchildren. Evan had been fighting a valiant battle against Alzheimer's disease but his general health had diminished as his mind slipped. He and Girlfriend had a special bond. Sabrina knew this was the time of the morning when Evan would be bathed and fed, if he was even still eating. Sabrina remembered the drill from when she took care of Ruth, her surrogate mother, when she was dying of lung cancer.

Sabrina considered slipping out of her robe and into the water for a quick skinny dip. No one would know, but it felt a little like stealing. Besides, she needed coffee more than a swim. She opened the door to the cottage with the spare key and entered the cool musty silence. She would make coffee and then call Henry. Maybe he would know something about the mysterious pool. But first, Sabrina went to the bathroom and removed several packages of paper towels from a shelf. Bingo, her keys were still there. She dropped them in the pocket of her robe and headed back to the kitchen to make the coffee she needed. The hum of the refrigerator told her the power was back on.

"Hello? Miss Salter? Are you back?" a man's voice called from outside. She hadn't had time to push the Keurig button.

She walked out the front door onto the stone patio, reeling

again at the sight of the pool. A man around fifty in khaki shorts and a navy tee shirt with KCC in green letters and shamrocks on the front stood under the arch.

"May I help you?" Sabrina asked. She felt chilled, aware that she was naked under her robe, and that there was a stranger about to come onto her property on an island where there had just been a murder. She had become so used to worrying that she might considered be a suspect, she nearly overlooked the possibility she could become a victim.

"Hi, I'm Troy Schaefer from Keating Construction. Were you surprised?" He stepped forward extending his hand to Sabrina who shook it.

"To say the least," she said, sure she had fallen down a rabbit hole.

"He knew you'd be," Troy said, grinning. He looked like he hadn't shaven for a few days, but otherwise appeared well groomed and respectable.

"Who is 'he'?"

"Neil, Mr. Perry. Isn't he here?" Troy's grin morphed into a frown.

"He's not back on island yet. Maybe you should explain," Sabrina said.

"You mean you don't know about the gift from the Keatings? I'm sorry. I thought the plan was for Neil to explain once you saw it. I'm sorry the wall isn't done. It's the only thing we hired locals to do and I guess their idea of a rush job is a little different from ours in California," Troy said. He shrugged as he pointed to the wall, which was about three feet high, leaving another four to make it even with the sides of the arch over the gate.

"Are you talking about Sean Keating's family?" Sabrina asked. The Keatings owned the eleventh villa she and Henry had added to Ten Villas. It tanked the first weekend it opened when Sean's bride had been murdered before their wedding. Sean's broken heart had hardened when his fiancé was revealed to be a manipulative fraud. Villa Nirvana was now on the market for sale, the end of a sad saga.

"Look, this feels awkward because I think Neil was planning to surprise you and explain how grateful the Keatings are for all you did for them during the tragedy at Villa Nirvana. They wanted to show their appreciation and asked Neil what you might like. Since they're in the construction business, he shared your pool plans with them. We made arrangements for me to bring a crew and get the job done while you were off island on vacation." Troy sounded a little winded to Sabrina. He was beginning to sweat around the neckline of his tee shirt.

"My pool plans?" Sabrina asked. She had no idea what plans he was talking about.

"I tried to follow them," he said.

"The pool is beautiful, but I can't possibly accept it as a gift. I'll have to figure out how to pay back the Keatings." Sabrina appreciated their generosity but it was way over the top. `What had Neil been thinking?

"Oh, I'm sure they won't hear of it. Here's my card if you have any questions about the pool. I left the written printout with maintenance instructions at Bar None for Neil. I'll be at Villa Nirvana for a few more days with my crew doing some work before we leave. It's not selling as quickly as Sean had hoped," Troy said, his hand out again, this time to say goodbye and end what Sabrina knew had been an uncomfortable conversation for both of them.

Back in her kitchen, Sabrina pressed the Keurig button before anyone else could disturb her. With her mug full, she opened the door to the screen porch, which was her haven and now had a poolside view. Sitting on a wicker chair, she kept hearing "pool plans" in her head. Pool plans. She had never had anyone draw pool plans. If she had, she would have had Mara Bennett, her friend and island architect, do them. What had Neil shown the Keatings? She stood looking at the pool and the wall beyond it. The young peach hibiscus and blue plumbago plants lining the inside of the wall felt familiar.

She walked inside beyond the open space combination living room and kitchen into her bedroom and opened the drawer to the nightstand next to her side of the bed. In recent months, Neil had often occupied the other side. Fumbling through lip moisturizer, tissues, pens, and a notebook, Sabrina pulled out a small sketchpad that she had been doodling on with colored pencils. Flipping it open, she arrived at a very primitive sketch of her dream pool with a gate, stonewall, and flowering shrubs. Just like the one outside her door now.

Chapter 5

"What was I thinking?" Henry said. He rolled over to see the time on his bedroom alarm clock. He had overslept and probably missed Sabrina leaving.

"You didn't want to be alone. We didn't do anything," David said. He sounded as if he had been awake for hours.

"Not you. I forgot to tell Sabrina about the pool. Neil was going to surprise her when they got home. And Evan. She doesn't know he's in hospice care. I have to tell her before she goes to see the Banks. Shit." Henry sprung out of bed and rushed into the bathroom. Grabbing a sarong from a hook behind the door, he trotted out to the hall and down to the guest room where the door was wide open and the bed had been made by a pro. He dashed back to his bedroom to find David half-dressed and grabbed his cell phone.

In the kitchen he told Siri to call Sabrina while he pulled two mugs out of a cabinet.

"Henn-err-rry?" Sabrina picked up on the first ring. She knew. Only Sabrina could make the name "Henry" into as many syllables as his mother had.

"I'm sorry, sweetie. I meant to tell you last night when I learned Neil wasn't with you. It slipped my mind, with the dead body and all, you know," he said. Henry placed the mugs under the double spouts on the gourmet coffee maker.

"I need to understand. It's going to have to be part of our conversation later," she said.

"Of course. Listen, I hate to be a bad-news-bear, but you should know hospice has been brought in to care for Evan. I think it's a relief to Lyla. She's been so worried she hasn't been doing enough." Henry heard Sabrina gasp. She'd developed a tough veneer necessary to cope with the challenges she'd faced in life, mostly alone. But Henry knew her interior was that of a gentle soul, who rarely complained even though she had more than most to wail about.

"I guess that was to be expected," she said

"And I've gotten text messages from our work crew. Both have been told to report to the police station first thing this morning for interviews, so we're without a work crew," Henry said. He handed David a mug with hot black coffee, pointing to the refrigerator to signal where he'd find milk and then to a sealed container for sugar.

"I forget. What are their names?" Sabrina asked.

"Tyler and Austen, the two kids we hired with Eric," Henry said. They hired so many occasional laborers, he also had trouble remembering their names.

"That means we'll have to do what they were assigned to this morning. At some point, I'll have to bring the file on Eric to the police station," Sabrina said.

"You grab that and I'll meet you at Villa Mascarpone in half an hour. I'll take the scooter since it's stopped raining for a change. We have lots to talk about. Wear your painting togs," he said, hanging up. Henry took his first sorely needed sip of coffee when his phone belted out his "It's Raining Men" ringtone. He'd gotten it partly to tease Sabrina who had been a television meteorologist in her former life. The caller I.D. told him it was Grace Armstrong, Sabrina's grandmother. He let it go to voicemail.

He would have to deal with Grace by the end of the day, but not now.

David sat barefoot on a stool, his long legs dangling. Henry envied his lean tall physique, while he knew David coveted his thick blonde hair. A moment like this when David's presence felt so natural was telling. Henry wondered where they were heading, unable to silence the sirens blasting warnings into his ears. Betrayal hung like an invisible curtain between them, an ever-present toxin contaminating their connection.

Henry was beginning to believe betrayal was inevitable in all human relationships. David had betrayed him. Sabrina's husband had betrayed her and died because of it. Her grandmother denied Sabrina's existence as a child, the cruelest of betrayals. He was certain Eric must have betrayed someone to end up murdered so viciously.

"I wish you could relax," David said, spooking Henry into suspicions of clairvoyance.

"The police don't think you butchered someone with your own machete," Henry said.

"I meant about me being here. Maybe I should go," David said standing up when the doorbell rang.

"Saved by the bell," Henry said, passing David to go to the door where he hoped he wouldn't find the police waiting. It wouldn't be the first time.

It was worse.

Henry knew the petite elderly blonde standing before his front door couldn't be Doris Day, although she was an amazing likeness. No, this had to be Sabrina's grandmother.

"I tried telephoning first," Grace said stepping forward so that Henry was forced back inside the entry where she passed him.

"I was on another call," Henry lied.

"Funny, it didn't go to voicemail," Grace said. Henry knew he was in big trouble if this octogenarian understood the difference between a missed call and one that was declined. Wearing navy blue and white polka dot capris and a white V-neck tee shirt trimmed in navy blue, there wasn't an ounce of fat to her and still some curves.

"How did you get through the gate?" he asked.

"Oh, at my age, you just wait for someone to come along who thinks you're a cute old lady and play it up. Some people," she said, shaking her head.

"Would you like coffee? I'm sorry I missed you yesterday. I got–"

"I know. One of your workers was murdered. I heard about it at breakfast this morning at Caneel, which was one of my last breakfasts there because they are closing the day after tomorrow for two months. That's why I'm here. That's why I wanted to meet you yesterday. I need to find suitable accommodations. Since your island seems to shut down for September and October, I need your help. The people at Caneel have tried finding me something but without success."

David handed Grace a mug of coffee while Henry led her to the living room, gesturing for her to sit down.

"I'm David Gilmartin," David said, offering Grace his hand.

"Nice to meet you. I'm Sabrina's grandmother, Grace Armstrong."

"Look, Mrs. Armstrong, I'd be happy to help you, but the truth is there's not much of anything available here during those months. It's hurricane season. Why don't you come back for a visit when the skies are sunny and clear and there are tons of rental options," Henry said.

"Henry, I'm not here to get a tan." Grace glared at him with disapproval. Although they looked nothing alike, Grace's expression was one he'd seen Sabrina wear more than once. He would hate to see them go up against one another.

"And please call me Grace." Henry thought "Your Grace" was more like it but nodded.

"Have you checked the Westin?" he asked.

"The Westin? That's so public," Grace said, her mouth

puckered as if she had sucked a lemon. Henry noticed she had remarkably few lines around her mouth and eyes for a woman her age and wondered how much work she had done. "I don't think that kind of visibility would be in my granddaughter's best interest," she added.

Henry had no idea what Grace was suggesting but decided against inquiring further. He had to get out to Villa Mascarpone to talk to Sabrina about Eric and what they needed to do. He hoped she had remembered to pull his job application from the file cabinet she kept in her living room for them to review.

"I'll see what I can come up with and call you later today," Henry said, taking the untouched mug of coffee off the table in front of Grace who stood, understanding the meeting was over. She took her cell phone out of the pocket of her capris.

"I'll expect your call, Henry. I can't imagine you'll run into another dead body today. Now, if you'll just give me Sabrina's number, I'll be on my way." Grace stood ready to punch the numbers into her keyboard with a perfectly manicured hand.

"Sorry," Henry said grabbing his own phone from his pocket. "You'll have to give me yours and I'll give it to her."

"Why not just give it to me and save a step?" Grace asked.

"Because I know very little about you, Mrs. Armstrong. What I do know is that Sabrina is my best friend and if she wants to talk to you, that's her decision, not mine or yours."

Chapter 6

"Well then, stop being silly. You already have my number. I called you. Remember?"

Grace Armstrong ticked off her telephone number to Henry and made him repeat it back to her. She wanted to say something to persuade Henry to have Sabrina call her, but she didn't have the words. She could see he was ferociously loyal to Sabrina, which gave her an odd rush of pride.

She told Henry she'd be at Caneel Bay and to please call her with news of lodging. She was surprised when David Gilmartin asked if she'd drop him at his house on the way.

"Do you mind? Henry's going in the opposite direction and on a scooter," David said.

"I suppose," Grace said. What she really longed to do was to ask David to drive her to Caneel. The first couple of days on St. John were sunny and bright and while driving on the left up and down forty-five-degree hills had intimidated her, she had handled the rental jeep admirably. It hadn't been until the deluge of rain that Grace wished she had a driver. That thought was preposterous, given how her entire life had been changed by a driver, although they had called him a chauffeur back in the day.

"Would it be easier for you if I drove until we reached my house?" David asked.

Grace handed him the keys, exhaling with relief. She wasn't sure who David Gilmartin was, but he seemed like an earnest fellow. His penetrating green eyes were accentuated by the fact he was very tall and his head was shaven.

Once she buckled her seatbelt, Grace got right to the point. She was direct by nature.

"So where do you fit it on this island stage, David? Are you a visitor, a resident? What's your story?"

David pulled out of the condo complex onto Gifft Hill Road.

"I live here. I moved to St. John a few months ago and bought a seaplane and cottage from a woman who had been recently widowed. How about you, Grace? What's your story?" he said keeping his eyes on the road.

Grace swallowed. People usually didn't dish it back to a woman in her eighties. David's tone had been respectful but pointed.

"I came here to sort things out with my granddaughter. I was brutal to her when she came to introduce herself to me," Grace said. She was ashamed of her behavior on that day and during the decades before.

They passed Gifft Hill School on the right. Grace wondered if children raised in the isolation of an island fared better than those exposed to the cruelty of the mainland. There had to be a serenity that came from being surrounded by the water. Her frontage on the Atlantic Ocean back in Beechwood had provided enormous comfort when she had lost her husband and Elizabeth. She had spent years trying to float above those losses and now she could feel the weight of them tugging her down.

"Why?" David asked.

"That would fill a book," Grace said watching goats scale a hillside. She had found encountering wild pigs, donkeys, and goats on St. John utterly charming in the short time she had been on island.

"Everyone on an island seems to be in escape mode. What are you running from?" Grace asked.

David looked over at her and smiled. Grace sensed peace within him.

"I'm done running. I did that the first forty years of my life, Grace. I'm not here to escape. I'm here to seek forgiveness for being a ruthless son-of-a-bitch to the man I love. I was vicious and nearly ruined him."

"Henry?" Grace asked.

David nodded.

"I see we have a lot in common," Grace said, leaning back and relaxing. She didn't know how confession was working for David, but it was making her want to take a nap. She had so much on her mind, so much she had to do on St. John.

On the right, The Last Chance Center was cordoned off with bright yellow tape announcing it was a crime scene. One lonely cruiser with blue lights flashing remained parked in front of it. A single cop sat in the driver's seat, windows up.

"You wouldn't think a place like this would attract murderers, would you?" Grace asked.

"Why not? We're here and we've both just admitted we're guilty of being pretty atrocious."

David took a left onto Centerline Road and after a short distance another sharp left. Grace could see a sweeping view of Cruz Bay and beyond to St. Thomas.

"Come in and have a lemonade. I'll show you my digs," David said pulling into a gravel driveway. Grace didn't have much else to do, so she stepped out into a light morning mist and approached the pink stucco cottage with a wraparound porch and blue corrugated tin roof. Her face must have shown her reaction to the color scheme.

"You're thinking a little cliché, the pink house, gay man?" David chuckled.

"Well, the thought did occur to me," Grace said. She liked David's ability for self-deprecation.

"It's all Cassie, the woman who owned it before me. Wait till you see the inside."

Indeed, thought Grace as she trailed David through a large open living/kitchen area with vaulted ceilings painted lime green. The walls were a warm shade of peach melba. Two roomy bedrooms off the living room were airy. Ceiling fans in all rooms were on high speed and yet the air remained still and heavy. And everywhere from the covers on the rattan chairs and couches to the bedspreads were bright floral fabrics screaming, "You have reached the Caribbean."

"I haven't touched a thing. Yet." David said, while Grace twirled in a circle taking it all in. One living room wall was covered with books, which she noticed were alphabetized. She couldn't stop herself from scanning to the H's and was pleased with the result.

"You're a big reader, I see," Grace said with approval.

"I am, but most of these were from Larry and Cassie, although I've gone through quite a few of them. Books I never would have expected to read keep jumping off the shelves onto my lap. Come see the pool," David said, leading Grace out the kitchen door to a deck and then through a hinged swinging door.

The pool was small but adequate with shady areas to sit in along the edges. It faced the driveway through a metal gate and fence on one side, which Grace guessed would keep the goats out. The other side had a sweeping view of Cruz Bay and St. Thomas beyond. A few tables with sun umbrellas and cushioned lounge chairs were scattered around continuing Cassie's propensity for lavish color.

"It should be gaudy, what she's done. But it's not. It feels happy, joyful, playful," Grace said without thinking. She noticed a small white structure at the rear of the pool with a periwinkle blue door and shutters, noteworthy because it wasn't bursting with tropical colors.

"What's that?" It reminded Grace of her garden shed but the

blue gave it an air of enchantment. The Victorian wooden t remained white.

"That was the start to what was going to be Cassie's art studio. She never got to finish it. Want to see?" David asked. Grace followed him around the pool where tiny raindrops made dents on the surface. Pots of flowering shrubs on wheels lined the way. Grace imagined David moving the plants in and out of the sun as need be. The moisture from the humidity lent a floral aroma.

David opened the door, which had a transom above it.

Grace gasped. Although it was only one large room, the studio appeared much larger with French doors opened on the opposite side suggesting the garden beyond was part of it. Everything had been painted a glossy bright white, from the floors to the ceiling, to several built-in cupboards lining the wall to the right. A small refrigerator and microwave were placed on a white marble counter. In the left corner there was a tiny bathroom with an exterior door to an outdoor shower. The only furniture was a long white Farmer's table with a chair and a white iron day bed.

The studio was a tabula rasa. A blank palette Cassie surely would have colored in, given the chance. Grace knew the opportunity had passed to her and she intended to seize it.

"I'll take it," she said to David who was leaning against the counter.

"Excuse me, Ma'am?" Grace detected a trace of a Southern accent for the first time. Ma'am was always such a giveaway.

"This is perfect. I'll rent it from you. You name the price." The only thing she thought she might need to add was a little lighting.

"Oh, this is too primitive for you, Grace. There's not even a television," David said pointing to the emptiness of the space.

"All the better. Now, let's have that lemonade you promised before we go collect my things at Caneel."

Chapter 7

Sabrina wasn't sure who looked worse. Evan Banks dozed on the lounge chair, a wiry man now skeletal, but with a peaceful expression on his tanned, still handsome face. Lyla's countenance told a different story, one of sleepless nights and fears about what was inevitable. Her hair poked out in as many directions as Sabrina imagined her mind was scattered. Lyla put on a brave smile to greet her.

Girlfriend's greeting had stunned Sabrina more than the deterioration of either Banks. She had expected her chocolate lab to pounce upon her and lick her face. Instead, Girlfriend had risen slowly from her place at the foot of Evan's lounge, wagged her tail, and lumbered cautiously over to her. Once Sabrina began stroking her, the dog let loose and sniffed and licked her. Sabrina understood she was being warned, "Don't think you can leave me behind casually and return on the same terms."

"I was hoping you might let her stay a little longer," Lyla said in a whisper sitting with Sabrina at the kitchen counter where they had shared many secrets over Margaritas and iced tea.

"Of course," Sabrina said.

"The kids are heading down this weekend from New York. Henry said they could stay across the road at Villa Mascarpone, which is wonderful. That way they can come see Evan when he's up to it and not worry about disturbing him. I can't thank you enough."

"You already have." Lyla and Evan had been the first to welcome Henry and Sabrina to St. John. They had offered unwavering loyalty and friendship when others on island would have preferred to see them exiled.

"How did the trip go, dear? I want to hear all about it," Lyla said.

"No, you don't. Not now." Sabrina wasn't sure who she was protecting from the ugliness of her story. She only knew that it was too painful to put into words. Having to describe what had happened meant having to experience the hurt again. Spitting out the details would only make her feel more undeserving of the love she desperately wanted but perpetually eluded her.

"You mustn't think you'd be burdening me. I still have room for you, Sabrina. Don't shut me out, dear," Lyla said, her eyes filling.

Sabrina marveled once again how she managed to inspire maternal feelings in women who did not give birth to her, yet she had been rejected by the woman who did when she'd abandoned her as a toddler. Even her maternal grandmother had been impervious to Sabrina as a child. She had no intention of wasting time speculating why Grace had come to St. John. It was too late. Grace wasn't getting another whack at her.

"Neil and I are over. My grandmother threw me out of her house, but now is on St. John. And I discovered the body of one of our workers who had been murdered yesterday," Sabrina said. "Those are the highlights, Lyla. They are all secondary to Evan right now. What can I do for you?"

"Nothing. I have more casseroles in my freezer and offers from friends to run errands than I know what to do with. Letting Girlfriend stay with Evan is more than I should ask."

Sabrina rose and bent to pat Girlfriend goodbye. The dog seemed confused about whether to follow her. Sabrina put out her hand and said, "Stay." Girlfriend obeyed, making Sabrina proud and disappointed all at once.

Across the road, she found Henry in the great room at Villa Mascarpone with a dry paint roller in his hand. "Oh good, you caught me before I started. Let's talk first."

"I love the color, even if she did pick it out," Sabrina said, referring to the villa owner, an obnoxious gourmet cheese shop owner from Chicago who was intent on making Villa Mascarpone look like an Italian villa. The warm shade of apricot caught the little light coming in from the double set of sliding glass doors on each side of the room.

Henry handed Sabrina a cold can of Le Croix pamplemousse seltzer, her favorite. She wasn't sure if it was the grapefruit flavor or the delicious French name for it she liked best.

"Austen called. The police asked him for the keys to our container next to The Last Chance Center. Like we would ever give keys to itinerant help," Henry said. He gave himself a mock dope slap to the forehead.

"Of course not, except maybe yesterday," Sabrina said, joining Henry's efforts to be light. "Remind me, which one of the other two workers is Austen?" she asked. She remembered hiring them, just not their names.

"The dude with the gorgeous blonde ponytail most women would kill for," Henry said.

Sabrina frowned.

"If Eric had the keys to the Ten Villas storage container, wouldn't the cops have found them on his body or nearby? By the way, I found my set right where they belong in my bathroom," she said.

"That's good. We'll need to decide what to do about changing locks. You have yours and I have mine, so we just need to find the set Eric had or call Love City Locksmith. I agree the keys should have been on his body, unless the person who killed him took them. I mean, why would the cops ask for keys if they already have them? That's pretty dumb," Henry said.

"Don't overestimate them. There was a recent study that showed the average cop on the VIPD is operating at the level of a fourth grader, Henry. But the real question is, why do they want the keys to our container?" Sabrina asked.

"Austen said they were asking him whether he knew if Eric was carrying a machete yesterday."

"Was he?" Sabrina didn't like where this was going.

"I don't know. I already told you, I was. I was the only one cutting away Catch 'n Keep from the exterior of the deck at Tide-away so the guys could paint it. I had them scraping as I cleared away the vines. I didn't see anyone else with a machete. They didn't need one," Henry said.

Sabrina's cell phone belted out her latest ringtone. She'd switched to Adele's

Turning Tables recently. The lyrics would never grow old. The caller I.D. said "anonymous," so she let it go to voicemail. Henry was frowning at the screen of his own phone.

"You are not going to like this. I know I don't," he said.

"What? Why?" She had hoped when she got back to her little piece of paradise, she could resume her unremarkable routine and lead an ordinary life. Every phone call, every text message seemed designed to prevent that.

"Your grandmother is moving into the studio behind David's house. I think he believes he's doing us a great favor. 'Don't worry about finding accommodations for grand-ma-ma. She's settling in here quite nicely.'" Henry rolled his eyes.

Sabrina put her phone on speaker and let the message from anonymous play.

"We need for you and Mr. Whitman to come to the police station immediately. Please bring the keys to your container and Mr. Hershey's employment file with you." Detective Hodge didn't bother identifying himself. He didn't have to.

"When will Neil be back? He's the only lawyer we've got," Henry said. Even though Neil wasn't admitted to the U.S. Virgin Islands bar, he'd been advising Sabrina and Henry informally when they had issues with the police. Neil had been granted a temporary courtesy admission during the Keating saga. The local cops respected Neil, which went a long way on an island where respect was more powerful than authority.

"I don't know. I haven't seen or heard from him in two weeks," Sabrina said. She finished her can of seltzer, which was no longer cold or fizzy.

"What? I thought you were spending three weeks exploring New England after you went to meet your grandmother. What happened?" Henry asked.

What had happened, Sabrina asked herself silently. How did she explain how betrayed she'd felt when she learned why he had chosen Vinalhaven as one of their destinations? They had a deal. The first week they would spend in Boston getting acquainted with her grandmother. The second week would be on an island in Maine that he selected. She got to choose the location for their third week. While she longed to return to Nantucket, Sabrina knew it would be impossible without the media finding out. Instead, she planned for them to tuck away on the obscure but nearby island of Cuttyhunk. It was the perfect plan.

"It doesn't matter, Henry. I learned I couldn't trust him," Sabrina said.

"He cheated on you? Neil? I can't believe it," Henry said. He shook his head emphatically. Sabrina worried he was thinking she couldn't inspire fidelity in a man. Her husband had cheated on her and now Neil.

"No, he didn't cheat on me. At least not that I know. Let's move on and figure out what we're going to do about the police summoning us."

"I get you guys had a falling out, but with Hodge back on the scene, everything else has to be secondary. You know how dangerous that man can be. I'm texting Neil. I hate going to the police station without him. It's even worse for you. We need an advocate," Henry said, his fingers flickering over the surface of his phone.

It was even worse for her, she knew. Nothing would ever change the fact that she had shot and killed her husband in Nantucket, not even an acquittal by a jury. The police would always view her with suspicion wherever she went. She needed Neil as much as Henry did. Like it or not, Sabrina knew Neil Perry wasn't out of her life for good just yet.

Chapter 8

At least she hadn't taken the keys to his truck, Neil Perry thought on the short cab ride to a local bar in Charlotte Amalie on St. Thomas where the owner let him park while he was away. Stranding him on Vinalhaven without a vehicle or an explanation had been enough. He was done with women. This time he meant it.

He'd meant it the last time and had kept to his word since coming to St. John, not an easy feat given the amount of women and alcohol available. But losing his only kid had killed any appetite he had for the kind of fun and carousing Neil previously had a reputation for.

Until he met Salty, who was even less interested in having a relationship than he was. With no agenda other than 'stay out of my way,' Sabrina Salter had become intriguing to Neil. Her nightly swims with her dog were the highlight of her day. She was fiercely loyal to friends and had bigger balls than most guys. He loved teasing her. He'd loved those rare tender moments they shared without words. He hadn't meant to fall in love with her. He just had.

But apparently it wasn't meant to be, so onward and upward, Neil thought as he got his pick-up truck and remembered he had purchased a round trip ferry ticket three weeks earlier. He headed to Red Hook where he hoped to avoid the afternoon commuter cluster and to catch the car barge. At least he was well rested after three weeks away.

Neil caught the three o'clock and celebrated by buying a beer for the trip. The ride was bit rough with the chop on the water, but he didn't care. He was happy to be home. He got off the barge and drove directly to Connections, the communications center in the middle of Cruz Bay where he found a parking space waiting for him, something that never happened in high season. He had so much mail, Cid, the owner and manager of Connections, gave him an empty box from Amazon and a little advice.

"You've got a lot of junk mail there, Neil, but I'd take the time to sort it thoroughly. You might just find something really important in there," she said winking. Neil could feel his face warming. Damn, that Cid didn't miss anything.

He threw the box in the back seat and drove the short distance to Bar None. He had chosen to stay open year-round because he wanted his bar to be a place where locals gathered, not just tourists. You can't be somebody's home away from home if you close two months of the year. He walked into a crowded bar, filled with locals and tourists, just like when he left.

"Boss is back," Mitch, his senior bartender, called out in good humor, grabbing a cold Guinness for Neil who took a spot at the bar and basked in the familiarity of what had become his home. He ordered a black and blue Beach Burger with bacon, American cheese and fries. He'd had so much lobster in Maine, he was almost sick of it. He knew he'd get a burger red enough to walk onto the plate at Bar None. So many restaurants were intent on protecting you from yourself.

"What's new?" he asked Mitch.

"I'm sure Sabrina told you about what happened to one of the guys who worked for them. Man, she and Henry can't seem to catch a break," Mitch said.

"Nope, don't know about it. Tell me." Mitch slid a plate with a burger piled high with fries in front of Neil. Neil was a little surprised Henry hadn't contacted him. He didn't expect to hear from Salty again. He looked at the screen on his phone. His battery was dead again. He hadn't paid much attention to his phone while he was away. He considered it part of his vacation. He pulled his charger out of his pocket and plugged in.

Mitch hesitated. "Um, a guy named Eric got killed up at The Last Chance Center."

"Did you know him?" Neil asked before taking a bite from where the bacon was sliding out of the bun.

"Yup. Kind of an asshole. Actually, he was a Masshole now that I think of it." Mitch used the term they had heard Sabrina and Henry and scores of other Massachusetts natives use to refer to jerks from their home state. "He liked to impress everyone with how smart he was, especially women. Although lately, the only one I saw him paying attention to was my friend Katie, who tends bar at the Tap Room."

"How did he get killed?" Neil asked.

"I'm not sure. I just heard it was bloody. Jay Callahan came in last night. He and Sabrina found the guy dead in one of the containers. Hey, how come you don't know this? Didn't Sabrina tell you? Where is she?"

"Don't know. End of story," Neil said, finishing the few fries on his plate. He looked at his phone, which had started to power up and saw a text from Henry waiting for him.

"Workers murdered. At VIPD w/SS. Can't leave. Worried. HELP!"

"Shit," Neil said, sliding off his stool. "I'll be in first thing in the morning, Mitch. Thanks for covering while I was away."

Neil went to his truck and reached into the back seat. He rifled through the mail he had picked up at Connections. Cid was right. There was a very official looking envelope from the Virgin Island Board of Bar Examiners with his name on it. He hadn't been sure when he signed up to take the bar exam if it was a good idea, which was why he hadn't told anyone, not even Salty. Man, if she thought he was holding back before, she would really rip him a new one when she heard this. He still didn't get why she had erupted when they were in Vinalhaven.

"What do you mean you were raised here?" she had asked after they had run into one of his cousins at The Harbor Gawker where they'd had lobster rolls.

"I mean this is where I come from, where I grew up. Why?" he had asked, wondering what the big deal was because Sabrina's tone made clear, it was a huge deal.

"When's the last time you were here?" she wanted to know. Women get so fixated with details, but he'd tried to remember.

"After high school, maybe once or twice. Once for my father's funeral. I can't remember," Neil had told her honestly.

"You mean you don't really come from L.A.? That was all bullshit?"

By then, he was getting annoyed.

"No, it's not bullshit. I lived in L.A. for years."

"But you don't really come from there, do you? You were raised in New England just like I was. You were on an island. I was on a peninsula. I've told you every bloody, gory detail of my miserable childhood, from my mother abandoning me when I was a toddler to my father's drunken neglect to my grandmother rejecting me to being taken in like a lost kitten by a kind woman. And you couldn't tell me you were taking me for a week for a return to your hometown? Where you knew people? Had family? Unbelievable." She'd stomped out of the restaurant. He'd followed her and argued in vain that he hadn't intended on shutting her out. But Neil had to admit he hadn't disclosed a material fact.

And he'd withheld information about taking the bar exam. But that was all, or mostly for her. Neil had felt impotent without a law license when she and Henry were under siege by the local police. He didn't intend to hang out a shingle. He liked being a barkeeper better than being a barrister any day, but if the occasion arose - and it seemed like it had once again - he'd be ready. He opened the envelope, pulled out the card and signed the back. Cornelius M. Perry, Attorney at Law. Salty would have a hissy fit when she discovered he hadn't disclosed his real first name.

Chapter 9

Sabrina sat on the plastic chair next to Henry in the waiting room at police headquarters. For a fairly new building, it was showing signs of aging prematurely. Cracks in the concrete floor and walls, paint peeling, and buzzing fluorescent lights lent a desperate atmosphere to the joyless building. They had come as soon as they'd received the message from Detective Hodge, although they hadn't yet been given a personal audience with him. As instructed, Sabrina had taken the key to the Ten Villas storage container and given it to the desk officer, who manned the lobby. She and Henry had been flattening their butts for over four hours. The only productive thing she had been able to accomplish was to text Love City Locksmiths to see what the chances were they could change every lock in each of their ten villas, plus in their own private residences and those entrusted by friends, as soon as possible. Sabrina knew the prospect was slim and that "ASAP" was a joke in island time.

There wasn't even a copy of *The Tradewinds* on the white plastic coffee table to peruse because the only weekly newspaper on island had recently gone digital. Sabrina didn't want to read it on her phone for fear she'd run out of juice and have no connection to the outside world. She and Henry didn't dare to talk candidly for fear their conversation could be overheard. They still hadn't had the chance to update one another about their respective adventures during the past few weeks. Even when Austen and Tyler, their other crew members, had emerged from behind the closed door that Sabrina knew from experience led to the interrogation room, they had carefully chosen to talk only about what task the two workers should tackle next.

"Head out to Villa Mascarpone and finish the interior painting. We've got Lyla and Evan's family coming in soon," Sabrina said. She wished she could ask them what had gone on during their interviews.

Sabrina expected she and Henry would be next to be interviewed, but another half hour passed before the door opened. Instead of someone summoning them inside, a young woman with pixie blonde hair in a tank top and jean shorts emerged. Her feathery earrings bounced as she walked over extending her hand to Henry, who stood to greet her.

"Katie, nice to see you again. Sabrina, you remember Katie Foster. Katie loaned her Suzuki to Eric yesterday so he could get to work." Sabrina nodded, getting the connection, also appreciating that the police were moving their investigation along more quickly than she'd come to expect. The Virgin Island P.D. was slow in more ways than one.

"Henry, I hate to ask here and now, so soon after Eric's passing, but can I have his job? I'm really experienced at painting inside and outside. I worked during summers when I was in college for professional painting companies. I'm also awesome at landscaping. I really could use the money. Bartending tips suck this time of year," Katie said. Sabrina was amazed how Katie managed to speak her spiel without taking a breath. She had that annoying habit common in younger people where their inflection rose at the end of each sentence, suggesting a statement was a question. Sabrina remembered how much the television station in Boston where she had been a meteorologist disdained the practice.

"What about your bartending job? Would you have to leave early to get to it?" Sabrina asked. She wasn't about to complicate life any more than it already was for a part-time seasonal worker, although it would help them complete their punch list.

"I don't have to be at the Taproom until 5:00 and they've cut me back to three nights until November," Katie said looking from Sabrina to Henry like a kid trying to play one parent against another.

"When could you start?" Henry asked.

"Right now. I don't work tonight," Katie said, her eyes widening at the prospect of getting Eric's job.

"Okay, head out to Villa Mascarpone where two other guys are painting. Do you know Tyler and Austen?" Sabrina asked.

"Sure. From The Taproom. Tyler rented one of my rooms for a short while," Katie said. She took a scrap of paper with the villa's location from Henry and gave him her cell phone number.

"I'm not sure that was smart," Sabrina said after Katie rushed out. "We don't know how connected she was to Eric, do we?"

"No, but at least we'll get some painting done and maybe we can pull some information out of her about Eric," Henry said. "I feel like we're missing something here. Why are they making us waste our time waiting instead of just telling us to come back later?"

The door to the right of the duty desk opened. Detective Vernon Hodge strutted over to Henry and Sabrina.

"I'll take you first, Ms. Salter. You shouldn't be nearly as long as Mr. Whitman. Do either of you have counsel?" Hodge asked. Sabrina cringed at the nasal tone to his sarcastic question. He knew how scarce lawyers were on St. John and took full advantage of it.

"Counsel? Why would I need counsel? I only found the body," Sabrina said. She knew she shouldn't babble but something about Hodge inspired her to chatter constantly.

"Right. The one that was killed with your partner's machete."

"Who was killed with what machete?" Neil Perry's voice boomed through the waiting room as he entered shaking rain off himself like a wet mutt. Sabrina felt her shoulders drop with relief and put her personal emotions aside. She had developed a gut instinct for survival, which she claimed was her birthright.

"Ah, Mr. Perry. No concern of yours. You just let the duty officer know why you're here and he'll take care of you." Hodge motioned for Sabrina to follow him. Sabrina waited to see what would happen next in the ongoing showdown between Hodge and Neil.

"Not so fast, Detective Hodge. Ms. Salter is my client. As is Mr. Whitman," Neil said.

"Since when do bartenders have clients?" Hodge chuckled.

"Since this," Neil said, whipping a small card from his pocket in front of Hodge's face. While it was too far away for Sabrina to read, Henry must have been able to decipher it because his face erupted into a huge grin.

"I'll need official verification of that," Hodge said, reaching to take the card from Neil who pulled it back from his reach.

"You may have a copy, sir, but I'll need to be present when it's made. Once you've gotten 'verification,' give me a call and I'll arrange for Mr. Whitman and Ms. Salter to come in."

Sabrina didn't know what was on the card Neil had shown Hodge. All she knew was it was a "Get Out of Jail" card and that worked for her.

Chapter 10

Henry held the umbrella over their three heads outside police headquarters while they decided where to meet. A steady downpour made Bar None impractical. Sabrina's cottage was too far, so she declared Henry's conveniently located condo once again the place to reconvene.

"Fine with me, Sabrina," Neil had said, sending a chill down her spine. She was no longer "Salty," spoken in a tease. He had called her Sabrina in a sardonic tone. She knew she hadn't played fair when she left him in the middle of Maine on an island without notice or a car. But dammit, she was the wronged party here. She drove in silence up Centerline Road passing the road where David lived and now hosted her grandmother. She turned onto Gifft Hill Road past the soggy scene of the crime and into Henry's complex, dreading the conversation that had to happen.

Henry had arrived ahead of her with Neil in tow. They assembled in the living room where they had gathered before on many occasions, most not as somber as this.

"How did the machete I was using yesterday morning end up being the murder weapon?" Henry asked, pacing the length of the living room.

"Whoa, buddy. Slow it down a little, will you? I can't help if I don't know what's going on. Have a seat and clue me in. Remember, you're among friends," Neil said, sinking into the chair next to him. Sabrina recognized the soothing tone Neil was using to calm Henry down. He'd used it on her successfully in the past. Now she wondered if that was how she had been lulled into trusting a man she obviously didn't know.

"Before we go there, what was the card you showed Detective Hodge, Neil?" Sabrina asked.

Neil sat quietly, then pulled it from his pocket and handed it to her.

Sabrina read the words, "Cornelius M. Perry, Attorney at Law, U.S. Virgin Islands." It was dated one week earlier. That meant Neil had studied for and taken the bar exam sometime earlier without ever mentioning it to her. He'd told her he cared about her, shared her bed, whispered "love you" to her, albeit so softly it could barely be heard. But he had never shared that his real first name was Cornelius, even after teasing her about why she was named Sabrina and nicknaming her Salty. He was a fraud.

Her hands shook as she handed Neil back the card.

"I guess there's even more about you I didn't know, Cornelius," she said, embarrassed by the hiss in her voice. Sabrina hated giving in to what she considered her catty side, but it was how she masked her vulnerability. If people didn't think she cared, maybe they would give up trying to hurt her.

"Stop. Truce. You two will have to knock it off until we deal with my situation. I'm sorry you've had a falling out. I don't know any of the details yet because I've been preoccupied with a murder, which apparently happened with my machete, making me a prime suspect, so that's where we need to focus. When I'm in the clear, you two can go at each other till your heart's content, but for now I am the priority," Henry said, his face paler than Sabrina could ever remember.

"Of course, Henry. I'm sorry," she said. Having been a murder suspect on island had been a terrifying experience for her. She should be empathetic, not bratty.

"Let's start with a summary of what's gone on," Neil said. Henry recounted the events of the past thirty hours in a few sentences. It had been that simple, Sabrina realized listening to him.

"Okay, that's sounds straightforward based on the little you know. But there are gaps, Henry. That's what the cops are filling in. We need to do the same. Let's do a timeline and a list of people who are involved, even tangentially," Neil said. Sabrina couldn't help but admire how organized he was. Neil definitely had the cognitive skills of a lawyer. He could distill a cloud of seemingly unconnected circumstances into a cogent set of facts.

Sabrina grabbed a pad of paper and a pen out of Henry's kitchen junk drawer and handed them to Neil.

In less than half an hour, Neil had recorded what they knew and what they didn't. Two uncontested facts glared at them: Henry owned the machete that killed Eric and he had no solid alibi.

"Who is this guy anyway? Eric's older than the average seasonal laborer, smarter by your observations, and a little too smooth to be on the Ten Villas crew. Why was he here? Where did he come from?" Neil asked.

"Allerton. We forgot to mention that he comes from Sabrina's hometown in Massachusetts," Henry said. "Although we don't know where he was before he arrived on St. John."

"Allerton? How can that be? How many people from a skinny little peninsula south of Boston can land on a tiny Caribbean island? Are you sure you don't know him?" Neil asked, looking at Sabrina.

She was about to go off on him, but stopped when she saw Henry looking at her, wanting her to be able to make sense of what seemed like a tragic farce. She hesitated, thinking back to the day when they interviewed Eric and she'd overruled Henry's objections to hiring him. It was just a few weeks before her departure to New England and she'd been distracted by concerns about her trip. Had she missed something familiar about Eric? It had been years since she'd lived in Allerton. She hadn't even attended the local public high school there. It had taken her a few minutes to recognize her former classmate Heidi, who worked for her grandmother, when she'd met her on her trip to New England. People changed. They go bald, get fat, lose pimples, get glasses.

"I only met Eric when Henry and I interviewed him. We've looked at his job application. It only gives a local address and lists his experience. There's nothing more than that and his cell phone number. I didn't know him before as far as I can remember. Sorry," Sabrina said.

"Could your grandmother have known him? I know that's stretching it, but her assistant was also from Allerton," Neil said. "It might be worth giving her a call, if she'll speak to me."

"No need to call. We can just drop by," Henry said, getting up from his chair.

"My grandmother is on St. John, Neil. She's staying in David's guest cottage," Sabrina said. She wasn't going to be able to avoid meeting Grace a second time.

Chapter 11

Neil was grateful the day was over. He could head on home to his trawler in Coral Bay where he would have a nightcap, then crawl onto a berth and let the waves rock him to sleep. They had agreed contacting Grace Armstrong first thing in the morning made more sense than besieging her that evening.

It had been rough seeing Salty. Add that to the mess Henry was in, and Neil wasn't sure why any of them believed St. John was the answer to their problems. He'd felt like a shithead when he handed Salty his new bar card. Was he shifty? Incapable of emotional honesty in a relationship? His ex-wife Sandra would say so. After being married to him for almost twenty years, Neil supposed she should know. But it had felt different with Salty. He thought they got each other without having to engage in endless dialogues about who had wounded them and how they'd been maimed.

Neil rounded the corner at Bordeaux Mountain wishing it were light enough for him to delight in the sight of Coral Bay below. He was home, thank God, even if it was to another murder and miserable weather. He had no clue about how he was going to bail Henry out of this one. Henry owned the murder weapon, his prints were all over it, and he had no alibi. Henry seemed to think the grocery store receipt he had that showed when he'd been at the store to buy the ingredients for the hors d'heurves he made for Grace Armstrong was a plausible alibi. Neil knew the cops would say Henry had plenty of time to shop, cook, and kill Eric.

Neil pulled into the drive passing Skinny Legs, tempted to have a drink, but that would mean making small talk and he had no room for it tonight. He just needed to be left the hell alone so he could refuel and fortify for the next day. He parked, lifted the box of mail and his duffel bag out of the back seat, and walked over to his dingy. When the motor turned over first try, Neil decided his luck had changed.

Within minutes, he pulled up to the *Knot Guilty*, the trawler he called home. He tied up the dingy, detecting a faint fragrance that didn't resemble the odors he normally associated with living on Coral Bay. The rain had turned into a light mist, a temporary respite Neil knew after spending several hurricane seasons on St. John. He flung his bag and then the box onto the deck and climbed aboard.

He wasn't sure why he knew someone had been onboard, but he did. Living in such small quarters after having grotesquely oversized homes in L.A., Neil had developed his own version of being a minimalist, which meant having few possessions. If he kept something, it was because it made his life better.

Nothing looked askew in the rear cabin of the boat, which he had converted into a study cum minibar. He'd put a couple of old leather chairs salvaged from an ancient courthouse on St. Thomas in the middle. Neil checked the minibar, thinking an intruder would hit it first but it was well stocked. He noticed a bottle of Gordon's gin, something he stocked at Bar None for the cheap gin and tonic drinking crowd but would never bring into his own home.

Neil hit the switch for the light for the small galley, which was neater than he remembered leaving it. He opened the refrigerator and found six containers of fruit yogurt. Yogurt disgusted him. So did the notion that someone had inhabited his tiny piece of the planet. The smell he had noticed while on the dinghy grew stronger as he approached the front stateroom. The curtain he never used covered the door. He was pretty sure he would find Goldilocks or some drunken bum from Skinny Legs sleeping in his bed, but just in case it was some armed robber, Neil slowly drew a crack between the two curtain panels.

Sure enough, it was Goldilocks, fast asleep on his berth, her blonde curls on his pillow. Her painted toes peeked from under the sheet. Browned calves made the white sheets look whiter. What the hell? All he wanted was a nightcap and his bed. Alone.

"All right, Missy. Up and out with you. I don't know who you are, but if I have to, I'll call the cops and find out soon enough," Neil said loud enough for Goldilocks to hear, but hopefully not to wake his floating neighbors.

She sat up suddenly.

"What? Oh, it's you," she said, resting her head back against the pillow.

"Wait a minute. Don't you dare go back to sleep. I want you out of here," Neil said, caring less about his neighbors than he had earlier. The woman wasn't as young as her blonde curls had led him to believe at first. The faint lines on her tanned face suggested she was fortyish. She looked vaguely familiar to him. Probably some barfly from Bar None who overheard he was out of town and took advantage of his housing vacancy. Squatting was the companion sport to couch surfing on St. John.

He could smell booze coming from her, combined with the sweet smell he'd caught earlier. Perfume made him sneeze. He'd been glad Salty didn't wear it. He wondered if he should leave and let her stay until morning. He'd always advised his male clients to be wary of situations in which they found themselves alone with women whom they didn't know well who had been drinking. But where would he go? Not to Salty's for damn sure. She'd throw him into that new pool of hers. Henry was on the edge. Everywhere else was closed or closing. Hell, he shouldn't have to go anywhere. This was his boat. His home.

"You need to get up and be out of here in five minutes or I'm calling the cops," he said leaning toward the woman, careful not to touch her.

"That's silly. You know the cops don't come to Coral Bay, Neil."

Her use of his name startled him, although he still couldn't remember her. He'd pretty much had been on his best behavior since arriving on St. John, so he didn't think she was someone he had a connection to. Her voice, smoke tinged and sexy, was vaguely familiar.

She sat up again, pulling the sheet up to her neck, and looked at him straight on.

He got it. The woman he and Sabrina had lunch with on that awful day after Grace Armstrong threw them out her front door. She had been Grace's personal assistant and had come to pick up her final check during Sabrina's aborted introduction to her grandmother. Neil tried to recall her name and understand what in the name of God she was doing on St. John in his bed.

"Why are you here? Remind me, what's your name?" Neil said, stunned and disarmed.

"I'm hurt you don't remember me. I'm Heidi. Remember? The woman you invited to visit you on St. John," Heidi said. She feigned a pout Neil knew was not genuine.

"Look Heidi whatever your last name is, I did not invite you to stay on my boat," Neil said, frustration creeping into his voice. He hated game playing with women, which was why he had been drawn to Salty.

"You did too. When I told you I'd love to see your boat if I was ever in Coral Bay, you told me 'Any time.' So here I am and this is how you welcome me?" Heidi's indignation compounded the absurdity of her affront. Neil struggled to remember more about Heidi. All he could muster was that she and Sabrina went through grammar school together and that she babbled throughout lunch. Sabrina hadn't recognized her until Heidi had reminded her of their connection.

"How long have you been here, Heidi?" Neil asked. The lawyer in him wanted a concrete answer to a concrete question.

"Oh, awhile. I've kept it nice and neat. I even cleaned inside the microwave and toaster oven. You get a lot of bugs down here, don't you?"

"Why are you on St. John, Heidi? You can't stay here on my boat," Neil knew it sounded more like a plea than a statement.

"It's just really hard to find a place to stay at this time of the year. Even Sabrina's company shuts down for a couple of months. I wish you guys had warned me." Heidi's voice dropped to underscore her innocence. Neil was beginning to remember their lunch.

Before her grandmother had summarily dismissed Sabrina, they had been interrupted by Heidi's appearance in Grace's library overlooking Beechwood Harbor. Grace had been indignant when Heidi entered unannounced. She demanded Heidi return her keys, which Heidi dangled until Grace handed her a check. On her way out the door, Heidi gave a parting shot to Grace Armstrong.

"You might not remember me, Sabrina, but we went to grammar school in Allerton together. I'm Heidi Montgomery, legally Heidi Hershey, but I never use my married name. Too many jokes about Swiss chocolate. I'm a professional woman and need a name that sounds more respectable."

Grace had shoed Heidi out the door admonishing her not to return. Grace then turned to Sabrina and Neil and demanded they leave. After Neil raced Sabrina away from her grandmother's brutal rejection, they found Heidi waiting for them in the driveway. She invited them to join her for lunch to "catch up." He had persuaded Sabrina to go, even though she was decimated by Grace's banishment. Neil figured they might learn more about Grace and why she had refused to acknowledge Sabrina from Heidi.

Neil looked at the woman who had shared some of Grace Armstrong's secrets with them, none of which helped Sabrina understand her screwed up family any better. He realized he hadn't appreciated what a lunatic Heidi was that day.

"Are you here for a vacation because hurricane season is no time for that."

"I told you I was looking for a place to start my own business, Neil. It turns out St. John is the perfect location," Heidi said, lowering herself back onto the pillow and closing her eyes. "We'll have to continue our conversation in the morning. I'm too tired to talk more right now." Heidi rolled over onto her side so that her face was against the wall.

Neil clenched his fists and then closed the curtains. He backed up into the galley and grabbed a glass. He opened the fridge and took a handful of ice cubes from a bag in the freezer and threw them into the glass.

In his study he poured a triple Widow Jane bourbon and sat back on one chair elevating his feet on the other, settling in for what was sure to be a long night after an even longer day. It confounded him how a man who had sworn off women ended up losing the one he loved, found another in his bed, and had to face a third, a crusty octogenarian, the next morning.

Chapter 12

Sabrina decided Henry needed company but knew he wouldn't admit it.

"Sleepover?" she asked once Neil had left Henry's condo. "Lyla texted the power is back out over in Fish Bay. I'm glad she and Evan have a generator." Sabrina rarely used her a/c, but tonight would have been an exception, it was so bloody still and hot.

When they first arrived on St. John, Sabrina and Henry would have marathon movie nights. Platonic friends who arrived wounded and lonely, they would gather to watch a couple of movies and eat fancy food their villa guests left behind. Neither of them knew anyone on island. The longer they lived on St. John, it seemed life grew more complicated. She and Henry had abandoned some of their simpler pleasures like movie nights.

"Please. The generator here is one of the reasons I pay extortionist rates for my condo fee," Henry said, looking relieved. Sabrina feared the wrinkles in his forehead would become permanent, something Henry would not tolerate well.

"Breakfast for dinner or grilled cheese?" she asked, pulling up the menu from prior sleepovers in her head.

"Breakfast for dinner. We had grilled cheese last night. Not that it was very good. How David can screw up grill cheese..."

They walked into the kitchen together.

"Are the Red Sox playing?" Sabrina asked. If they were, no further discussion about the evening's entertainment was needed. The Red Sox always preempted old movies.

"No. Cinderella?" Henry asked.

"Yes. Drew Barrymore or Lily James?" Sabrina and Henry were closet Cinderella movie freaks. Sabrina attributed their addiction to the isolation of island living.

"Can't deal with *Ever After* tonight. Too sad. Lily," Henry said. He stepped over to the section of his kitchen set up as a bar, while Sabrina opened the refrigerator and took out eggs, cream, butter, and a chunk of cheddar cheese.

"Screwdrivers or whiskey sours?" Henry asked.

"Whiskey sours for sure." Movie night called for retro cocktails. Sabrina hoped Henry was finding their exchange as comforting as she was. She was concerned about Henry and the inference finding his machete was the murder weapon conjured. She was furious Neil had concealed his real first name and that he had studied and sat for the bar exam without sharing it with her. She was sad because it would have been such fun calling him "Cornelius" when he called her Salty if their relationship hadn't gone south. If he could just talk openly and seriously once in a while and have an adult conversation instead of constantly bantering and teasing, they might be together still.

"Agreed. I need to belt one down before I call your grandmother." He pulled out a bottle of Jameson. "Grab me the cherries, will you?"

Sabrina found the cherries and then reached for some sausages and English muffins in the freezer. She handed Henry the jar and then placed the sausages and muffins on the griddle on the stove on low. She walked over to the kitchen counter where Henry was sitting, looking at his phone.

"Do you think your grandmother might really know anything about Eric?"

"It's worth a try, Henry. You might as well take advantage of her being here. I'm okay with it, if you're worried about upsetting me," Sabrina said. She slid onto a stool and took the first divine sip of the cold tart cocktail Henry made better than any bartender on St. John, which said a lot.

Henry tapped his fingers on his phone screen, putting the phone on speaker, so Sabrina could hear it ringing. She started at the sound of her grandmother's voice, which she'd only heard once before.

"Grace Armstrong. Please leave a brief message."

Henry left a rambling message, telling Grace he'd like to talk to her with his attorney about some information she may have that would be helpful to him and asking her to return his call "ASAP." Sabrina's relief when Grace didn't answer was palpable. She returned to the stove, liberally buttering the English muffins, and placed them back on the hot griddle below the sausages that smelled faintly of maple syrup. She had loved breakfast for dinner as a kid. Ruth, her surrogate mother, had owned a diner and made breakfast a feast.

A ping interrupted her memories. Henry looked down at his telephone screen while simultaneously emptying his glass.

"Cannot talk right now. What kind of information are you looking for? Who is your attorney and why will he be present?" Henry read aloud to Sabrina.

"Damn, your grandmother is tough and quite a techie for her age. I'd better answer her questions if I want her to help."

Sabrina began scrambling eggs furiously. The woman who had rejected her for four decades had dared to invade Sabrina's island and was now calling the shots.

"I will see you and Neil Perry at my new home at 10:30 tomorrow morning after I meet with Sabrina here at 10:00." Henry read Grace's statement as if it were a question.

"Do you have a meeting with her at 10:00? What's she

talking about?" Henry asked, looking up from his phone screen. He grabbed the shaker out of the refrigerator to refill both of their glasses.

"No. She's telling you that I have to meet with her as a prerequisite for her meeting with you and Neil." Sabrina noted how quick and clever her grandmother was with mixed feelings. Grace's self-assurance and technical adroitness irritated her, yet she admired both and hoped they were hereditary.

"Well, that's bullshit. I'm not throwing you under the bus," Henry said.

Sabrina reached for his phone on the counter and tapped in the words, "Fine, see you at 10:00. SS"

Henry looked at the sent message.

"What are you doing?" he asked while Sabrina returned to the stove and poured the eggs into a warm buttered skilled. She sprinkled grated Cheddar cheese on top, breathing in the comforting smell of melted butter and memories of Ruth.

I, Sabrina am not afraid. I, Sabrina, am fearless. The words Ruth had ingrained in her that first night when she rescued four-year-old Sabrina down off a roof from a ladder rang through her head. A night that had changed her life forever.

Grace Armstrong would meet the granddaughter she had tossed out of her Beechwood mansion three weeks before. The granddaughter who was no longer afraid of her. The fearless one.

"So, tell me," Henry said. Sabrina knew she couldn't postpone telling Henry about that horrible morning when she and Neil had appeared at Grace's front door. The heavy oak carved door was so richly stained and polished that Sabrina could almost see her reflection in the sheen. Dressed in her carefully chosen Beechwood appropriate Talbot's outfit, Sabrina stood erect when Neil had knocked at the door.

It swung open almost immediately, startling Sabrina who was standing so close to Neil she could feel the heat from his body.

"You're early. I wasn't expecting a pair," the petite blonde matron had said, opening the door for them to enter.

"We prefer to think of ourselves as a couple," Neil said. Sabrina observed he was wearing that charming grin most women found impossible not to return. Not Grace Armstrong.

They followed Grace through an impressive entrance hall with a stone floor covered by a deep blue hexagonal Persian rug. A bouquet of hydrangeas in a bowl on a mahogany table in front of a mirror next to an umbrella stand caught Sabrina's eyes. She had always loved hydrangeas, especially in her garden in Nantucket. They moved forward into a huge room with floor to ceiling French doors that overlooked a pool surrounded by lush gardens and beyond to the Atlantic Ocean Sabrina had spent her youth swimming in. To the left was an enormous fieldstone fireplace with floor to ceiling bookshelves on each side crammed with books spilling off the shelves. To the right, Sabrina saw a huge desk cluttered with pens, notebooks, papers, and more books. Paintings covered the wall. A floral chintz sofa sat in the middle of the room beside a matching stuffed chair with an ottoman in front of it. One night when she was in her teens, Sabrina had spied upon her grandmother sitting in that chair.

Sabrina's eyes had darted throughout the room searching for photos of her mother. She almost tripped over an open cardboard box filled with multiple copies of the same book, "Beach House Destiny."

"I won't pay wages for two of you. If you want to split the work, that's your business," Grace was saying to Neil.

"You've misunderstood, Ms. Armstrong," Neil said, when another blonde woman had appeared in the doorway.

Sabrina turned to Henry to explain. "It seems I went to grammar school with her in Allerton. I didn't remember her. She apparently worked for my grandmother and had recently been fired. Before I knew it, Grace insisted that Heidi give her the keys she was jingling and leave. Heidi told her she wouldn't leave without her severance pay. Grace went to her desk to get an envelope, when Heidi looked at me and recognized me. Grace returned with the envelope just in time for Heidi to shriek, " 'Of course, Sabrina Salter. You're Grace's long-lost granddaughter.'"

"Neil tried to introduce us, but by then Grace had freaked out and was screaming for us all to leave."

Sabrina poured what was left in the whiskey sour pitcher into their glasses, careful to share evenly between them.

"Honey, I'm sorry. That's awful," Henry said. Sabrina saw his eyes were moist.

"Then we had lunch with Heidi who told us my grandmother was a 'bitch on wheels' to work for and that she had been writing romance novels under a pen name for years." Sabrina ate the orange slice at the bottom of her glass, handing the cherry to Henry. Bing cherries were delicious, but Maraschinos looked better than they tasted.

"What's her nom de plume?" Henry asked with a slightly drunken French accent.

"Eliza Higgins," Sabrina said.

"Beach House Destiny? Your grandmother wrote Beach House Destiny? Be still my heart."

"Henry, are you coming out of another closet? One for trashy beach readers?" Sabrina asked.

"This one I'm guilty, as charged," Henry said, blushing.

September 4, 2017

Hurricane Irma

Latitude 16.8N
Longitude -52.6W

805 miles from St. John

Chapter 13

Neil left Heidi a note telling her to be packed and ready by 9:00 if she wanted a ride to Cruz Bay with him. He left her to figure out how to get to the dock. She'd managed without him until now. In any event, he told her she was to vacate the premises or he'd be charging her with trespass.

He headed over to Pickles for coffee and breakfast and to grab a newspaper, returning to his pre-vacation morning routine. He ran into Crustacean, who slapped him on the back and welcomed him home.

"Dude, where you been?" asked the man with a long white beard and a faded red bandana wrapped around his head. Crustacean had been living in Coral Bay since the 70's. No one remembered why he was called Crustacean or what his real name was. He could play a mean banjo and often did at open mike on Wednesday nights. He was probably the smartest person on St. John. At least it seemed that way on Trivia Night.

"I spent some time up in Maine. I hear you killed someone over at the Last Chance Center while I was gone, Crusty. What's up with that?" Neil laughed, hoping to cajole some information about Eric's murder out of Crustacean, who was the best source for local news in Coral Bay.

"Yeah, man, I heard about that. The guy was a know-it-all. No loss. He didn't spend much time in Coral Bay."

Crustacean continued to work his way through a stack of chocolate chip pancakes.

"You know anything about him? Like why people didn't like him?" Neil asked. All he knew was that Henry hadn't wanted to hire Eric when he and Sabrina were trying to get out of Dodge and head for New England. Sabrina had insisted Eric was okay for the job they were hiring him for. He doubted Grace Armstrong knew him, but since she was on island, it was worth a try. Crustacean's insights about Eric might be helpful.

"Besides him being an arrogant, pretentious asshole, no." Crustacean picked up his own copy of the Virgin Island Daily News Neil was sure had been retrieved from the trash and buried his face behind it. Crusty was done sharing, or so he thought.

"Hey Crusty, one more thing. Do you know anything about a woman staying on the *Knot Guilty* while I was away?"

Crusty dropped the paper enough so Neil could see his rheumy blue eyes reddened by more Buds than Neil would ever sell at Bar None.

"You mean the desperate blonde? Just that she drinks way too much. Doesn't know how to pace herself. I thought she was your cousin, man. She's just about had her ass carved into a stool at Skinny Legs since she got here."

"Not my cousin. Just a squatter," Neil said, resenting Heidi even more. His egg and bacon with cheese on a Ciabetta roll arrived, a miraculously simple breakfast he appreciated after he'd been fed more Maine blueberry pancakes soaked in Vermont maple syrup in the past week than he'd eaten in his whole life. The fact that he was sick of lobster was a statement about his family and its proclivity for excess. If only Salty had stuck around to enjoy the fun with his cousins.

After he'd soaked the last of his roll into the egg yolk and downed the final sip of coffee in his mug, Neil was sufficiently satiated to face Heidi and the rest of his day. He figured the "interview" with Grace would take less than five minutes and then the only hurdle remaining was Henry's interrogation by Hodge, whom he hadn't heard back from.

Neil put a call in to Mara Bennett who was a personal friend of Leon Janquar, the other ranking detective on the V.I.P.D. He needed to find out where Janquar was and why the arrogant and incompetent Hodge seemed to be in charge. Gavin Keating had filed a big fat law suit against Hodge and the department a few months earlier for misconduct. Neil had heard Hodge was under close watch. If Hodge served in any other police department in the country, he would be suspended, but things didn't work that way in the Virgin Islands. Neil's call to Mara went straight to voicemail. He left a message and proceeded to pick up his squatter.

She was waiting at Skinny Legs where the bar hadn't opened yet. Neil figured someone must have given her a ride in from the *Knot Guilty* since Heidi wasn't wet. Something about her irritated him.

"I thought you were moving here," Neil said looking at the one small suitcase on the bench next to Heidi, who looked even more worn on an overcast morning. He didn't want to consider how she'd look under the harsh brightness of the Caribbean sun.

"I am. I shipped the rest," Heidi said, handing Neil her suitcase as if he were her porter. Neil slung it in the bed of the truck and got into the driver's seat. Heidi hadn't closed the door when Neil took off and headed up the steep winding hills of Centerline Road at a clip meant to share his displeasure with the company he was keeping. Heidi grasped onto the handle above the passenger window until her fingers turned white.

"Where to?" Neil asked when he got to the intersection of 104. He pulled over in front of the Myrah Keating Smith Clinic so Heidi could instruct him.

"Hmmm, I don't know." Heidi said, sounding more stupid to Neil by the moment.

"Well, you don't want to go down Gifft Hill Road. Some poor bastard got himself killed with a machete there two days ago," Neil said, enjoying the fear in Heidi's eyes. He'd barely slept sitting up in a chair last night and resented Goldilocks commandeering his cozy berth.

"He got murdered? That's awful. With a machete? I thought St. John was one of the safe islands," Heidi said.

"So did Eric," Neil said, hanging his head in mock regret.

"Eric? Eric who?" Heidi asked.

"Eric Hershey. Why do you know him?" Neil asked. Then he remembered she was also from Allerton and her joke about Swiss chocolate. Shit.

"He's my almost ex-husband," Heidi said banging her head repeatedly against the headrest on her seat.

Chapter 14

Grace slept through the night for the first time in weeks. Although the cottage was warm, the small fan David had provided her created enough of a breeze to sweep from one end to the other. The constant hum soothed her until the power went off and then it went back on. The flow of electricity was as unpredictable as everything else on St. John.

David's initial reluctance to rent her the cottage studio quickly dissipated once Grace engaged him in errands and activities. They first fetched her belongings from Caneel Bay Plantation, where the staff seemed relieved to learn she had found new quarters. They assured her she could return as soon as they reopened in November. By then, Grace intended to be fully settled in permanent quarters.

Next, David had taken her to Mongoose Junction to shop for a few household necessities, even though he had graciously offered to lend her linens and other staples. But Grace had enjoyed picking up soft bamboo sheets at Nest, dishes and glasses with coastal themes at Portico, and rich tapestries at Bamboula. She bought lots of throw pillows, knowing she'd be sitting on her bed until she could purchase a reading chair and stool. Grace hadn't felt so alive in years. Coming to St. John had given her a fresh start. Whether her granddaughter would cooperate with her renaissance was another question.

After Grace's shopping excursion, she treated David to lunch at The Lime Inn, which he told her would soon join the list of other restaurants that closed during September and October. Sipping Isola Bellinis made with Prosecco and mango puree, Grace and David surveyed the menu like an old married couple.

"I think I'll have the Brie en Croute. It's too bloody hot to eat much more," Grace said. She gazed around her at the lime green open-air restaurant that was devoid of air conditioning and cooled only by overworked ceiling fans. There was no natural breeze.

"Not me. Pretty soon, there will only be a few restaurants open. I plan to eat like a bear and store my fuel for hibernation. I'll have the short rib burger with caramelized onions, cheddar cheese, and their secret sauce on brioche. Save some room. They have the best key lime pie on the island," David said.

"The grocery stores must stay open, don't they?" Grace had lived in one of the wealthiest coastal suburbs in Massachusetts since her marriage to Charles Armstrong where the best stores and restaurants flocked to vie for the patronage of the wealthy.

"Sure, but I don't cook."

"Then how do you survive?" Grace was shocked that a man in his forties didn't cook. Even Charlie, her late husband, had at least known how to grill.

"I eat out a lot. This is my first hurricane season here. It should be interesting," David said. He signaled the waitress to bring another round of drinks.

"Well maybe that's where I can be of help to you." Grace had loved to cook and entertain until she no longer had a family to care for.

"David, tell me what do you know about Sabrina?" Grace was embarrassed she had to ask a man she barely knew about her own granddaughter, but she had to start somewhere.

The waitress placed their meals in front of them. David took a bite of his short rib burger and groaned with delight. Grace wasn't certain if there really were any vegetarian men. Maybe some pretended, but that groan David had emitted upon his first bite seemed primal. She picked up an apple slice and spread some Brie on it, politely waiting for David's carnivorous orgasm to pass.

"I only know her through Henry and Neil. She's very bright, poised, and can be funny. I think she's kind and I also know she's been wounded. A lot."

Grace winced, knowing she was the source of many of her granddaughter's wounds.

"Can you be more specific?" Grace had to know as much as she could so she could try to make amends for her portion of Sabrina's pain.

"Well, you have to remember, I'm not in the inner sanctum. Henry will only see me occasionally for dinner or a drink at a public restaurant. I'm not invited to hang out with them at his condo or Sabrina's cottage. Even if I stumble upon them, I'm not necessarily invited to join them." David put his burger on his plate and stared at it. Grace felt guilty.

"You must be lonely," she said, reaching over and patting David's tanned hand. He nodded. Grace was learning more about David than Sabrina, but there was time.

"Henry did tell me about what happened with Sabrina's husband. You must know about that. It was in the papers everywhere, not just in Boston. And that Southern blonde screamer with the helmet hairdo on television was like a dog with a bone about the case," David said.

"Faith Chase." Grace had occasionally watched in horror when she could bear the guilt and shame. The rabid pseudo-journalist who pandered to the masses had made Sabrina's misfortune a nightly event, inviting her viewers to join the public lynching.

"The husband betraying her was the other bad part according to Henry. The son of a bitch was the only family Sabrina had and he cheated on her," David said, his eyes opening wider as soon as the words were out of his mouth. "I'm sorry, Ma'am. I didn't mean to say that."

"That's okay. We'll get along fine as long as you and I are honest and direct with one another, David. What about Neil? Do you know what happened between them? Did I cause their breakup?" Grace asked. She figured she needed to know what she had broken if she was ever going to fix it.

"Nondisclosure, I'd say." David took a big bite out of the middle of his burger. Grace suspected he hoped a full mouth might spare him more of her questions. But she could wait.

"Meaning what?" Grace had no idea what David meant or what Neil had done.

"Meaning, I think, Neil kept something from her. From what I've seen, if Sabrina sniffs even a whiff of concealment, she's done. She has no tolerance for anyone she can't trust. Neither does Henry. They don't distinguish sins of omission from those of commission."

"I guess that's why we're both screwed," Grace said.

Chapter 15

Sabrina met the Ten Villas crew at Villa Mascarpone, pleased to see all three had arrived and were holding brushes or rollers in their hands. She walked into the kitchen, put a pot of coffee on, and found a plate to place the lemon poppy seed muffins she had taken out of her freezer on the long table in the great room. The power had gone back on, but the muffins would never be the same after being refrozen.

"Hey, coffee break time. We need to regroup a bit here. Join me at the table," she called.

Katie arrived first, apricot paint spots already splattered on her tee shirt. She sat on a chair not designed for yoga with her long, tanned legs in lotus position. She was barefoot with a tattoo on her right ankle. Even though Katie was only about five years younger than her, Sabrina felt like her matronly aunt. She had barely known Katie before now, only to say hi to when she went to the Taproom for a drink or ran into her while grocery shopping at Starfish Market.

The one thing Sabrina did know about Katie was that the guy she had moved to St. John with about ten years before had dumped her rather dramatically. An artist and talented musician, Geoffrey had been playing open mike at Indigo Grill in Coral

Bay one night when a young female tourist offered to do a duet with him. They brought down the house with a spontaneous version of "Say Something," which by the end of the song had torpedoed Geoffrey and Katie's relationship. Katie was left with a half-built island shack and a stack of bills the next day.

"Everything working out okay with you and these two slugs?" Sabrina asked, gesturing toward Austen and Tyler who had joined her at the table.

"I'm working on straightening them out," Katie said with a half-hearted chuckle.

The two young men, who sat opposite one another, devoured the muffins within minutes. With Sabrina at the head of the table, it felt like a meeting of the board of directors.

"Guys, I want to say that I'm really sorry about Eric. I mean, I guess he could be a jerk, but still what happened to him-" Sabrina was cut off by Austen who was more animated than she'd seen since she met him.

"The dude didn't deserve to have his neck hacked by a machete, no matter how big an asshole he was," Austen said, shaking his head downing his coffee in gulps.

"Maybe he didn't deserve it, but it might be why he got himself killed," Tyler said, reaching for the last muffin.

Katie sat silently staring at the mug of black coffee she had yet to touch.

"Did the cops tell you that's how he died?" Sabrina asked, wanting to confirm what had been hinted at by Hodge, but not fully disclosed.

"Yeah, that's why they wanted us to identify the machete. It was in a plastic bag, but you couldn't miss Henry's initials on it." Austen said.

Leave it to Henry, fastidious about the care of his tools, careful not to let them walk away with the last person who borrowed them, he wrote "H.W." in black Sharpie on every tool he owned.

"Not that Henry had anything to do with what happened to Eric," Tyler said.

"Right. Henry had finished using it before Eric went to The Last Chance Center to get more primer," Austen said.

"Did you see if Eric took it?" Sabrina asked.

Tyler and Austen both shook their heads.

"Sorry I can't be of help. I wasn't there. I was only trying to get my car back so I could go to work," Katie said, finally taking a sip of her coffee.

"He was staying at your place, right?" Sabrina asked, hoping to invite some insight from her.

"Yeah, he had been staying on my couch. He had plans to open a business on island," Katie said.

"What kind of business?" Sabrina asked. Eric was such a blowhard, he was probably trying to impress Katie or buy time to pay his rent.

"He told us that, too." Austen moved his thumb in Tyler's direction.

"Yeah. He told us he was going to start an 'upscale tropical horticultural consultancy,'" Tyler said in a feigned aristocratic accent.

"Well, speaking of upscale businesses, let's get the work done here today and move on to the next villa tomorrow. I have to head into Cruz Bay and have a chat with the police myself. Let's keep each other up to date on the murder. It's too small of an island for someone to hide for long. I want everyone to be safe," Sabrina said, grabbing the empty plate and mugs off the table.

"Wasn't he from Massachusetts, Sabrina?" Tyler asked. Sabrina looked and him and wanted to say, "And your point is?" but didn't.

"Yes. There's no shortage of Massholes on St. John it seems," Sabrina said, ending the inquiry, but detecting an accusatory tone in Tyler's voice.

"He wasn't. A Masshole. He was an okay guy, just getting his shit together like everyone else who comes to St. John," Katie said. She sounded so solemn, Sabrina felt chastised for speaking ill about the dead.

"Fair enough, Katie. No one deserves what happened to him."

Chapter 16

Neil didn't stop driving for the wailing. Heidi continued to blubber the rest of the ride to Cruz Bay. He handed her the roll of paper towels he always kept under the front seat to use as tissues. After a few honks, Heidi resumed weeping, though more quietly now.

Neil knew he'd have to be gentler with her now. She was a much better source of information about Eric than Grace Armstrong. Usually, ex-wives were only too happy to dish about the cads who left them or behaved so badly they got dumped. From the amount of tears Heidi was shedding, Neil would bet money she was the dumpee.

"Heidi, let's get you a room at the Westin. I'm pretty sure there are vacancies. You can settle in there until you figure things out. I'm sorry I shocked you with the news about Eric. I knew where he was from, but I didn't connect him with you or that you had been married to him," Neil said cutting across Gifft Hill past the scene of the crime, which he didn't point out to Heidi. He drove past Henry's complex, hugging the slippery curves and hills with his pickup truck. He noticed how slick they were after a day of rain, which now had diminished into a fine mist.

By the time he took the left into the entrance to the Westin, Heidi's sobs had morphed into hiccups. She wouldn't be the first one to check into the hotel with hiccups, Neil knew. More than once, he'd to get a cab to take an inebriated patron to the hotel for the night.

"Sit tight. I'll go see what I can do about getting you a room. Do you have a credit card I can use?" Neil asked.

"I've got one coming. All I have is cash right now," she said, reaching into her purse.

"They'll want a credit card. You can pay me back what they charge you," he said through his teeth. He marveled how Heidi had managed to ingratiate herself into his life, but he needed to let it go. There were too many dots he had to connect without being distracted by her shenanigans.

Within five minutes, Heidi was settled into a room overlooking the pool and was ordering room service.

"I fell asleep before I ate dinner last night," she said to Neil who didn't need an explanation. He was an expert on how drunks forgot to eat dinner. That's why he served food at Bar None.

"Tell me a little about Eric," Neil said, sitting in a chair while Heidi lounged on the bed propped up against two puffy pillows. She started to cry again.

"We were going to make a go of it. I know we'd have made it. We just needed a new place to make a fresh start. And our own business, of course. That would work better this time too, but now he's g-ooo-nnnn-eee. Who would do this to him?"

"I'm sorry for your troubles, Heidi, I really am. Look, I've got an appointment I'm already late for. Why don't you eat, take a nap, and I'll come back this afternoon and check on you," Neil said, rising to answer the knock on the door.

"Okay. Maybe you could take me to dinner," Heidi said. Neil wasn't fooled. She was already working his sympathy.

He opened the door and let the man delivering room service

in. Neil couldn't imagine meeting Grace Armstrong could be worse than dealing with Heidi Montgomery.

Chapter 17

Henry paced up and down the hall that extended from the front door all the way to the living room in his condo. He wished he were wearing his Fitbit because he was sure he had already topped his record for steps.

Sabrina was on her way back from checking in on their work crew. Neil was due to arrive. Both were late. Henry hated being late. He'd been awake since 4:00 a.m. when the roosters started crowing. Normally he didn't hear them, but when he had finally fallen asleep after midnight, it was into a state a mere notch above dozing.

All he could think about was his machete. The words, "my machete," were incongruous with his old life. He had never seen, let alone used a machete until he came to St. John and encountered thick brush like Catch 'n Keep. He had borrowed a machete and found it effective, so naturally he bought his own. Henry liked to have his own tools and prided himself on taking excellent care of them, unlike the sloths they usually hired who would leave paint brushes soiled and tools outside to rust in the moisture. Of course he'd written his initials on all of his tools. He had tried to persuade Sabrina to do the same. "I'm anal enough as it is, Henry. Don't go encouraging me," she had told him.

Henry knew he hadn't given the machete to Eric. He must have taken it. Or someone else grabbed it, perhaps Tyler or Austen. Why would they do that? He couldn't picture Eric taking it just to mess with him. He was arrogant, but not mean. Unless he took it to use it, Henry pondered. He couldn't figure out why would Eric need a machete at The Last Chance Center.

Henry doubted Grace Armstrong would know anything about Eric. Neil was just covering his bases. It didn't seem enough to warrant Sabrina subjecting herself to a potential second round of rejection and humiliation.

He heard the door being unlocked and knew it was Sabrina. Thank God, they each had a set of keys and a spare, which he was now using. They shared keys to everything. Houses, cars, vans, gates. They knew each other's passwords, secrets, and inner demons. Sabrina's willingness to see her grandmother meant two things. The first was that she was truly the best friend he'd ever had. The second was that she thought he was screwed with the police because of the machete.

"There you are. Let's go. The cops just dropped the van off. I'll drive," Sabrina said not opening the door fully. She was wearing her "meet and greet" the villa guests at the dock outfit. Black sleeveless dress, black flip-flops, and large Jackie O sunglasses. On sunny days, she added a straw hat with a black grosgrain ribbon around the brim.

"We have to wait for Neil. He got delayed. He says he has some important information he should share before we go to David's to meet your grandmother. How crazy does that sound? We're going to my ex-boyfriend's to meet your grandmother, Cruella."

"I'm not waiting for him," Sabrina said, even as Henry could see Neil stepping behind her in the doorway.

"You already did, Sabrina," he said, using her proper first name, which sounded more like "bitch" to Henry.

"Good morning, Cornelius," Sabrina said.

Henry hated how these two could go at it. St. John wasn't big enough to contain the sparks they could raise.

"Okay, kids. Do I have to remind you again? This is about Eric getting killed with my machete and us finding out more about him so we can figure out who really killed him." Henry had dropped his voice just enough to convey how serious the situation was.

They filed down the hall to the living room. Henry decided against offering coffee. He wanted Neil to spit out his news and to head to David's to get the meeting over with. He knew he would be summoned to police headquarters again before the end of the day.

Neil sat at the edge of a chair, while Sabrina and Henry sank onto the sofa.

"Quickly, here's what I've learned. One, Mara Bennett emailed me to say that we are stuck with Detective Hodge for another day or so until Detective Janquar returns from the states. He took his daughter to her first semester at Mount Holyoke. He's staying with Deirdre and Sam Leonard."

Henry felt a moment of comfort. The Leonards were lovely people who had been guests at Villa Mascarpone. Deirdre had come to St. John to reclaim her children after their father had kidnapped them. Janquar had helped them. She and Sam were the kind of people who would reach out to return the kindness and help a kid from St. John adjust to an elite stateside campus. Deirdre and Sam both taught at Mount Holyoke.

"So we're stuck with Hodge for a few more days, but then Janquar should resume command?" Henry asked. He could end up arrested by then.

"Yes. Next, Heidi Montgomery is on island. I've just left her to check in at the Westin."

"Who's Heidi?" Henry asked.

"My grandmother's personal and professional assistant. The

one who came to pick up her severance check when I went to meet her," Sabrina said. "Why is she here?"

"I'm not exactly sure, but it sounds like it was to make a go at reconciling with her ex-husband," Neil said.

"Who was?" Henry's head hurt from the permutations the Allerton connection conjured.

"Eric Hershey," Neil said.

"Well, that's good news. We can get what we need to know out of Heidi. Now you don't have to go meet with Cruella," Henry said to Sabrina.

"We still want to hear from Grace. I don't suggest we keep her waiting. But you needn't join us, Sabrina." Neil stood and walked toward the hall.

"Now I need to fill you in," Henry said to Neil and explained how Grace would agree to meet with him only after she had a private meeting with Sabrina. He watched Neil's expression when he looked over at Sabrina. There was no disguising the admiration Neil had for her, even if they were at war with one another.

"You need to learn what you can from both of them. Let's go," Sabrina said. "I'll take the van by myself if you don't mind, Henry."

Chapter 18

Within three minutes, they reconvened in David's driveway. David stood in the front door with a mug of coffee in his hand waiting for them. Sabrina walked ahead of Henry and Neil, entering David's colorful living room, which looked to her like someone had bombed Georgia O'Keefe's studio. She could hear Henry gasp but couldn't tell if it was from admiration or shock.

"Cassie had quite a sense of color," David said, laughing.

"I'm getting kind of used to it," Neil said. Sabrina knew he was the only one of the three of them who had been to David's home.

"Where is she?" Sabrina asked, looking around. She could feel her respirations becoming shallower with anxiety as she waited once again for the moment she had rehearsed in her mind countless times. Meeting her grandmother. Her mother's mother. They would embrace and weep and forgive. They would scream and cry and blame. They would regard each other with unforgiving silence and turn away from each other.

But Sabrina had never expected Grace would summarily eject her and Neil along with her former personal assistant on that sunny Saturday just weeks ago. It had seemed so impersonal, it was worse than anything Sabrina had imagined.

"She's in the guest cottage, which was formerly Cassie's artist shed in the works. She talked me into renting it to her. She's not easy to say no to," David said. He sounded apologetic to Sabrina.

"You seem to have that problem with women," Henry said. Sabrina watched Henry glare at David. She knew he was referring to what Henry called David's gutlessness with his ex-wife.

"I'll walk you over," David said to Sabrina, pointing to a door at the back of the kitchen. Outside, Sabrina admired the pool surrounded by plants and chairs and chaises with bright cushions on them. He ushered her to the back of the pool toward a white shed with blue shutters.

"She's in there," David said. He placed a hand on her shoulder while pointing toward the periwinkle door with his other. Sabrina experienced a short rush of gratitude at the gesture sensing David knew how difficult this was for her.

Sabrina walked toward the door. Instead of knocking, she pushed it open. She wasn't going to ask permission from this woman to reject or abuse her ever again. Her grandmother was sitting behind a long white table with a laptop open on it. Grace looked almost like a child, small, sitting on a white chair. She wore a pair of white capris and a navy-blue Bar None tee shirt. She was barefoot. Her toenails were painted in playful sky- blue polish. She looked up as Sabrina entered the one room cottage.

Sabrina didn't speak. She had no intention of initiating a conversation she had no interest in. The time had come and passed for amends.

Grace was also silent. Her blue almond shaped eyes seemed to take in every detail of Sabrina. Sabrina didn't care. She no longer needed the approval of the grandmother she once longed for, fantasized about.

"Thank you for coming," Grace finally said in a voice lower than Sabrina expected or remembered from that morning in

Beechwood. She stood and pointed to a white plastic chair that matched the poolside furniture. "Please, sit down."

Sabrina sat, offering no words, hoping her face didn't belie the somersaults her belly was doing. She wanted to be cool, void of emotion toward her grandmother, who deserved nothing more. She tried not to notice that in her early eighties, Grace was beautiful. Her long neck, high cheek bones and vibrant blue eyes were reminiscent of Sabrina's blurred recollections of the mother who had held her, rocked her, and read to her decades before. It almost felt like an insult that Sabrina looked nothing like either woman. She was tall, with thick dark curly hair and eyes as green as the emerald island that claimed her as its own. Her father's daughter, people had said. Hugh Salter had a full head of black hair and dark brows the mark of the Black Irish. Where the porcelain skin and widow's peak he had shared with Sabrina came from remained a mystery Sabrina wasn't ready to unravel. Her mother's legacy was mystery enough.

"Can I offer you coffee or icedbn tea?" Grace asked. She was so formal, Sabrina half-expected her to ask, "Shall I pour?"

"No. No, thank you. You have exactly ten minutes," Sabrina said. She placed her cell phone on her lap with the timer on the screen. She wasn't about to let Grace convert their conversation into a tea party. She didn't even intend it to be a conversation. What Sabrina wanted from Grace was a monologue with answers about what happened to her mother, where she was, and why her grandmother had ignored her.

Grace wasted no time.

"I want to start by apologizing for my abominable behavior when you came to my home with Mr. Perry several weeks ago. There is no excuse for it. I was startled when my former assistant, Heidi Montgomery, burst into the house right after you arrived. I had fired her several days before and became unraveled when she let herself in through my back door. I thought she had returned all of her keys."

Sabrina watched Grace pause and look to see Sabrina's

reaction. Sabrina sat expressionless with her hands wrapped around her phone on her lap. It was a position she had learned well when she sat next to her defense attorney when she was on trial in Nantucket. No, Grace would have to work harder than this to break her.

"I was already stunned and then became totally dismantled when she said who you were. I couldn't think of anything but to get the three of you out of my house. I felt as if I were having a mammoth panic attack. I had many visions of what it might be like to meet you, Sabrina, but none of them were like that. I am truly sorry."

Grace hadn't been able to totally excise Sabrina from her world. She had thought about meeting her. Sabrina took small comfort in that but was insulted if Grace felt it was all she had to apologize for.

"If that's all you have to say, you don't need ten minutes. I think it's time you go talk to Henry and hold up your end of the bargain," Sabrina said. She was having difficulty reining in her rage. She had practiced many versions of the same speech. The moment when she would finally confront her grandmother and make her accountable for her heinous neglect after her mother had abandoned her when she was a toddler. Oddly, when she'd gone to meet her in Beechwood, it had been with an olive branch in hand. Sabrina had been inspired to attempt the reconciliation by Carmen Perez Pagan, a woman who had lost a daughter twice. Sabrina had gone to meet her aging grandmother before she ran out of chances.

"Of course, that's not all I have to say. I barely know where to begin," Grace said, her throat thick with emotion, her cheeks flushed.

"Well start at the beginning then and get on with it," Sabrina said. She was no longer able to mask her exasperation. Grace's eyes widened in dismay.

"It began long before you were born when I decided to join a writers group at my local library. Your mother was in her first year at Wellesley and I no longer felt needed. I met a number of local people who were aspiring authors, including your father. He was a talented short story writer and poet but wasn't able to support himself by writing. He'd come over from Ireland a few years before and had been a waiter, bartender, that kind of thing. When my husband, your grandfather, could no longer drive because he had lost most of his vision from a rare form of macular degeneration, I persuaded him to hire Hugh as a driver. Charlie was CEO of Blade and could have had a company paid driver even when his eyesight was 20/20, but he resisted hiring one until after he became ill because it was an acknowledgement that he was legally blind. Somehow hiring Hugh felt more like an act of charity than a concession."

Grace stopped and caught her breath. Sabrina was spellbound by what she had heard so far. She had no idea her rogue Irish father had been in a writers group with what he called her "callous, evil grandmother." She knew nothing more about Charlie than she had read in his obituary, which had been more about his role in Blade, the leading national razor manufacturer. Sabrina wanted to ask questions but knew it was better to let Grace go on at her own pace. She was mindful that Henry was also waiting to hear what Grace had to say and that his questions were more immediate than hers.

"I could take days telling this story, but I'll get on with it and let you decide if you want me to fill in the details. We hired your father and let him take the apartment over the carriage house that served as our garage. It never occurred to me that Elizabeth would find him attractive and fawn all over him like a schoolgirl, but of course, that's what she was. He was more than ten years her senior. When she came home for her summer break, I noticed she went out less often and would find her way near the garage ostensibly painting a seascape whenever your father was around. Did you know she was an artist?" Grace looked at Sabrina to see if she did. Sabrina nodded. About all she had from her mother were a few photos and a watercolor of Nantasket Beach.

"Elizabeth flirted shamelessly and from what I could see from the house, he was enchanted. When she dropped the boy she had been dating through her first year in college, I became concerned and planned to talk to her. She told me she was spending Labor Day weekend with some girlfriends. The last hurrah before she was scheduled to return to college. Your father had weekends off. I didn't put it together until they reappeared together on Monday night to announce they had eloped. She was nineteen years old." Grace reached for a glass of water sitting next to her laptop and took a sip.

"I know this part. Tell me something I don't know and make it fast. Henry needs to talk to you about something that is important and that isn't ancient history." Sabrina knew this wasn't fair. Grace didn't know what she had learned from her father. But it wasn't fair that Grace hadn't intervened and shared this information with Sabrina decades ago. Sabrina was terrified that if Grace managed to crack her open, the lifetime of grief and flattened fantasies she had struggled to contain would escape like the air from a child's balloon.

"Sure. I think they thought Elizabeth could simply move into the carriage house with Hugh, commute to Wellesley rather than live in a dorm, and carry on. She obviously didn't know her father well. He was livid. He told Elizabeth that she had made her bed and now she could lie in it. If she wanted to go to college, she'd have to figure out how with her new husband. That was it."

"What do you mean, 'that was it'?" Sabrina asked. The words were out of her mouth before she could stop them.

"I mean, Charlie was so furious, he relegated them to a life on their own, one that Elizabeth was hardly prepared for. We were quite wealthy. Charlie's family came from Beacon Hill. He went to Harvard. Blade was the largest shaving product company in the country and paid him more money than we could ever spend. We hadn't been able to have more children so everything we had or did focused on our Elizabeth."

This was her mother Grace was talking about. The mother Sabrina never knew. She was learning more in the short time Grace had been speaking than in the forty years before. It was a tease. The more she heard, the more she longed to know.

"They moved to Allerton. Charlie insisted we cut our ties with her. You have to understand. He was heartbroken. So was I, but I knew estrangement would only compound the pain. I had to sneak around to find out where they lived. It wasn't in a great area. I heard Elizabeth was working at Stop and Shop as a grocery cashier. I was terrified of seeing her there, but I would sit in the parking lot hoping to watch her walk in. I never did. I stopped seeing friends socially because I couldn't bear hearing about my daughter's life second hand. I found out she was pregnant from our mailman, who learned it from a carrier he knew in Allerton. Your father had gotten a job with the post office there."

Sabrina glanced at her phone. Grace had under a minute to finish her story. Sabrina wanted to stop the clock. No, she really wanted to reverse time.

"I tried reasoning with Charlie, telling him we couldn't change what happened. We should make the most of it and take comfort in the grandchild we were about to have. Charlie said he'd lost his daughter and his eyesight, and he didn't want to lose his wife on top of it. I was shocked. But the message was clear. I had to make a choice."

Charlie sounded like a prick to Sabrina, who wondered why Grace didn't stand up to him.

"I agonized about what to do. I was being asked to choose my husband or my daughter. I know Charlie sounds heartless, but you have to understand his illness had resulted in more than blindness. We both knew he was withering and his time was limited-"

Sabrina knew she had to pull the plug. No wonder her

grandmother wrote books. She didn't seem to know the Cliff Notes version.

"Look, Grace, or Mrs. Armstrong, or whatever you expect me to call you, time is limited. I have a friend who needs your help more than I need to hear a sob story I've waited my entire life to learn. Let's just break here and have you do your part of the quid pro quo you insisted on."

"Will you let me tell you the rest later, Sabrina?" Grace asked.

"Maybe," Sabrina said, even though she knew she would. She had to know the rest.

"That's more than I deserve," her grandmother said, rising from her chair. "Give me a moment and I'll come to David's."

Chapter 19

Sabrina left the cottage, shutting the door behind her. She thought she heard Grace swallow a sob and then water running from a faucet. She hesitated. The child buried deep inside, the one who had developed an attitude of indifference to family connections and wore it like invisible armor, wondered if she should go back to her grandmother and embrace her. Grace was old and there couldn't be much time left for them to heal and try to be a family, even a tiny one. But Henry deserved her loyalty first.

She entered the door David had led her through a short while before, knowing she was no longer the same woman she had been then. Now she had a family history, albeit a totally messed up one. Sabrina walked through the kitchen into the living room where Henry, David, and Neil sat drinking lemonade. No one was talking.

"Are you okay?" Henry asked.

"Sure," Sabrina said, but her knees were shaky. She sank into the empty chair next to him.

"Let me get you a lemonade," David said, rising.

"I'll take one as well," Grace said, slipping in from the kitchen.

"I'm having mine with a little drizzle of bourbon on top. Care to join me?" David asked Grace. Sabrina noticed her eyes had a slight suggestion of redness.

"Better yet, make mine bourbon with just a drizzle of lemonade on the top," Grace said. She found her way to the one chair that wasn't occupied.

Neil jumped in. Sabrina knew he was good at sensing emotional turmoil and even better at avoiding it.

"Mrs. Armstrong, there's a slight chance you might know some information that could help Henry. It seems the local police are trying to implicate him in the murder that took place two days ago. Before we go to headquarters for an interview, I'd love to know if you might know Eric Hershey from Allerton."

"Eric Hershey? Of course, I know him. He was my landscaper before, well before he left Beechwood abruptly. I know his mother. We both belong to the South Shore Garden Club. We've been members and friends for years," Grace said. She accepted a glass from David that was more amber than yellow. "Why do you want to know?" Her eyes darted from Neil to Henry and back again.

Neil said nothing for a moment. Sabrina had watched him use silence as a buffer for bad news before. He seemed to let people anticipate what he was about to tell them before he had to say the words. It was gentler that way.

"You aren't saying Eric was the man killed yesterday, are you?"

"I'm afraid so," Neil said. "I'm sorry."

"Margaret will be shattered. He's her only child." Grace gulped from her glass. Sabrina felt a rush of sympathy for her grandmother. Now she knew how devastated Grace had been when she'd lost her only child and imagined not knowing if she was still alive intensified the pain. She wondered if Elizabeth had intentionally hurt Grace or if she had just been a callous selfish young woman who abandoned the people who loved her. Like Grace. Like Sabrina.

"Tell us about Eric," Neil said.

"I didn't actually meet him until a few years ago when Margaret mentioned he was a very talented landscaper, although she had talked about him incessantly at garden club. My landscaper, who'd been with me since my husband died, had retired. I interviewed Eric, let him show me the ideas he had to rejuvenate my grounds, and hired him. He proved indispensable. He plowed and shoveled snow for me in the winter. When he married Heidi, I let them move into the apartment above my carriage house, which had been vacant for a long time." Grace looked at Sabrina. They both knew just how long.

"That would be Heidi Montgomery, right?" Neil asked.

"None other than," Grace said through pursed lips.

"What was Eric like?" Neil asked.

"Well, he was a charming, nice looking man. A bit full of himself on the outside. I'd say he was one of those men who compensate for their lack of confidence with swagger. I noticed that more when he was around people he didn't know well. I had many conversations with him when we were in the garden digging together and he seemed genuine and thoughtful. But that may just have been how he talked to someone my age."

Sabrina could see Henry squirming in his chair. She knew he was growing impatient with the pace of Neil's questions. She would have to caution him, just as he had to remind her often, that was Neil's very effective style of questioning witnesses.

"How long did he work for you? Why did he leave?"

Grace took the last sip of her drink. She put the glass down on a coaster and sat back in the chair.

"He left last winter after working for me for at least five years. After he and his wife, who by then had become my personal assistant, had a terrible row, not their first. I had to call the police. There was more than screaming this time. I heard things being thrown. I was frightened someone might get hurt. Heidi claimed Eric had been violent with her and took out a restraining order. He had to vacate the premises until there was a court date, which was scheduled for ten days later. He didn't wait for the court hearing. He hated winter and had talked about moving to the islands whenever the temperature dipped below freezing. He took off for the tropics and a new life and left Heidi behind. I never heard from him again. I only know this much from Heidi. She was obsessed with him. She couldn't believe he would leave her. They had what I'd call a love addiction in one of my novels."

Sabrina could see that Grace was tiring. Her voice wasn't as animated as it had been earlier. The bourbon probably didn't help, but Sabrina hadn't had a drop and also felt exhausted.

"Well, here's the interesting part. Heidi has shown up on St. John and is grief stricken with the news Eric is dead. I dropped her at the Westin earlier after finding her squatting on my trawler last night," Neil said.

Sabrina noticed that Grace didn't flinch.

"She blamed me for him leaving. She said it was my fault for calling the police, that it had been just a lover's spat. She claimed I exaggerated the incident. I later learned she had been the one throwing things at him," Grace said.

"Pretty ugly," Henry said, breaking his silence.

"I made the mistake of underestimating her. She is a clever woman. Heidi can charm you and convince you she's naïve and vulnerable. She is really a calculating, pathological liar. I fired her so I wouldn't have to put up with her. This island isn't big enough for both of us and I'm not leaving," Grace said, crossing her arms.

Neil's cell phone rang. He put up his index finger to silence everyone. He looked down at the floor saying, "I see," several times.

"This is outrageous. We demand an immediate arraignment and bail hearing. If you do this, I'll have you before a judge by the end of the day," Neil said.

Everyone had moved forward to the edge of their seats, straining to hear the words being spoken on the other end of the connection. Henry was paler than Sabrina had ever seen him. There was little mistaking what was happening.

"Henry, I'm sorry. Detective Hodge has asked me to have you surrender voluntarily. He plans to charge you with first degree murder."

Chapter 20

"No," Sabrina said. "He can't do that. Henry hasn't even been interviewed. Neil, you have to do something."

Henry sat next to her shaking, unable to believe the words Neil had just spoken. He had no words. He was going to be taken into custody. He didn't want to think about what might happen to him in jail. He had heard too many stories about the horrific treatment prisoners received from guards and other inmates. Sabrina reached an arm around him to pull him closer toward her. Henry knew she understood what he feared. She'd been there. He looked at Neil who was rubbing his temples. Neil's expression alarmed Henry more than his words had.

"Tell me what I can do to help," Grace said. She no longer seemed tired as she sat up tall in her chair.

When David burst into tears, Henry thought he would lose it.

"All right, everybody. Let's pull ourselves together here. We need to be smart and strong for Henry. We can emote and wallow later. Hodge told me to bring my client in, but he didn't say when, and I didn't say I knew where he was. We've got a little time here."

"How much?" Henry asked.

"A couple of hours at least. Maybe more at the rate Hodge moves. I wish Janquar were back on island." Neil said.

Henry liked Lee Janquar better than any cop he'd ever met. He knew Hodge was jealous of Janquar and would like to arrest someone for Eric's murder before Janquar got back from Massachusetts.

"Call Lucy Detree," Sabrina said. Detree was another police officer Henry respected. She had aligned herself with Janquar during a division among the police department ranks.

"I'll try," Neil said, pulling out his phone. "I'd like to make this call in the kitchen. She's more likely to talk if she doesn't think I have a bunch of people listening in."

Henry could hear him saying hello to Lucy from the living room where the rest of them sat in silence trying to hear. There were a lot of "uh-ha's" and "I see's" and then "Yes, I know her. What do you want with her?"

Henry didn't like the expression on Neil's face when he returned to the living room. Neil sat down. He looked exhausted for a man who had just returned from a three-week vacation.

"She knew nothing about Hodge charging you, Henry. That's just weird. She's directly under him and should certainly know if he is about to charge someone with homicide. I don't know if he was just trying to scare the bejesus out of you before he interviews you or bust my chops because of the bar card. He's a gutless bully."

Henry felt oddly relieved. He knew from experience Hodge was corrupt and would stoop to any level if it would benefit him. It helped to have it confirmed by one of his own officers, if only tacitly.

"This is good, isn't it, Neil?" Henry asked. If Hodge was bluffing, they might still have time to find who had killed Eric before he was arrested.

"I think so, buddy. But we need to proceed very cautiously and make you unavailable to Hodge until I get more information. I'm just not sure what's going on here. By the way, Lucy asked me if I knew you, Grace. When I told her I did, she asked if I would have you contact her," Neil said.

"What?" Sabrina said. "That's just too crazy. How would Lucy even know my grandmother is on island?"

"She never said she knew Grace Armstrong was your grandmother. She just wanted to know if I knew Grace and could I tell her to contact her. She wouldn't say why. I don't know why she thought I would know you, Grace."

Grace sat silently looking from Henry to Sabrina to Neil. Henry wondered what she had done that the cops wanted to talk to her. She was too old to be a criminal. Then he remembered Whitey Bulger. But Grace was so genteel, aristocratic. He couldn't imagine what the police wanted to talk to her about. He knew it couldn't be about him because he had just met her.

"I may have given your name and Henry's as on-island references at the hotel when I was trying to find somewhere to live. You'd better give me her contact information, Neil," Grace said, pulling out her phone to enter the data.

"Is there anything else you haven't mentioned, Grace?" Neil asked passing her his phone with Detree's information on the screen.

"If there is, you won't hear it unless I know the conversation is privileged," Grace said.

Chapter 21

The plan was for Henry to go off the grid for the rest of the day. That meant staying away from his condo or any of the Ten Villas' properties.

"That's easy. He can keep Lyla company. She could use someone besides Girlfriend to help her out," Sabrina said.

"We're off to St. Thomas. From the sound of the forecast, we're in a direct line for a couple of tropical storms that have serious potential to become full hurricanes. I'm heading over to Home Depot to get a generator and Grace needs a printer and some other stuff for her writing. Anyone want anything?" David asked. Sabrina noticed he had collected himself after his emotional outburst. David seemed calmer when he was busy doing something productive, often for someone else. Maybe he was a good match for Henry, but how would she know? She was no expert when it came to relationships.

"I'll head over to Bar None and see if I hear anything. Lucy will know that's where to find me if she wants to talk," Neil said.

Come on. I'll drive you to Lyla's so you can duck if we happen to see a cruiser," Sabrina said to Henry. She avoided driving to Fish Bay past the scene of the crime on Gifft Hill where she expected cruisers and cops would be stationed. She drove through town, up Jacob's Ladder and past the Westin.

"What do you make of Heidi being on St. John?" Henry asked after several moments of silence.

"I don't know. I don't remember much about her from elementary school, other than I think she may have been kind an odd duck. I didn't recognize her at my grandmother's house until she introduced herself. I barely remember the conversation during lunch that day. I was shattered after all of those years fantasizing about meeting my grandmother."

"Poor baby. That had to suck," Henry asked as he stretched his neck to look beyond Ditleff Point where the sky was a heavy metallic gray. "You think we might get a hurricane?"

"Nah, we meteorologists always warn people to be on the safe side, but most of the time storms change direction or fizzle. What will be will be. Let's focus our energy on getting Hodge off your case. Hopefully, Janquar will be back and on the trail of the real killer in a day or two," Sabrina said.

She felt more confident that there was little chance a hurricane would hit St. John than she did about Henry evading Hodge. She didn't plan on waiting for Janquar's return to spare Henry even a short spell in jail. She would do whatever she could to prevent that. Sabrina couldn't imagine Henry enduring what she knew went on in the overcrowded barbaric Virgin Island prisons. A white gay male didn't have a prayer.

"Why do you think Lucy asked for your grandmother to call her?" Henry asked. Sabrina had been wondering the same thing. Just when it seemed Grace was becoming less of a mystery to Sabrina, Lucy had lobbed a curve ball.

"No clue."

"How did your chat with her go?" Henry asked. Sabrina was surprised it had taken him this long to ask her. She guessed he hadn't asked before because he was preoccupied with his own troubles. She told him about the conversation.

"How did it feel?" he asked. Damn Henry, he wouldn't accept

a sound bite. He wanted the drama beneath every story. Sabrina hesitated before replying. She'd barely had time to consider the short surreal conversation with Grace.

"I felt like I handed her a box of crayons and a coloring book with pictures of my family in it. Every word she spoke colored in the empty images of my mother, my grandfather, and her. Even my father. I learned more from Grace in ten minutes about my family than I had during my whole life." Sabrina swallowed, afraid she might tear up. This was not the time. Henry had to be the focus.

"Do you want to know more? Did you let her have it?" Henry asked. Sabrina pulled into the Banks's driveway at the farthest end of Fish Bay high up on a hilltop so close to the clouds it made you feel like you could reach out and touch God. But only if you believed in him. Sabrina did not.

"Maybe. Sort of."

She deposited Henry with Lyla, who was grateful for the company. After a few smooches from her pooch, she drove across the way to Villa Mascarpone to join her work crew do the final touches before Lila's family arrived.

Sabrina nearly tripped over Austen as she slipped through the sliding glass doors. He was lying on the floor finishing the trim with Michelangelo precision. She spotted Tyler on the deck across the living room on the other side of the house. From what she could see, they were nearly done. Sabrina was surprised and impressed.

"Where's Katie?" Sabrina asked. She suspected Katie had been the one cracking the whip.

"Um, in the bathroom. She's been puking most of the morning. Probably tied one on last night. Can't blame her. She knew Eric the best. Saw his better side," Austen said from his supine position.

"What better side? Just because he's dead doesn't mean he wasn't an asshole," Tyler said coming through the sliders opposite Austen.

"Come on, man. You know, his 'softer side.' She said he read her poetry. You're just pissed because he threw you out of her house," Austen said.

"You don't know what you're talking about. About the only poetry Eric knew was Poe's The Raven. He wouldn't know Shelley or Dickenson if their poems were on a beer bottle," Tyler said.

Sabrina laughed at their immature banter. They were so young, so obnoxious, so beautiful in their own innocent bravado. Tyler with a bandana around his chin length curly brown hair flecked with gold strands from the sun. Austen, long and lanky, with a blonde mane most girls would kill for. Sabrina smiled. She was happy for them. She had never felt that young. She scolded herself for the irritation she had with them previously. It was hard not to be jealous of people who could be fearless and carefree when launched into adulthood after a stable childhood. She vowed to work on it.

Sabrina found Katie sitting on the floor in the master bedroom bathroom straddling the toilet. She looked pale and clung to a washcloth she held against her forehead.

"Are you okay?" Sabrina asked.

Katie nodded. "I should have known better."

"Sure, we all should. But we don't. I'm sorry. I didn't realize you and Eric were friends. I thought he was just another roommate," Sabrina said, unsettled to see Katie's eyes filling. She seemed a little too mature to be tying one on the night before she had to work, but Sabrina understood losing a friend might cause her to overindulge.

"Well, of course you would think that. I was such a cold bitch. He was barely dead before I grabbed for his job. I was in such a panic. Two of my other housemates are off island for the summer, leaving only Eric and Mackenzie to help me make the mortgage. Then Mac decided Colorado looked better during the summer than St. John. I've been living on the edge ever since Geoff left me. All I can think about is losing a half-assed, half-finished house. I've turned into an emotional robot," Katie said, starting to sob and then heave.

Sabrina put her hand on Katie's shoulder. "That's okay, honey. Survival comes first. Let me drive you home."

"I'll be okay. Just give me another five minutes," Katie said. She blew her nose into a piece of toilet paper and closed her eyes.

Tyler and Austen were cleaning and putting paint supplies away when Sabrina returned to the living room.

"What's next boss?" Austen asked.

Sabrina looked out the large glass doors at the steady rain falling. The annual conundrum. Ten Villas was closed for three months because of the unpredictable tropical weather, giving them plenty of time to do repairs and maintenance. Except they couldn't do repairs and maintenance during tropical weather. She checked the two weather apps on her phone to see what the rest of the day looked like. Not good. Nor tomorrow. A tropical weather watch had been upgraded to a tropical warning. Even though it was likely to be reduced to a tropical watch again, Sabrina had to take the current readings seriously. If she was worried about the chance that the missing key ring might fall into the wrong hands and cause loss or damage to Ten Villa rental properties, she had better take a tropical warning seriously. Normally under the circumstances, she and Henry would set out to each property and make storm preparations. But this wasn't "normally."

"I have something important I'd like you two to do for us. I don't really think we're going to get hit by a storm, but people trust us with their property, so we need to be cautious. Henry's preoccupied with the police investigation and I really need to stick by him. I know you understand," Sabrina said. Tyler and Austen nodded somberly.

"I'd like to entrust you with my key ring with keys for each of our villas. I want you to head to each one, except for Tideaway which Henry secured yesterday, to make sure doors and windows are latched, pool furniture is secured, you know anything that looks like high winds would affect it needs to be addressed. Call me if you have any questions." Their expressions were so serious, she half expected them to salute her. Sabrina had never entrusted any of the help to do storm preparation before. But she couldn't rely on the weather to hold out long enough for her and Henry to get to the job.

By the time Katie emerged, Tyler and Austen were on their way and Sabrina had the living area ready for guests.

"Do you feel well enough to empty the dishwasher? I threw the coffee pot and a few other things in yesterday," Sabrina said.

"Sure," Katie said.

Sabrina heard the ringtone from her cell phone and saw Henry was calling. Good boy, she thought. She had told him not to risk walking over to talk to see her at Villa Mascarpone just in case Hodge sent a cruiser out looking for him at their villas. Sabrina doubted the cops would bother the Banks.

"Hey, Lyla thought you'd want to know. Her kids' plans have changed. Jet Blue has cancelled their flight and a whole bunch more because of the weather," Henry said.

Sabrina told Henry she had dispatched Tyler and Austen to do storm prep.

"I think that was the right thing to do. When the airlines start canceling flights because of weather, it's time to pay attention. Money talks," Henry said.

Sabrina looked out the glass doors again. She couldn't distinguish the gray sky from the silver sea below, but she could hear waves crashing ferociously. For the first time since her husband's death in Nantucket, since she hung up her meteorologist credentials, she had the urge to check the NOAA radar.

Chapter 22

Henry left Lyla napping on the couch while the hospice nurse tended to Evan in the bedroom. As much as Lyla needed sleep, she resisted. "I want to be here for him, Henry, you know, when..." Henry mused what a better place the world would be if everyone had someone like Lyla loving him. He longed for the kind of relationship Evan and Lyla had shared for decades but didn't dare consider if he and David would ever find commitment and peace together. His future was too unsure to think about anything beyond eluding Hodge.

Henry knew before he entered Villa Mascarpone Sabrina would not be happy to see him.

"You're supposed to be out of sight, Henry. Why not just call me again?" she asked. Henry noticed Katie was in the kitchen wiping the counters.

"I'm jumping out of my skin, Sabrina. I'm about to be arrested and picturing what will happen to me in jail. I'm scared." Henry spoke quietly, hoping Katie couldn't hear him confess his fears, but knew the open room plan made that unlikely.

"I know, Henry. I understand what you're going through," Sabrina said. She gave him an uncharacteristic hug he knew she reserved for rare moments when someone was in deep shit. Henry's fear grew, although the gesture from his best friend was touching.

"Do either of you happen to know where the spare set of keys to my car are? Eric had them, but they weren't in the car when I picked it up," Katie said. Henry understood she was announcing her presence before bursting in on the hug.

"No," Sabrina said.

"Maybe it was in his man bag. Did you ask the cops? We're missing a set of keys too," Henry said.

"Man bag? Eric carried a man bag?" Henry thought Sabrina seemed surprised. "What else did he have with him when he stayed at your house, Katie?"

Katie slumped into a wicker chair, leaning over as if she were about to faint.

"Are you okay?" he asked.

"She's a little under the weather, Henry. She had a rough night," Sabrina said.

Katie sat up. Her face was a shade of green Henry recognized and occasionally wore.

"When he came to stay at my house, Eric had a backpack, a duffel bag, and yes, a man bag. He told me that was all he owned in the world. He left the duffel at the house and sometimes the backpack, but he always had that man bag with him. I used to kid him that it was nicer than any purse I ever owned."

"Katie, did the cops come to check out your house and go through Eric's stuff?" Sabrina asked.

"No, they were going to, but when I told him he didn't have his own room, that he was just couch surfing, they had me bring in his duffel bag when they interviewed me yesterday. There wasn't anything interesting in it. Just his clothes and his Jungle Bag. T-shirts, jeans, shorts, socks, you know. I did his laundry." Katie started crying. Henry didn't understand why Katie broke down at the mention of Eric's laundry.

"What's a Jungle Bag?" Sabrina asked.

Katie laughed. "Eric came to St. John prepared to rough it for a while. He didn't have a lot of money, he told me, but said that would soon change. The Jungle Bag is a tropical sleeping bag with insulation to keep you cool in the humidity. It even has a built-in mosquito net. Eric loved that it rolled into a ball the size of a coconut." Katie's eyes drifted off to a place neither Henry nor Sabrina could see.

"What about the man bag and the backpack? Do you know if the cops found them? And maybe your keys?" Henry asked, bringing her back. He wondered what Eric had been carrying in his man bag. Since Henry owned more than one, he hadn't jumped on Eric for carrying a man bag. Although man bags had long been common in Europe, a growing number of American guys had discovered having a portable compartment for your important stuff was a great idea that women had known forever.

"I asked the cops if they had my keys and that horrid detective told me they didn't, but even if they did, they wouldn't hand them over to me because the keys would be 'evidence.' Eric wasn't killed with keys, for Christ's sake. They'd already told me about the machete. I think he enjoyed telling me how it severed Eric's carotid artery. I didn't offer any information to him about his belongings or anything else after that. Let them figure it out. I answered questions 'yes' or 'no' and got the hell out of there. Well, you saw me," Katie said.

"So you don't know if the cops even know Eric had anything other than a duffel bag?" Henry wanted to be clear so he could share the information with Neil.

Katie shrugged. "As far as I know."

"Go back to the Jungle Bag for a moment, please. When did Eric arrive on St. John? Did he camp out?" Sabrina asked.

"He got here at the end of March. He didn't want to spend the money to camp at Cinnamon Bay, so he found places where he could bunk in his Jungle Bag."

Henry grimaced. Most St. Johnians loved mongooses, bugs, and iguanas, but no one wanted to sleep with them.

"How long did Eric camp out?" he asked.

Katie looked at him. "I know. It didn't last long. Eric was pretty resourceful. He found one decent place to stay before he came to my place that didn't cost him anything."

"Where was that?" Sabrina asked. Henry was grateful she was on top of things. He hadn't gotten past the image of sleeping on a beach and finding a crab crawling over your face.

Katie put her hands over her face. If she was going to lose it again, Henry figured he would too. Sabrina was the only one who had her composure.

"Where?" Sabrina pressed.

"Where he died. In the furniture container."

"How did he get the key to it?" Henry asked. He had to give Eric credit for being resourceful. The furniture container was dry, almost always had a couch or mattress in it he could sleep on and was vacant from mid-afternoon until early morning.

"Jay Callahan gave him one. He felt sorry for Eric. Eric promised to give it back when he got a place to live," Katie said.

"Did he?" Sabrina asked.

"I don't know," Katie said.

Chapter 23

Grace got out of David's jeep and stepped into the heavy sea mist that sprayed the car ferry. The fine spray felt cool on her bare arms. The downpours they had endured in St. Thomas had let up and the sky had a hint of brightness, enough to make her put her sunglasses on.

She remembered the countless times she had stared into the Atlantic Ocean in Beechwood searching for answers. She walked over to the railing and looked down at the white caps on the surface of the water. The wind from the south created a healthy chop on Pillsbury Sound, where the Atlantic Ocean and the Caribbean Sea met.

David approached her from behind and handed her a bottle of Island Hoppin' IPA wrapped in a koozie. She took it gratefully, although she couldn't remember the last time she had a beer.

"Looks the weather might break," David said squinting into the distance.

"Maybe. Nothing we can do about it, either way," Grace said. She found the cold ale David had stashed in a cooler in his Jeep an odd but not unpleasant combination of malt and citrus. Maybe she'd been wasting her money on pricey Pinot Grigio.

"Why does that detective want to talk to you, Grace? Are you in some kind of trouble?" David asked. He leaned against the bannister next to her seemingly as mesmerized by the passing swirls as she. They had talked about everything but the conversation at his house during their shopping trip. She now knew more about generators than she'd ever thought possible and he had become an authority on which printers were best for writers. His question sounded kind, not accusatory.

"I'm not sure. I paid my hotel bill, so don't worry about me skipping out on you," Grace said.

"How did it go with Sabrina?" David asked.

"She was tough. I can't say I blame her. I'm not sure she'll continue the conversation, although it was really a monologue. I was trying to give her information about why we had severed ties with Elizabeth so she'd understand. But I guess I was really putting up an affirmative defense. There is no defense for what I did," Grace said. She hung onto the railing as the ferry navigated across a series of large waves.

David took her by the arm. "We'd better get back to the truck. It's getting rough."

They pulled off the ferry just in time for the sun to come out.

"I bet we'll have a great sunset tonight," David said.

"Drop me at Starfish, dear. I'll pick up some groceries and cook you a decent dinner. You were so kind to take me with you today," Grace said.

David hesitated. "I can go in with you or wait in the Jeep."

"Nonsense. You want to unload that heavy generator and maybe carry the printer out to cottage for me. I'll get a taxi."

"Are you sure?" David asked. Grace sensed he was on to her, that he suspected she had a hidden agenda. He just didn't know what was on it. She did. She was going to confront Heidi Montgomery and put an end to her chicanery.

As soon as Grace was certain David had left the Starfish Market parking lot, she found a cab waiting outside the largest grocery store on the island. The cab had a sign on top of its cab that said, "Westin." Grace had learned early that the sign meant nothing. It was intended to lure tourists who were staying at the Westin to believe the cab was "official." Almost all of the cabs on island had identical signs.

The taxi hurried up over the hill known as Jacob's Ladder before she had time to become frightened. The nearly perpendicular road reminded her of the old wooden roller coaster in Allerton. She wondered if her granddaughter ever got to ride on it before it was demolished. There was so much about Sabrina she didn't know, that she needed to find out. Her chat with Heidi Montgomery was pivotal.

Grace entered the reception area located in an atrium filled with towering potted tropical plants and found the front desk. A beautiful young West Indian woman with a hibiscus tucked over her ear stood playing with her phone.

"Good afternoon, I'm here to see Heidi Montgomery. I'm her grandmother and forget what room she told me she is in," Grace said. She took a breath in, preparing to elaborate on the lie, hoping Heidi hadn't checked in under her married name.

The woman looked up, turned toward a keyboard, and clicked a few keys. "Three twenty-three, Ma'am." The woman was back on her phone before Grace could thank her.

Grace walked past the nearly empty enormous geometrically challenged pool, which had small islands within it. The sun had extracted moisture from the pool making the air unbearably steamy. Grace was tempted to jump in fully clothed, or at least to join the half-dozen people sitting at the bar sipping tall frozen drinks.

She arrived at the row of rooms facing the pool and the beach beyond which was labeled "Rooms three-twenty to three twenty-nine." She was grateful the "Three" referred to the building number and not the floor.

Grace found a small empty terrace that had a door with Heidi's number on it. The drapes on the windows were pulled. She knocked, not quite sure of what she would say to Heidi, but confident that the words would come as they always did ultimately and that she would get her message across. This was no time for writer's block. She knocked gently a few times, then harder. She got no response. Grace turned and checked to see if she had missed Heidi back at the pool or the bar. No Heidi.

Each unit had a small passageway to the side with a second door where Grace assumed housekeeping and other hotel staff entered. She turned down it and found a door toward the rear with "323" on it. She knocked again. This time the door pushed open as she hit it.

Grace knew Heidi and Eric had been heavy drinkers. After Eric's departure, Heidi's drinking had escalated. When Heidi had first worked for her, she had offered to make Grace a cocktail for "Happy Hour" before leaving for the day. Soon, Heidi was joining Grace for a glass of wine and not long after, a few martinis long before the sun was down. Grace had to rein Heidi in. "I'm not Hemingway, you know. I need to be sober to write."

Heidi probably had too much sun and too much to drink, Grace decided. It would give her an advantage if she had to be awakened when Grace confronted her with what she had to say. She pushed the door open and walked in, almost falling over a tray on the floor with dirty dishes and glasses. Grace figured Heidi was too lazy to put the tray outside the door. A faint odor filled her nostrils.

Surprised the clatter hadn't awakened Heidi, Grace took a few steps forward where she could see tousled bed clothing. She hoped she wasn't interrupting a tryst, a tried-and-true plot technique she wasn't above using in her books. The room was dark with light coming in only from a small gap between the curtains and the window on each side. Grace could see someone wrapped in a sheet facing away from her toward the opposite wall. A liquor bottle with amber liquid sat on the nightstand next to her with two glasses and an ice bucket. Grace panicked at the sight of the second glass and glanced over at the closed door she assumed was the bathroom. The glass must belong to someone who was in the bathroom.

She turned and rushed out the door, down the passageway, and sprinted past the pool and bar. Gasping for breath, Grace hopped in yet another idle taxi with a "Westin" sign, where she directed the driver to take her back to Starfish Market and to wait for her. She bought two steaks and salad makings that cost almost as much as the filets, which was another of the ironies about island life she was learning. She grabbed a bottle of Four Roses Small Batch bourbon and a bag of ice. She had learned quickly that ice didn't go far on St. John and you could never have enough.

Within twenty minutes, she was standing barefoot on the patio lighting David's grill with a bourbon on the rocks in her still shaky hands. Grace wasn't sure what had spooked her. The prospect of confronting Heidi hadn't been pleasant, but Grace wasn't intimidated by someone she considered an unworthy opponent. No, something else had frightened her. It had been the prospect of being discovered by the person she imagined was in the bathroom. She had no idea who lurked behind the closed door, only that Heidi's companion probably didn't want to be discovered.

David approached her with a salad bowl in hand. "It took you longer to buy groceries than it did for you to buy a printer." He chuckled and showed her the salad he had tossed.

"My contribution to your purchases. It's about the only thing I don't fully ruin." He placed the salad bowl on a table and then raised the umbrella above it. "Just in case," he said, winking at her.

"Shall I toss that for you?" Grace asked, knowing David stocked only bottled ranch dressing, a fate no salad should suffer. She dashed back to the kitchen and grabbed a lemon and some olive oil and doused the wilting lettuce. The sun was relentless even as it prepared to set.

The sunset turned out to be a fiery finish to a gray day. The flames dashing across the ember sky rivaled those burning in the grill.

"You never know," David said. He sat forward in his chair and raised his glass to the sky.

"You never do," Grace said.

Chapter 24

Sabrina waited for ten minutes to emerge from the bathroom, first peeking through a crack of the door. She listened for the sound of anyone in the room, even Heidi snoring. The only sounds she could hear were from a distance. She imagined them to be coming from the pool, even though it hadn't been crowded when she had walked by on her way to find Heidi. The tray from room service still lay on the floor, although a plate and some silverware had slid onto the carpet. Whoever had been in the room hadn't been room service.

It had been foolish to come here. Sabrina knew that. She wasn't certain if she had come wanting to get more information to help Henry or to just tell Heidi off. It didn't matter now. Heidi had clearly passed out and a visitor had nearly discovered Sabrina in her room. She'd ducked in the bathroom just in time to avoid meeting whoever had come to see Heidi. Sabrina half expected it was Neil. He was a free agent now. She remembered how Heidi had flirted with him at lunch in Beechwood, even though it was clear they were a "couple." That's what Neil had told her grandmother. It was a public pronouncement, one she had never heard him make before. She had cherished his barely audible occasional whispers that he loved her. Now Sabrina wondered if she imagined them.

Sabrina didn't consider waking Heidi. She ran out the bathroom door through the exit without taking a second glance toward the lump in the bed. Rather than pass by the bored young woman at the front desk who'd given her Heidi's room number, Sabrina exited to the right of the door entering a small rear passageway used by housekeeping behind the units. She reached the Ten Villas jeep she had parked near other service vehicles just in time to catch a red-hot sunset sizzling over St. Thomas in the distance. If only she could be in the moment and simply enjoy it instead of worrying about her next stop at Bar None to share the new information she and Henry had learned from Katie. Perhaps her side trek to see Heidi had been a way to avoid it. She lingered in the tranquil air-conditioned van and tranquility reluctant to leave, when she caught the sight of a tall blonde woman with a blue and white striped towel over her shoulder walking toward a ratty red vehicle next to a few shiny rental Jeeps. Katie. Katie in huge sunglasses she didn't need at this time of the day.

She watched Katie place the towel and something she was carrying beneath it on the front passenger seat. Katie was wearing a beach cover up over what Sabrina guessed was a bathing suit. She wondered if Katie was doing what many island folks did when they wanted a dip in a pool but didn't own one. Islanders salvaged the iconic Westin blue and white guest beach towels left on beaches or bargained for them from hotel staff. They would casually enter the pool area with a towel over their shoulders as if they were registered guests staying at the hotel or in one of the time-share units. They bought drinks and ordered food and no one seemed to notice or care they were trespassers. The timing seemed odd to Sabrina, although it was bloody hot and Katie had been upset and hung-over. Maybe she needed to chill, but Sabrina still thought it out of character.

Sabrina didn't want to go to Bar None and talk to Neil, but

she knew she had no choice. Procrastinating and pondering why Katie was at the pool wasn't going to help Henry. What she and Henry had learned from Katie might be important and if Neil was going to help, he needed any information available. Henry had to lay low, so it was up to her to convey it.

The lights in Cruz Bay had begun to twinkle as she cruised down Jacob's Ladder. Pine Peace Market bustled with locals shopping after work. She passed Starfish Market where the tourists shopped and thought she saw Grace leaving in a taxi. It had been a long day. Sabrina didn't have room to ruminate about her meeting with her grandmother that morning. She had little left to give and it belonged to Henry.

She found a parking space first try, a sure sign it was off-season. She saw Mitch tending bar and felt a twinge of regret that things weren't the way they used to be. Easy, not awkward.

"Hey, Sabrina. What can I get you?" Mitch asked without hesitation, just like always. She took the bait.

"The usual, Mitch. How've you been?" Sabrina said sliding up on a stool while she watched him mix a lemon drop and pour it into a martini glass after swirling the rim in sugar.

"Not too bad. I could do without the humidity," Mitch said. He slid a Bar None coaster in front of her and placed the drink on top. She leaned over to take a sip so it wouldn't spill. Mitch definitely knew how to pour a drink.

"Perfect, as always. Say, is Neil around? I need to give him some information," Sabrina said. She normally wouldn't need to say why she was asking for Neil, but just in case Mitch had been instructed by him to keep her at bay, she made it clear it wasn't a social call.

"Sure thing. I'll go tell him," Mitch said as he stepped through the break in the bar.

The sound of Bob Marley's One Love drifted across the bar filling Sabrina with melancholy. She sipped the velvety smooth lemon drop as she watched a group of young men enter and sit at the other end of the oval shaped bar. Tyler waved to her, elbowed Austen, who followed suit. Sabrina slid off her stool, a little surprised to feel the effects of half a lemon drop and went over to them.

"How did it go today?" she asked. She was still surprised herself she had entrusted them with the keys to the villas. She rationalized that the threat of rough weather warranted her breach of security, but when the sun returned later in the day, Sabrina chastised herself for overreacting. She was always overreacting.

"Fine, I think. We even finished early," Austen said, handing her the ring of keys. Sabrina felt ten pounds lighter when she felt the cool metal ring in her hands. She took an involuntary deep breath and realized how much the stress had affected her.

"Just couldn't fit all of that lawn furniture up at Villa Bella Vista inside, so we tied it together and down," Tyler said.

"That should be fine for now. The weather's looking a little better. Thanks," Sabrina said. "Let's meet at the North Shore Deli in the morning at 7:00 and regroup."

Sabrina walked back to her stool to find Mitch delivering a plate of onion rings, her favorite item on the Bar None menu.

"Boss says he'll be with you as soon as possible. Something about getting some documents that might be helpful."

"Thanks," Sabrina said, as she watched Mitch make her another drink. She glanced down the bar and saw Tyler and Austen perusing menus as they nursed bottles of beer.

"Hey, Mitch, can you go over to Tyler and Austen and tell them dinner and drinks are on Ten Villas tonight? They've more than earned their keep today."

"Of course," Mitch said. Sabrina watched and waved back when her workers acknowledged her gesture.

"That was nice," Mitch said when he returned and entered the order in the restaurant computer system.

"They seem more reliable than most of the kids we hire," Sabrina said.

"I hear you. Same problem here at the bar getting help. So

immature. Although Austen's no kid. I never would have guessed he did five years for white-collar crime. He looks like the rest of that crew over there," Mitch said gesturing toward the group of guys who had entered with Tyler and Austen and were now joined by a few young women.

"What? You're kidding me?" Sabrina felt for the key ring she had placed back on the loop of her purse.

"You didn't know? Sorry. It was just some bogus mortgage scam from what I hear." Mitch shrugged an apology.

"Don't tell me Tyler's got a shady past too, please Mitch." Sabrina was serious. She needed to know if she had botched all three of the Ten Villa hires before she left for Massachusetts. She hated to think she had been so excited about the trip her judgment had been impaired. Ten Villas only hired independent contractors, which meant they were responsible for paying their own taxes, so the information Ten Villas collected was minimal. No one on island ever thought of checking criminal records for casual labor.

"No worries there. The only thing Tyler is guilty of is being young and impressionable. He's got a huge crush on Katie, the bartender over at The Tap Room. She's probably fifteen years older but he doesn't care," Mitch said. "Hey, Neil's waving for you to join him. I'll bring you another round."

Sabrina declined a third drink. The thought of joining her former boyfriend in the tented cubicle at the corner of Bar None that served as his office without her wits made her feel vulnerable. He stood waiting for her on his side of the table they had shared so often as she slid onto her spot opposite him. He had a pile of paper placemats marked with the typical pencil scribbling she had to work to decipher.

"Sorry to keep you waiting, Sal-Sabrina," he said. She wanted to respond with, "No problem, Cor-Neil," but bit her tongue. Part of the attraction they had shared was a keen ability to banter. Whatever remnants of their relationship remained, if any, had no place on the agenda tonight.

"Henry and I have learned a few tidbits we thought you should know. I'm assuming you haven't heard anything more about bringing him in from Hodge, so he's still staying with Lyla," Sabrina said, quickly getting down to business.

"No, Lucy told me Hodge was called over to St. Thomas, so we've been given a little reprieve. I suspect the lawsuit Sean Keating filed has Hodge over there answering some questions from the brass. In the meantime, I've been collecting some interesting data about Eric and Heidi, although I'm not sure how relevant it is," Neil said, pointing to his notes.

"You go first," Sabrina said.

"I called an old buddy of mine who practices law in Boston and asked him to see if there were any public records on Eric and Heidi. His paralegal turned up quite a bit of information in little time. It seems that after Heidi was issued a temporary restraining order against Eric early last March, a hearing was set for ten days later so he could respond. He never showed, which is what Grace told us. Instead, he had a lawyer file for divorce and serve Heidi outside the courthouse the day of the hearing. One of the documents Heidi was served with, in addition to a complaint for divorce, was what Massachusetts calls an automatic financial restraining order, which essentially freezes use of marital accounts for anything other than ordinary use," Neil said.

"Which means what in English, Neil?" He was beginning to sound like a damn lawyer to Sabrina, which pissed her off, although rationally she knew he had talked like one even before passing the V.I. bar.

"It means that he tied up the money they had in both their individual and joint accounts. But it also seems he drained the one joint account they had before he filed because the financial restraining order is mutual. According to the court documents, it was only a couple of thousand, but I'm guessing that's what funded Eric's trip down here. Heidi also alleged that he cleaned out their safe deposit box."

Sabrina considered Neil's information with what she had learned from Katie.

"Okay, that makes sense. Katie was apparently more of a friend to Eric than I realized. She told Henry and me that when Eric arrived, he was sleeping rough in what she called a coconut sleeping bag," Sabrina said.

Neil laughed.

"I had one of those I used on the *Knot Guilty* I used until I bought some sheets." His look told her that was when she began spending occasional nights with him there. Sabrina would miss the quiet evenings she spent with Neil sitting in his study on the old-cracked leather chairs, sipping drinks and eating take-out from Indigo Grill down the road. The gentle sway of the *Knot Guilty* had been hypnotic. Sabrina rarely felt as relaxed as she did on Neil's trawler. She drew in a breath and focused on what he was telling her.

"Wait, back to the divorce. Was it ever final?" Sabrina asked. She was mystified why Heidi had shown up on St. John if she and Eric were divorced.

"No, there's a six month wait in Massachusetts before you can even schedule a contested divorce hearing. There's a pretrial conference scheduled for September that Heidi won't need to attend now that she's a widow. Good thing for her because Eric was looking to split what he alleged was a hefty amount of dough she'd siphoned into her individual account during the marriage."

"So why did she come here?" Sabrina asked.

"I'm not sure," Neil said. "I'm afraid I'm going to have another conversation with her about that and more. I need to make sure she's switched the hotel bill to her own credit card. She just makes me so damn uncomfortable."

Neil's candor surprised Sabrina. It was the kind of sharing she had been looking for in their relationship when there was still a chance for one. Still, she couldn't help but respond.

"Would you like company when you visit her?"

"Yes, please," Neil said with atypical brevity that felt awkward to Sabrina.

"The other thing Katie told us, Neil, was that Eric carried a man bag with him all of the time. The cops have his phone, which was on his body, and they have his duffle bag, which Katie brought to them. But his man bag and his backpack seem to be missing," Sabrina said, filling the uncomfortable moment with more information.

"Man bag? One of those affectatious sissy sacks European guys wear over their necks and on their cute little hips? Eric?"

"Yep," Sabrina said, trying not to smile while she pictured Neil carrying a man bag.

"I've got more documents coming on Eric and Heidi tomorrow. That was just the court stuff they could easily pull off public records," Neil said.

"The only other thing we learned from Katie was that after a few nights of sleeping rough, Eric got his hands on a key to the furniture container at The Last Chance Center. He slept there until he started renting her couch."

"You mean, where he was murdered?" Neil asked, as his dark bushy eyebrows arched.

"Yes," Sabrina said.

"Where did he get his hands on the key?" Neil asked.

"Jay Callahan gave it to him. He felt sorry for Eric and said he could sleep in the furniture container until he found a place to live," Sabrina said.

"Sleep, those little slices of death — how I loathe them."

"Huh?"

"Poe. Edgar Allen," Neil said.

Poe again. Twice in a day, was two too many for Sabrina.

Chapter 25

Henry looked at the crossword puzzle on Lyla's kitchen counter. Twenty-seven down, Super Bowl XIV Champs. If it wasn't the Patriots, who cared? He tossed the pencil Lyla had given him before she went with the hospice nurse to tend to Evan. He was stir-crazy. Sitting and waiting for Sabrina to speak to Neil so Neil could talk to Lucy Detree was more than frustrating. He needed to feel as if he were part of the team. It was his skin on the line after all.

Lyla had left him Evan's keys when he mentioned he might run into Cruz Bay for a few items. She had arched her thin gray eyebrows when she said, "You're a big boy, Henry. You don't need my permission to do what you have to do." There was never any fooling Lyla. She knew.

Henry doubted the cops would look twice at him driving Evan's ancient Volvo wagon. He would drive slowly, like Evan. And he would don a disguise. He grabbed a Skinny Legs baseball cap from a peg on the kitchen wall next to Lyla's straw sunhat. No one had ever seen Henry Whitman, the Ralph Lauren of the Caribbean, in a baseball cap. Henry slid his sunglasses on and headed for the car.

The glare of the late afternoon sun stung his eyes even with sunglasses. After the steamy gray rain, it felt insulting, too late to salvage the day. Evan's car was as meticulous as the man. No trash or sand on the floor. The windshield clean and shiny, save for a few dried raindrops. Henry would miss Evan.

He approached Tide-Away, where he and his crew had been working the day of the murder, just before the plum-red sun began to set over St. Thomas in the distance. Henry and Sabrina often marked the end of their workday watching the sunset, marveling how no two were ever the same. But there was no time to revel in the magic of the red-hot ball melting into the water tonight. Henry needed to poke around Tide-Away to see if Eric had left behind either his man bag or backpack before darkness fell.

The aging Volvo climbed a treacherous curvy hill where more than one water delivery truck had taken an instant dive into oblivion. Henry drove along the road above Klein Bay and looked over toward Boatman Point. The neighborhood consisted mostly of opulent villas, which were short-term rentals owned by wealthy investors. They were almost entirely unoccupied during the scorching months of August and September. A vehicle was descending the road leading to Tide-Away. Henry stopped and watched as the small pick-up truck crawled down the steep hill leading to the villa. He strained to see who was driving it, cursing his foolish vanity. Why hadn't he gotten glasses? Anderson Cooper looked so smart in them.

Henry fumbled through the glove compartment, hoping he knew Evan as well as he thought he did. Bingo. He pulled out a black leather case holding a pair of Bushnell waterproof binoculars. Through them, Henry watched Austen get out of the truck and walk around the front of the villa where Henry had tangled with the catch-n-keep. Austen walked onto the front deck where he and Tyler had been priming. He disappeared toward the back of the villa for a few minutes, then returned and looked at the front again. Henry kept his eyes fixed on Austen's movements with the only light left after the sunset's after-splash.

He watched Austen get into the truck and back out of the driveway.

Henry put Evan's car into drive and hustled past the road from Tide-Away before Austen exited. He didn't know whose vehicle Austen had been driving or why he had been at Tide-Away. He just knew it was better if Austen didn't know he had been watching him.

He drove past Chocolate Hole scolding himself for not knowing the answers to those two questions when he reached the entrance to the Westin. On impulse, he turned left. When the security guard at the tiny booth asked if he could help him, Henry said he was visiting a guest. The guard signaled him to drive through with no additional questions. Henry drove to the parking lot, enjoying the cool air flowing from the air-conditioner. He would go introduce himself to Heidi Montgomery and offer condolences for the loss of her husband and Henry's employee. He wished he had a gift, a bottle of wine or flowers, but his charm would have to do. Maybe Heidi would share information about Eric that would help find his killer and get him off the hook.

The woman at the desk barely looked up from her Kindle when he asked for Heidi Montgomery's room number. He didn't need the excuse he cooked up for why she should give it to him. Instead she said, "Room 323, well past the pool, nice and quiet, just like Mr. Perry requested."

Henry was glad the clerk hadn't bothered to look at him. She might remember a guy who wore sunglasses in the dark. He hurried away, on past the pool and nearly deserted bar toward Building Three. He removed the sunglasses as he approached the door to Heidi's room. No need for a disguise with her when he planned to introduce himself and play his way into her confidence.

When he arrived at the door Henry noticed it was several inches ajar. He held the doorknob while he tentatively knocked, not wanting it to fly open and scare the woman inside. She'd been through enough. When there was no answer, he knocked again. No response.

"Ms. Montgomery? Heidi? Are you in there?" There was no light coming through the crack in the door. Maybe Heidi was sleeping. But who takes a nap in a hotel without locking the door, especially when there's been a murder on island, Henry wondered?

He knocked again, this time louder, as he held the door in place by the knob.

"Are you okay? Can I help?" Henry asked because his instincts told him Heidi needed more than condolences. He couldn't help but speculate whether she had decided to join her husband or ex-husband, whatever. He knew it wasn't smart, but smart wouldn't matter if something happened to this woman if he could have prevented it.

He pushed the door open and stood still, waiting for his eyes to accommodate the darkness. The quiet was deafening. A faint odor reached his nostrils, one he couldn't identify other than as unpleasant.

Henry reached toward the side of the door for the wall. He felt several switches and slid them all in the opposite direction of their present position. The room blazed like a movie set. His eyes moved toward the bed where white linens shrouded a long form.

"Miss Montgomery? Heidi?" Henry pleaded with her to respond, speak, move. Anything.

Nothing.

He moved toward the bed where he could see blonde curls over the top of the covers. He moved slowly past the foot of the bed and up toward the face of the woman, who was lying on her side. Her face in the garish iridescence looked lifeless. Henry placed his hand under her nostrils. There was no flow of air. Her arms were beneath the bed covers. He didn't want to move them so he could take her pulse. He remembered from his days as a flight attendant a doctor on board checking a passenger's pulse on his neck. Reluctantly, he placed his index and third fingers where he believed he might find a pulse. The woman, who must be Heidi, was cold. There was no pulse.

He was an idiot. Coming here had been a supreme act of stupidity, of egotism, especially considering he was under suspicion for murdering the woman's husband. He needed to leave and never tell anyone, not even Sabrina, he had been here. And he needed to see David. Not to share what he had seen, but simply to put his eyes on him. To consider, pretend, fantasize that there was hope for a future.

Henry covered the doorknob with his tee shirt and pulled it closed.

Chapter 26

Sabrina picked up the cardboard box filled with mail from the front seat of Neil's pickup truck to make room for her when she noticed a small unopened heavy cotton envelope addressed to him in elegant cursive. The engraved return address read, "Armstrong." Sabrina seethed. After her total absence for almost four decades, her grandmother was everywhere.

"New pen pal?" she asked, handing him the envelope.

Neil frowned as he read the address and ripped open the envelope slashing his address in half. He opened the notecard, which Sabrina could see had an "A" in Edwardian script in classic navy-blue ink on the front.

"Here," he said and gave her the notecard.

Dear Mr. Perry, Please forgive me for my atrocious behavior when you came to my home. I plan to ask for your forgiveness in person shortly when I arrive in St. John, but I could not let a day pass without expressing my remorse and regret for my uncivilized conduct. Respectfully, Grace Armstrong

"If I got that much of an apology, she ought to write you a whole book," Neil said. He placed the box in the back seat usually reserved for Girlfriend. Sabrina doubted her chocolate lab would ever ride to the beach with them again. It seemed about as unlikely as creating a relationship with her grandmother. She wondered if she'd received a note from Grace in her absence and when she would ever get to go through her own mail.

They rode in silence, although not as companionably as before. One of the things Sabrina had enjoyed about her relationship with Neil was that neither of them had felt compelled to fill the air with words. They reserved conversation for when they had something to say, unless they were teasing each other. How quickly things had changed.

The guard at the Westin waved Neil through without asking why they were there. Neil parked the scratched and battered pick-up truck right next to a shiny new rental jeep, apparently not feeling compelled to park in the area reserved for service vehicles Sabrina had used earlier.

Walking next to him through the pool area, now lit with soft faux-Tiki lights, it felt unnatural to Sabrina that Neil didn't reach for her hand, although she would have rebuffed him if he had. She looked over at a few stragglers at the bar and wished she was having just one more lemon drop rather than going to confront a woman she didn't like and whoever had been in the hotel room with her earlier. She felt a little deceptive not sharing her earlier visit to Heidi's room with Neil, but she didn't know how she could explain why she had gone there. Some things were better left unsaid.

Neil led her to the side door rather than the sliders, which were covered with drawn drapes. Sabrina remembered he had been here before when Heidi checked in. He knocked on the door without hesitation. When there was no answer, he pounded and called out, "Hey, Heidi. It's Neil. Let me in."

Sabrina remembered Grace's description of how heavily Heidi and Eric drank and assumed Heidi was still out cold. Impatient with Neil's newfound manners, she reached for the doorknob, turned it, pushed it open.

"Age before beauty," Sabrina said, gesturing for Neil to go ahead of her.

Neil didn't hesitate. He stepped into the room and onto the tray of empty dishes waiting for room service to pick up. The clatter didn't rouse Heidi.

"Heidi, it's Neil," he called out. He walked over toward the bed where Sabrina could see a form under the white bed clothing, which appeared ghostly in the faint light falling into the room between the cracks in the curtains. Sabrina followed him past the foot of the bed and up toward the pillow where Heidi's motionless head lay. Her blonde tresses partially covered her face

"Shit," Neil said. He flicked on a lamp on the nightstand next to two glasses and a bottle of bourbon. Neil placed a hand on Heidi's neck on one side and then the other. He drew back the bed clothing. Her partially tanned body outlined by the bikini she wasn't wearing was reclined on a foul-smelling smear of excrement. Sabrina knew people become incontinent upon death. Heidi was dead. But still, she had to ask.

"She's dead, isn't she?"

"She sure is," Neil said. He dropped the sheet over her. "Don't touch anything. Exit the room." Sabrina was insulted by his condescending attitude. She had discovered enough dead bodies to know she shouldn't touch anything. But it didn't matter. Once again, she had been the first person to find a dead body, but at least this time she wasn't alone.

Out in the passageway, Neil pulled out his cell phone.

"I'm calling Lucy Detree on her cell. The last thing we need is for Hodge to show up here if he's back from St. Thomas."

"Shouldn't we call hotel security?" Sabrina asked.

"What for? She's dead. The real cops can deal with the toy cops. You saw how vigilant they are when we entered the hotel complex." He tapped on his cell phone and spilled the details to Lucy Detree. Sabrina wondered if Heidi had taken pills with booze so she could join Eric rather than live without him. She really hadn't seemed the suicidal type to Sabrina, but they'd only had lunch together on the day when Sabrina had been leveled by her grandmother's rejection.

"They're on the way. Lucy wants us to wait right here. I'm sorry you had to be here. I know you don't need this and came only as a favor to me. The one consolation is that at least Henry isn't here. That would really nail him," Neil said. Sabrina realized that Neil was babbling, something he did only when he was nervous, which didn't happen very often.

Sabrina nodded her head, agreeing with Neil. She heard the faint sound of sirens in the background. Within minutes, Lucy Detree was standing in the passageway with Neil and her, after entering the hotel room and confirming what Neil had informed her. Heidi was dead.

"I'm treating this as a crime scene, Neil," Lucy said.

"I understand," he said solemnly.

"Well, I don't. She'd been drinking, probably taking pills. She was a mess, and may have even done this intentionally," Sabrina said. The thought of Heidi's death complicating Eric's murder when Henry was the focus of the police investigation terrified her.

"I think we may find she was suffocated, Sabrina. The victim's face has petechial hemorrhages consistent with suffocation. We'll see what the medical examiner has to say after an autopsy."

Detective Detree began choreographing the scene of the crime, sending officers to isolate it with gaudy yellow tape, just like on television. Sabrina watched the horrified hotel manager try to persuade Lucy it wasn't necessary, that they could keep hotel guests away more discreetly, but Detree wasn't having any of it.

"Listen, you two can go sit in the hotel lobby. I'll send someone up to take your statements shortly," she said.

"We don't know anything more than what Neil told you,"

Sabrina said. She wanted to get as far away from the Westin as she could on an island nine miles by three.

Lucy Detree raised an eyebrow at Sabrina but said nothing. Neil took Sabrina by the elbow.

"Come on. They have bar service in the lobby. I'll buy you a drink."

Sabrina grunted, but a drink sounded in order. She started to walk toward the main building where the lobby was located when it occurred to her the woman at the front desk where she'd inquired earlier about the location of Heidi's room might recognize her. What if she said something in front of Neil or later to the police? Sabrina agonized about whether she should just come clean with Neil, but it felt oddly humiliating. Sabrina knew now why she had gone to see Heidi. It wasn't because she thought she should clear the air and tell Heidi off. It wasn't even because she worried Henry would end up in jail. It was because she was jealous of Neil's shiny new bar card and how it might enable him to find Eric's killer without her. Before, she had been part of a duo with him. Now, with "Esquire" newly emblazoned after his name, he needed no one. She was too proud to admit how shallow she had become. She'd take her chances that the hotel clerk found her unmemorable.

Chapter 27

Henry sat at the bar at the Tap Room nursing a beer he didn't want. The Summer Pale Ale crafted by St. John Brewers was excellent and his favorite. He just wasn't thirsty or hungry. He'd ordered six of the personal sized pizzas he knew Lyla loved to go, although he'd only bring two to her. He would deliver the other four he'd ordered to Grace and David. He would drop by and hand them to Grace as an apology for standing her up the evening he had invited her for drinks and apps at his condo. "And because David doesn't even know how to light the grill," he would add.

It was a pathetic sham so he could stop by and see David for a few moments. He couldn't come up with something better. The fear he might be arrested and end up in a cell may have paralyzed his creative side, but not his dominant self-destructive one.

"Aren't you supposed to be laying low, Henry?" Katie asked from the other side of the fairly empty bar as if on cue.

"I was going crazy and Lyla loves these pizzas." How lame was he, using Lyla as an excuse.

"They're such a cute old couple. I love it when they come in," she said. Henry noticed Katie had the color back in her face.

Half-way down the stairs to the main floor of Mongoose Junction, the complex where the Tap Room was located, Henry encountered Tyler and a couple of guys he recognized but didn't know by name. Austen was not with him. Where had Austen gone after leaving Tide-Away? What was going on that led him back to the villa?

"Where's your buddy, Austen?" Henry asked.

"The last time I saw him was at Bar None. He's got a hot date at Woody's, or so he says. I don't care as long as he stops giving me shit about having a crush on Katie just because I'd rather drink here than at Woody's," Tyler said. Henry agreed. Woody's was a shit-show with people spilling out on to the narrow street where oncoming traffic tried to avoid hitting them.

"You drink where you want to, Tyler. There are enough bars on this island to please everyone," Henry said, letting Tyler pass him.

Henry placed the pizzas on the floor of the front passenger side of Evan's Volvo. It seemed sacrilegious to be bringing pizzas in a car owned by a man who wouldn't get to eat them. Henry felt like shit it and a lot of other things, but it didn't stop him from heading to David's on a pretense.

Just as he turned off Centerline Road, Henry heard the blare of sirens that rivaled those he'd heard at The Last Chance Center just a few days earlier. When he had been a flight attendant flying out of Logan Airport, the honks and screeches from emergency vehicles were so common he had become immune to them. In St. John, people stopped and paid attention to the sound of sirens. For Henry, tonight it meant the cops were busy pursuing something other than his incarceration and that was fine by him. That it was likely the discovery of Heidi's death didn't matter to him. He had nothing to do with it and could do nothing about it.

He practiced the little speech about why he was dropping by as he pulled into David's driveway for the second time in one day. Twinkling tiny white lights lined the roofs to the house and Grace's studio lending a magical touch to the pool area, which was filled with tropical plants, also illuminated. Henry felt like an intruder.

They were seated by the pool at a round table under an umbrella. The citronella candles cast a soft light that made Grace and David appear angelic in front of their empty plates. Clearly, they had demolished porterhouse steaks and a garden salad. An empty bottle of Pinot Noir sat next to a half-filled one. Henry felt stupid carrying the four pizza boxes toward them.

"And here I thought David might be starving you, Grace. He must have taken some grilling lessons. You can reheat these for lunch tomorrow," Henry said, setting the stacked boxes on the table.

David stood and asked Henry to sit down, but there were only two chairs at the table. He stumbled over to a group of chairs closer to Grace's studio and dragged one over.

"I can't stay. I didn't mean to burst in and interrupt. I just felt bad about standing you up the other night when I'd invited you to my home for drinks," Henry said looking into Grace's sharp blue eyes. The old girl wasn't missing a trick, he could tell by the tiny upward curl of her mouth.

"Why Henry, that was so sweet of you, dear. I know fully well you couldn't help but miss our appointment that evening. If I'd known you'd be stopping by I would have picked up a third steak. I'm the grillmeister here, you see. David is just my sous chef, but he's learning." Grace turned to smile with pride at David as if she had given birth to him.

"But there is plenty of key lime pie to share," David said, rising and heading toward the kitchen. Henry knew he should decline and return to Lyla's but he couldn't. David's backyard under the now clear sky felt more comforting to him than the regrettable pall hanging over Lyla's home. He would have a piece of pie and a glass of wine before returning to Fish Bay where the Grim Reaper sat beckoning Evan.

"Aren't you supposed to be in seclusion?" Grace asked. Henry decided she was clairvoyant on top of her other talents. She seemed like a genuinely caring person, which made her indifference to Sabrina as a child even more perplexing.

"Lyla and the hospice nurse were tending to Evan's evening rituals, so I decided to break out for a bit before I went mad waiting to know if I'm going to be thrown in jail," Henry said. "I got pizza for Lyla too. It's her favorite." He sounded lame. He wasn't fooling anyone. He was here to see David.

The pie and wine went down surprisingly easy after the ale he'd had at the Tap Room, which was right after he found Heidi dead. This new "normal" felt as frightening as what he once considered to be abnormal.

David cleared the table and brought out a third bottle of wine and set it on the table.

"No more for me, David. You'll have to carry me over to the studio if I have more," Grace said.

"You may want to reconsider when you hear this," David said, uncorking the bottle, while a new stream of screaming sirens began in the background.

Henry knew what was coming.

"They've discovered the body of a woman at the Westin. I just heard it on the scanner in the kitchen when I was grabbing the wine" David said, holding up the bottle of Josh Cabernet.

"No, what happened?" Grace asked. Her baby blues bulged out of their sockets. "Who is it? Do they know?"

Henry was surprised by Grace's intensity, but then he already knew who the dead body was.

"They talk in code. I only monitor it so I know what's going on at the airport in St. Thomas. All I caught was that it was a woman and at the Westin. Hey, isn't that where Neil said Heidi was staying?" David asked.

"It was," Henry said, pushing his empty wine glass toward David.

"Pour," said Grace, following suit.

Chapter 28

Once Sabrina had a few sips of the Chardonnay Neil ordered for her, she decided it would be better if Henry heard the news that Heidi was dead from her. The island coconut telegraph was remarkably speedy on the rock where everything else moved slower than tourists believed possible. She knew he'd been drinking as soon as he answered her call. She wondered if Lyla and Henry had just had their fill of misery and were drowning their sorrows together while the hospice staff was there.

"Any news about when Lyla's kids will get a flight out of New York?" Sabrina asked before plunging into the news about Heidi.

"Yeah, they should be able to get out in the next day or so when the backlog falls off. The tropical storm that was heading our way, the one that put David in a panic, veered to the northeast so New England got hit instead of us. It wasn't a hurricane, just enough wind and rain to screw flights up for a few days."

Sabrina marveled how airline people understood weather as well as many meteorologists. The same seemed to be true of sailors. She guessed that if you are drawn to the air or sea, you develop a sense about what may be looming. She wished she had more time to consider what weather was headed their way. In her old life as a meteorologist, she would linger over screens and charts, comparing the European to other computer models. Sabrina had loved weather since she was a child living in a shabby motel complex overlooking the fickle Atlantic Ocean where she swam every day from May until early October. Ruth bragged to her teachers that Sabrina knew when a Nor'easter was coming before the weathermen on television.

"How's Lyla doing?" she asked. When Henry hesitated to answer, Sabrina had an epiphany. Henry wasn't sipping tequila with Lyla. Henry wasn't with Lyla at all.

"Where the hell are you, Henry? I thought we agreed you'd lay low until Neil could figure about why Hodge says he's going to charge you with Eric's murder when Lucy Detree knows nothing about it. What are you, self-destructive?" Sabrina immediately regretted scaring Henry, who was already terrified, but she was angry that he was being reckless. She had taken great pains to keep him off Hodge's radar. Then she remembered how stupid and impulsive it had been for her to visit Heidi earlier. If Henry knew she had gone to Heidi's room, he could accuse her of the same recklessness, so Sabrina let up.

"Are you somewhere safe?" she asked.

"Yes, I'm at David's. With him and your grandmother."

Sabrina groaned. She pictured the three of them, drinking red wine, or maybe margaritas because it was so hot

"Do you know what's going on at the Westin?" she asked. Neil was far enough away from her in the lobby that Sabrina was sure he couldn't hear what she was saying. She knew he'd get all lawyerly and tell her to stay quiet. When Henry didn't take the bait, Sabrina filled him in.

"Neil and I just found Heidi dead in her room. Lucy Detree thinks it may have been intentional."

"Like she'd been murdered?" Henry asked. The incredulous tone to his voice said she'd gotten his attention.

"Yes," Sabrina said. "It was awful, Henry. Almost worse than seeing Eric. At least he could see what was coming. Heidi may have been suffocated when she was sleeping or passed out. It seemed more cowardly, unfair." She hadn't meant to blurt out how upset she was at the sight of Heidi.

"Sabrina, I have to go now," Henry said, suddenly sounding sober.

Sabrina knew she had pushed him too far. He didn't need to hear how awful it had been finding Heidi dead with Neil.

"Why? What's wrong?" she asked

"Detective Hodge just drove into David's driveway," Henry said.

Sabrina heard the voice she now knew belonged to her grandmother through the phone. It had been calm, reasoned, and deliberate when Grace revealed a sketch of her family's history earlier that morning. Now, it sounded alarmed and commanding.

"Go into David's house before he sees you, Henry," Grace said. It wasn't a request.

"Henry, do what she says. Just do it," Sabrina said, trusting her grandmother for the first time in her life.

Chapter 29

David pulled Henry out of his chair before he could say no and led him toward the kitchen. Grace took two of the wine glasses off the table and placed them under the tablecloth, which fortunately touched the ground. She refilled her wine glass and sat tall in her chair.

"Hello, may I help you?" Grace called out to the man approaching her from the driveway. He passed through the gate omitting any of the polite pleasantries islanders are known for. No "Good evening" or even "Inside" to see if he might approach.

"I'm looking for a woman named Grace Armstrong, who recently stayed at Caneel Bay," Hodge said.

"That would be me. And who are you?" Grace asked, although it was clear she was addressing a man wearing a badge. She wondered how Henry had known recognized him from his car until she saw that the emblem on the squad car identified his office.

"I am Detective Hodge of the United States Virgin Islands Police Department. I have some questions to ask you," Hodge said. He took the chair Henry had been sitting in without being asked.

"Please sit down, Detective," Grace said, after Hodge had

plopped his body into the chair. "What kind of questions do you want to ask me? Do I need my attorney present?"

"I'm not accusing you of anything, Ma'am. I'd just like to know if you knew Eric Hershey or Heidi Montgomery. Both lived in Massachusetts before they came to St. John. You live in Massachusetts, don't you Mrs. Armstrong?"

"The last I heard, living in Massachusetts hasn't been a crime since George McGovern ran for office," Grace said.

"No but harassing and threatening a new resident in the Virgin Islands is," Hodge said.

Grace looked at the man sitting across from her. His face was barely lit by the candlelight that minutes ago had seemed playful. Now, his sneer made it appear menacing. She hadn't understood the entire conversation that morning, but the upshot had been that Hodge was more than a buffoon. He had the power to put Henry in jail without much evidence. He was someone Neil Perry avoided very cautiously. Grace knew she must measure her words and not lash out, even if she was tempted to show Hodge what a moron he was.

"I'm not sure I understand, Detective."

"A woman filed a complaint with our office claiming you were harassing and threatening her," Hodge said.

"I've only arrived on your island recently, sir. I don't know anyone well enough to harass or threaten. I'm a writer. I usually use my pen to deal with people I find annoying. I find inspiration everywhere," Grace said staring directly into his eyes.

"Well, this particular woman has just been found dead at the Westin Hotel, Mrs. Armstrong. Detective Detree had been looking to find you earlier today to ascertain whether you had indeed been threatening Heidi Montgomery. It seems like she didn't look hard enough and that she was tragically too late. This kind of thing happens way too frequently when I am called to administrative duties on St. Thomas." Hodge shook his head in overstated regret.

"I beg your pardon. Are you suggesting I had something to

do with that wretch's death? You are way out of line, Detective. I think I will have to summon my attorney," Grace said. She took a sip of wine wanting to spit it in the despicable detective's face. During their short conversation, she had ascertained that she was dealing with a small-minded despot. Hodge thrived on power, but it didn't compensate for his lack of intelligence.

David stepped out of the kitchen and approached the table. His stride was long and confident, assuring Grace that reinforcements had arrived.

"Grace, are you all right? I heard your voice rise and saw that a police van was in the driveway. Is your visit here connected to all the sirens we heard? Is Mrs. Armstrong's granddaughter okay?" David asked, turning to Hodge, who seemed perplexed by his appearance. Grace was impressed by David's performance.

"You must be David Gilmartin. The owner of this house, the guy who operates the seaplane, right? I'm here to ask Mrs. Armstrong some official questions, Mr. Gilmartin. There's no need for you to get involved. Now, Mrs. Armstrong, I didn't know you have a granddaughter on island. Who would that be?" Hodge asked Grace directly, his back to David.

"Sabrina Salter, Detective Hodge. That's the last question I will answer without counsel." Grace folded her arms in front of her on the table. She could see that her answer had surprised Hodge, who slumped back in the chair. He sat back up attention, ready for another go.

"If you believe that's necessary, Ma'am, we can continue this inquiry down at the station. Who's your attorney?" Hodge asked. Grace knew he was calling her bluff and doubted she had an attorney on island since she was just a tourist.

"Neil Perry. You can contact him directly to make the arrangements to question me further. Now, I'm tired and upset and would like you to leave. David, will you please turn off the outdoor lights as soon as Detective Hodge has left. They seem to draw insects to my cottage during the night."

Grace rose and placed her hand on David's shoulder in silent gratitude and walked toward the tiny artist's bungalow she now called home. Just as she reached the door, she heard Hodge call out, "Hey, isn't that Evan Banks's Volvo in the driveway? I thought he was on the way out. Who's driving it?" Just when she thought Hodge had been distracted from any notion that Henry was present. He would know how close Sabrina and Henry were to the Banks.

"I am. His wife was kind enough to loan it to me so I could return my rental jeep until I can purchase a car of my own. That was your bonus question, Detective Hodge. Good night."

David turned off the exterior lights once Hodge was in his cruiser. Hodge peeled out of the driveway into the darkness that had set in.

Grace reversed her direction and headed toward the kitchen door to David's house using the flashlight she pulled out of her pocket. She had lived alone long enough to know a flashlight was the first line of defense at night.

David waited outside for a few minutes until Grace heard the sound of Hodge's cruiser enter Centerline Road. He joined her in the kitchen, calling out to Henry that he could come out of the spare bedroom.

"Thanks, guys," Henry said looking sheepishly at Grace and David.

You're welcome, Henry. Now you'll just have to explain to Neil Perry that he's my new attorney, to Lyla Banks that she's loaned me Evan's car, and to Sabrina that you've outed her as my granddaughter," Grace said, chuckling.

"Maybe I should just turn myself into Hodge," Henry said.

Chapter 30

Neil resisted the urge to suggest he stay with Sabrina on her couch for the night. With two murders on island in as many days he didn't like sending her home to her isolated cottage. He'd have felt better if Girlfriend were with her.

But he kept his mouth shut. She made it clear where they stood when she left him stranded on Vinalhaven a few weeks before. He had been wrong thinking they understood one another.

Lucy Detree's abrupt dismissal of them had Neil more concerned than if she had stuck Sabrina and him under glaring light bulbs for interrogation. Something was amiss with the investigation. Maybe he'd learn what it was when he and Sabrina reported to the police station together at 9:00 the next morning as ordered.

By the time Neil arrived at Coral Bay, it was last call at Skinny Legs. Exhausted, yet restless, Neil decided to have a drink. He spotted Crustacean at his favorite barstool and took the empty one next to him.

"I start the day having breakfast with you and end it having a nightcap next to you. People are going start talking about us, Crusty," Neil said, slapping the old man on his back.

"Looks like you got bigger things to worry about, my friend. That cousin of yours was found dead a few hours ago at the Westin." Crusty raised his fingers in italic signs when he said "cousin."

"Jesus, Crusty don't even kid about me being related to her. I knew she was trouble when I met her in Massachusetts, but I didn't know how much trouble." Neil said. He took the bourbon the bartender had poured him and downed it. He slid it back for another. It was the first time he'd felt right all day.

"Me too. I've been watching women like her use guys for decades. But somehow she still managed to con me into doing favors for her. Still, she wasn't bad enough to die so young. Do you know how it happened?" Crusty asked.

Neil was too tired to avoid the question, plus Detree hadn't said her suspicions Heidi had been asphyxiated were confidential.

"Asphyxiation. Maybe suffocated with a pillow." Neil sipped his second bourbon more slowly. He'd already gotten one extra after last call. He was surprised to hear Heidi had been able to finagle Crusty into doing anything. Neil thought Crusty was well past that.

"Well, that's not the worse way to go. Better than the guy who took it from a machete," he said.

"That was her husband," Neil said. He realized as he said it, how unlikely it was that the two deaths were a coincidence. He would need to give that more thought, but not until the morning when he'd cleared his brain of the alcohol and got a decent night's sleep.

"No shit. She told me she was divorced. Said her husband had run out on her, but that it was another woman's fault."

This was the first suggestion Neil had heard that sounded like Eric had been cheating on Heidi. Although Crusty's earlier description of Eric as a womanizer was consistent with what

Heidi claimed. But maybe Heidi meant Grace was to blame for calling the police.

"Did she talk to you a lot?" Crusty might be a better source of information about Heidi than Neil initially considered.

"She yapped a lot one day when I drove her to Cruz Bay and never shut up at Skinny's. I swear, people bought her drinks just to keep her mouth busy. I tuned her out mostly. She would go on about buying a villa and where she thought the best sections on the island were. Crap like that. She didn't have enough money to rent a jeep so how was she going to buy a villa? I figured she wouldn't last six months on island," Crusty said. He finished his beer and put a dollar under the bottle. Neil knew this was the extent Crusty tipped, even after taking up the bar stool all night.

"When's the last time you took her to Cruz Bay?" Neil was surprised to hear Heidi had left Coral Bay after landing on the *Knot Guilty* and taking up residence at Skinny Legs.

"I only took her once. Hmm, it was whatever day it rained really hard. I had to pick up a prescription at Chelsea Drug or I wouldn't have been driving. My tires are pretty bald, but I take heart medication. So I figured I had a bigger chance of having a heart attack than I did of going off the road. Catch you later, my man."

Neil savored the last sip of his drink. Heidi was turning out to be as big a mystery as her husband. Maybe the bartender would know more about her, but he was closing shop and it would have to wait.

Chapter 31

Leaving the Westin without being interrogated left Sabrina wired. She had wanted to get the questioning over and to learn whether the police knew she had been to Heidi's room earlier. Instead, she and Neil had been dismissed by an exhausted Lucy Detree, who seemed to know she could trust them to show up the next morning. "I'm more concerned about keeping the scene clean for forensics than I am in hearing what you two have to say," Lucy admitted to them when she finally let them leave the lobby.

Neil drove her to Bar None, where she picked up her vehicle and decided to drive directly out to Fish Bay. She wasn't sure where Henry was, but since he'd seen fit to leave the refuge she had come up with for him and gone to David's, he was on his own. David and Grace would have to babysit him tonight. The utter exhaustion Sabrina felt after discovering Heidi's body with Neil was more visceral than mental. She was spent.

Her head throbbed as she reviewed the events of the evening on her way up over Jacobs Ladder for the third time in one day. Heidi had been alive that morning. Neil had driven her to check into the Westin. Sabrina couldn't be sure if Heidi had still been alive by the time she went to visit her before heading to see Neil at Bar None. She had no idea who had entered Heidi's room while she hid in the bathroom or who may have visited her before. There had been two glasses next to the liquor bottle. Sabrina hadn't thought to check whether the tray from room service had plates for more than one meal. She was horrified by the idea that Heidi may have been suffocated while she hid in the bathroom.

If Lucy Detree was right, and Sabrina had confidence in the young policewoman's instincts based on her past performance, Heidi had been murdered. But who on St. John, save Eric, had motive to kill her? He was already dead. It seemed more logical to suspect Heidi of killing Eric than vice versa, except she had been stuck on the other side of the island when Eric was murdered and had flipped out at the news of his death.

The muggy night air felt like a blanket suffocating the island. Sabrina hadn't wanted to go home alone to her empty cottage. She had been tempted to suggest Neil camp out with her, on the sofa, of course, rather than drive all the way over to Coral Bay. He had to be at the police station with her at 9:00 the next morning. It would be natural, but no it wouldn't. Not now.

Sabrina drove by Klein Bay and looked up at the top of Fish Bay where she could see lights coming from the Banks' villa. The other two homes were vacant with Mara Bennett being away and Villa Mascarpone unoccupied until Lyla's kids arrived. There were few homes in between those and hers, which sat on a hillside below. She wished Girlfriend were with her. The night was just too damn hot, dark and quiet for her.

When she rounded the turn toward her cottage, Sabrina remembered she had a new beautiful, heated pool waiting for her. Perfect. She would shed her sweaty clothes and indulge in a skinny dip. Then she would pour a tall glass of lemonade with vodka, which was so much better than with bourbon, and read for a while on her sweet little porch to soothe her nerves.

Sabrina pulled in front of her new stonewall when the entire front yard, pool area and garden, lit up like a stage at a theater.

Sean must have included sensor lighting with the pool. That's when she noticed a man sitting with his feet dangling off the side of the pool, dipping in the water.

"What are you doing here?" Sabrina gasped as she pushed the gate open.

"Sorry, I didn't mean to frighten you," Austen said looking up at her.

"Well, you did a good job of it any way," she said. She remembered hearing from Mitch just hours before that Austen had been in jail for five years. True, it wasn't for a violent crime, but still.

"I just wanted to talk to you alone and that's next to impossible at work. I thought it would be easier to come here," Austen said, his white teeth shining against his tanned face under the garish outdoor lights.

"How did you get here?" Sabrina asked.

Austen nodded over toward some Genip trees where a small white Toyota pick-up truck sat. Even from under the outdoor lights, Sabrina could see dings and dents and chipped paint.

"In my new wheels. Just bought her today. No more pleading for rides. That's why I'm here," Austen said while he beamed toward the truck like a proud new papa. Sabrina began to relax. Austen didn't sound like he'd come to murder her.

"Congratulations on the truck, but I'm not following you. What's that got to do with you coming here to talk to me after hours?" Sabrina asked. She was letting Austen know that no matter how excited he was to have wheels, coming to see her at her private residence late at night was inappropriate.

"I'm sorry," Austen said, pulling his feet out of the water. "It's just so damn hot. I don't know how I resisted the temptation not to jump in."

His apology sounded hollow to Sabrina. Austen needed to spit out why he'd come and leave.

"Why are you here, Austen?"

Austen stood to face Sabrina. She was taller than him. She was taller than a lot of men.

"Eric owed me money." Austen sounded a little angry now.

"So..." Sabrina said, wondering what that had to do with her.

"He said he had it in an envelope, in his purse, you know that guy-bag. Did you find his bag? Katie says the cops didn't even know he had one," Austen said.

"No, I'm sorry. How much did he owe you?"

"Three hundred. He borrowed it a while ago. Nothing in writing, but I knew he needed the money bad. He didn't tell me why, but he did say it was going to change his life. The other day I told him I needed it back soon, that I finally had a chance to buy some wheels. I bought Fat Betty's truck – you know her, don't you? The skinny cook at The Lyme Inn. I told her I'd buy her truck for $750.00. I gave her $450.00 I've been saving and was supposed to give her the three Eric was going pay me today. I feel bad. She trusted me and let me take the truck," Austen said.

"I see," said Sabrina, and she did.

"The last day we worked together, the day he got killed, Eric said he was getting some money, a lot of money very soon. He said would pay me back out of his pay from last week because he'd have a lot more than that real soon. But now he's dead, my rent is due and if I pay it, I don't have the three to pay her. I probably shouldn't be telling my boss this, but I got into some trouble with money before. Legal trouble. I'm really trying to start over, that's why I came here. I don't want people thinking I'm a low-life."

Sabrina shook her head. Austen's tale was an all too common one on island, where the one percent owned opulent villas they rarely set foot in and the rest of the ninety-nine lived paycheck to paycheck.

"I'm sorry, Austen," she said once again, hoping to end the conversation on a sympathetic note.

"I know, me too. Listen, I had one other idea. Since Eric

worked the first three days of the workweek, do you think you could pay me the three hundred out Eric's wages?" Austen's throat had thickened and his mouth sounded dry. Sabrina imagined it would be difficult for someone who went to jail for swindling to be humbled to the point where he was asking for a dead man's wages. But it was better than stealing.

"No, I can't do that. His wages go into his estate, whatever that means. But I'll lend you the cash if you'd like and take it out of your weekly pay $25.00 a week for the next twelve weeks," she said.

Austen put out his hand. Sabrina shook it.

"Thanks, you are not nearly the bit- I mean," Austen stammered without finishing his sentence.

Sabrina laughed. "Yes, I am, Austen. Just ask around."

Austen slipped into his flip-flops and headed for the gate, when Sabrina thought to ask him a question.

"Hey, Austen. Where was Eric getting the money to pay you? Did he mention where the money was coming from?" Sabrina asked.

"Karma. He said Karma was paying him a visit."

Sabrina waited five minutes till she heard the sound of the truck struggling down the hill before she stepped out of her clothes and into the cool water in the pool she didn't own. She let her head sink beneath the silvery surface because she knew you never fully cooled off until you did.

Karma. What did Eric mean? Did it matter?

Not tonight, it didn't.

Chapter 32

Grace asked David to drive the Volvo to Lyla's while she rode in the front passenger seat. Driving on St. John in the daylight had been challenging enough, but at night with occasional rain and no streetlights, it was treacherous She'd tucked Henry in the back seat with instructions to duck if she or David said so.

"You're the second one to tell me that today," Henry said, sitting with the two small pizzas he had bought for Lyla on his lap.

"Well, you should have listened to the rest of her instructions," Grace said. Henry had admitted that he abandoned Sabrina's sensible plan to keep him off the police radar until Neil could point the cops toward a credible suspect who killed Eric. Grace wasn't cutting him any slack. He had been reckless leaving Lyla's.

Lyla greeted them at the door where Henry introduced Grace.

"So you're Sabrina's grandmother. Well, well, well," Lyla said letting the threesome through to the cheerful kitchen, where Grace felt immediately welcome, even if she wasn't clear what "Well, well, well" meant.

"How's Mr. Banks doing, Mrs. Banks?" David asked. Grace was grateful for his manners. It was awkward coming to the home of a woman whose husband was about to die and complicating her situation.

"We're not here to bother you. You must be exhausted. We just needed to return Henry and ask for what I hope is a small favor," Grace said.

"Please sit and give me some non-hospice company for a few minutes. I can make some tea, or if you'd like something stronger?" Lyla asked. Grace thought Lyla was probably a little younger than she, but she was of the same generation where manners never went on vacation.

"Tea would be fine," David said. "Can I make it?"

"Let me, otherwise we'll be chewing tealeaves," Henry said.

"Evan is at the back of the house, sleeping quite well thanks to some magical potion the nurses administer. Girlfriend is next to him," Lyla said, sitting on a stool at the kitchen island. She patted the one next to her, signaling for Grace to come sit. "I've learned it's best to let these two work it out," she whispered conspiratorially gesturing toward David and Henry.

Grace sat down. She wondered what to say next. She supposed Lyla was a mother figure for Sabrina, and a lovely one at that. Twinges of jealousy began to rise when Grace remembered she deserved what she was getting. And more.

She watched Henry pour water from a bottle out of the refrigerator into a bright yellow kettle. Cistern water wasn't great for tea, she'd learned. Lyla's unreserved welcome disarmed Grace. She found herself blathering to the woman she had just met.

"What I did, or didn't do, was unforgiveable. I know that," Grace said, looking directly at her.

"I'm not one to judge," Lyla said gently.

"She was a child, an innocent child. I couldn't see past the pain of losing my only daughter, even though it was obvious she had lost her mother. When my husband forbade me to connect with Sabrina, I didn't have the courage to stand up to him. I let myself believe I had no room to love again, that I wouldn't be able to survive more pain or loss, and I retreated. I was a coward." Grace could not understand why she felt compelled to confess to Lyla, only that she did.

Lyla nodded, but kept silent. The only sound in the kitchen was David shutting cabinet doors after taking out bold-colored pottery mugs.

"By the time Charlie died, I was so ashamed I pretended it was too late. That Sabrina was better without me. I'd failed in my relationships with my daughter and my husband. I hid in my house writing silly books about beach romances no one believes could ever happen, but for some reason everyone wants to buy." Grace continued with the truth, a truth she had never spoken out loud, before she lost the courage.

"I was horrid to her and her friend when she came to my house. She must have told you," Grace said. She hoped Sabrina had laid it out with all the bloody details so she would be spared recounting her horrid behavior.

"No, she didn't. You tell me," Lyla said.

Grace sighed. It felt lopsided that she was unloading on Lyla while Evan lay two rooms away dying. But she also sensed Lyla wanted to listen, to help where she might still be able to do some good, so she pressed on. Grace spared her nothing.

"I can see why you're not feeling very good about that," Lyla finally said to Grace. Grace was grateful that she did not cushion her words.

Henry interrupted them by placing a mug of hot Earl Grey tea in front of each of them. He returned to the counter next to the stove where he had set David's and his cups, giving the two older women some space to continue their conversation.

Grace mixed a spoonful of Coral Bay honey into the hot tea, swirling it around until it had dissolved. She took a sip and shuddered.

"That's why I'm here. I came to make things right. No, wait.

I know I can't undo the past. But I want Sabrina to know it wasn't because of her or anyone else that I didn't step up to the plate when she was a child. It's entirely my fault. I'd like her forgiveness, of course, and even more so a relationship with her."

Lyla put her mug down. "Well, maybe you'll need a little patience for that."

"Sure, at my age, patience is about all I've got left," Grace laughed.

"Grace, I don't know what to say to you except that your granddaughter is one of the kindest human beings I know. She's got a tough veneer. Who can blame her after all she's been through? But I know she desperately longs for family. Give it a while."

Lyla finished her mug of tea, signaling the end of the time she had to spare from Evan. Grace appreciated how generous she had been.

"Now, just so you know what a hard-hearted bitch I am, I really came to tell you I'm stealing your husband's car for a while."

Lyla chuckled and squeezed Grace's hand.

Grace started to explain what she had told the police, but Henry jumped in to explain how he'd foolishly left Lyla's and what happened afterward, including the news about Heidi's murder. He finished with a grand bow and a presentation of her favorite pizzas.

"Well, Grace, we'll have to keep this from Evan. He never loans his car, not even if it is to keep Henry out of jail. Not even in exchange for Girlfriend spending time with." Lyla laughed.

At the sound of her name, Girlfriend began to whine from the back bedroom. She rushed into the kitchen, her nails sliding across the clay-colored tile floor, looking around at everyone. She sniffed and walked over to Grace and placed her head in Grace's lap. Grace leaned over and kissed the chocolate lab on the top of her head.

"I guess it will all have to come out, won't it sweetheart?" she whispered into the silky brown fur.

September 5, 2017

Hurricane Irma Category Five

Latitude 16.7N
Longitude -57.8W

470 miles from St. John

Chapter 33

If the sound of pouring rain hadn't awakened Sabrina at 5:30, she might have forgotten she had set a breakfast meeting with her workers at 7:00 at Mongoose Deli. Henry texted her at 6:30 to say he was sorry he would have to miss the meeting because his partner was secreting him at an undisclosed location. She texted him back, "Very funny," but she was pleased to hear Henry got it. With luck, she and Neil would learn the police had discovered who killed Eric when they went to the police station.

Austen was the first to arrive for breakfast, which Sabrina had anticipated. She had gone to the ATM to get the cash she had promised him. Sabrina had surprised herself when she agreed to advance the money. She knew there was a good chance Austen wouldn't work for Ten Villas long enough to repay it, but it had felt right. If he didn't pay it back, she'd make good with the company what he didn't.

Sabrina handed him the cash in a bank envelope. She had taken an extra one at the ATM and written the terms of the agreement on it for Austen to sign, which he gladly did.

"Here, take a picture of it with your camera so we both have a copy. I'm surprised you didn't do that with Eric."

"I know. I don't usually lend money. Since I got into trouble a while back, I try to keep from borrowing or lending, but it's not easy on an island where you don't know what's going to happen from one minute to the next. Eric told me he needed the loan from me to show someone he had changed his life. I kind of get that," Austen said, sitting across from Sabrina. He'd bought them each an ice coffee while they waited for Katie and Tyler.

"Tell me about it," she said.

He must have thought she meant it because Austen began talking about how he had landed in prison for five years after graduating from Wharton with honors. He recounted how his eagerness to pay off hefty student loans led him into some dodgy real estate deals with predatory mortgages in Hartford, Connecticut.

"So here I am, a convicted felon with a Wharton pedigree. My family pretty much doesn't ever want to hear from me. When Tyler told me he was heading to St. John on a self-discovery mission, it sounded good to me."

"Hey, you're not the first guy who graduated from Wharton to mess up, you know. I didn't realize you and Tyler arrived on island together. Where did you meet him?" Sabrina wondered for the second time if Tyler had done time too. Although she had to admit, this year's crew was proving more reliable than others.

"Starbucks. He was a barista and I was a guy sitting all day in front of a computer looking for a job that called for a felony conviction on his resume," Austen said. He sucked down the last sip of his iced coffee just as Tyler landed at the table.

"Sorry I'm late, but looks like I'm not the last one. Where's Katie?"

Tyler asked, his eyes searching the deli.

Sabrina's stomach growled. She could smell the slow roasted meats Demetri cooked daily for sandwiches. She couldn't wait to eat for Katie to arrive and asked Tyler to place their orders.

Katie sauntered in just as the server placed the tray with breakfast sandwiches for the three of them on the table.

"Sorry. I had unexpected early morning company," Katie said after telling the server she wasn't ordering.

"Are you sure? It's on me," Sabrina said. She understood eating meals out, even breakfast, might not be in the budget of a worker who worked two jobs on St. John as most did.

"I'm not very hungry, but thanks," Katie said.

"Who came to visit it you?" Tyler asked. Sabrina thought his question sounded stern, almost patronizing, but Katie didn't seem to notice.

"That idiot Hodge. I thought I heard he was being suspended after the uproar over how he had conducted the investigation out on Ditlieff Point. I only wish." Katie offered no more, but Tyler wasn't satisfied.

"What did he want? You shouldn't be alone right now, Katie. Especially since there's been another murder. I'd be happy to bunk in one of the empty rooms again until things quiet down," Tyler said leaning forward and looking into Katie's eyes as if Sabrina and Austen weren't there.

"I'm fine, Tyler. I'm even locking the doors at night. For the first time in the ten years since I've lived on St. John, but I get it. I'm not stupid. Hodge just wanted to know if I knew a couple of women on island."

Sabrina's ears perked up.

"What women?"

"Someone named Grace and a woman who died at the Westin," Katie said.

"Do you know either of them?" Austen asked with a yawn. Even with two coffees, he seemed half asleep.

"I don't know anyone named Grace. The other woman, I'd only heard of." Katie shifted in her seat, looking uncomfortable at the direction of the conversation. Sabrina shared her discomfort. She didn't like Hodge asking about her grandmother. She liked it even less that she felt protective toward Grace.

Sabrina pulled out three index cards with a rainy day "to do" list on each. She handed one to Austen, Tyler, and Katie.

"Here are your marching orders. Call me on my cell when you're done, please." Sabrina watched Tyler and Austen head out without even looking at what they had as tasks before them. Typical. Now if they had questions, they'd have to call her. She watched Katie read hers before leaving. Smart woman.

"Hey, how did you know about Heidi Montgomery? Sabrina asked. Katie looked up from the index card, her blonde eyebrows arching.

"From Eric. Sorry, I need to use the restroom," Katie said, looking pale as she rushed away, her hand over her mouth.

Chapter 34

Sabrina regretted not agreeing with Neil's suggestion that they meet at Bar None and go to the police station together. Her pride would be her downfall. Wait, she'd already had her downfall. It was only supposed to get better after that.

She entered the lobby to the "new" station that already looked as shabby as the old. The orange plastic chairs and tables were scratched and dingy. Mercifully, it was air-conditioned. Even during rain, St. John felt hot and oppressive in August.

There was only one person sitting in the lobby waiting for her and it wasn't Neil. Her grandmother perched on an orange chair with her legs crossed at her ankles, as if she were the queen on her throne. She was making notes in a smooth navy-blue leather notebook with a gold fleur-de-lis design on its cover. Her short sleeved white blouse and khaki capris looked as crisp as Grace did. She wore the humidity well. Another gene Sabrina regretted missing.

"What are you doing here?" Sabrina asked, hearing how rude she sounded.

"Responding to an invitation hand-delivered by Detective

Hodge last evening," Grace said. "And writing in my journal, something I've done every day since I was a very young woman."

"You mean he wasn't looking for Henry at David's?" Sabrina asked.

"Why would he? Henry wasn't there," Grace said, winking one eye as she nodded toward the desk officer who appeared impervious to their conversation as he flipped through the Daily News.

Sabrina sat down in a chair as far away from Grace as was possible in a room with only six chairs and two end tables. Her face flushed with embarrassment after Grace demonstrated she was more discreet about protecting Henry than Sabrina was. Where the hell was Neil? It wasn't like him to be late for a meeting with the police. She hoped he was okay. Hodge had them so caught up in minutia, it was easy to forget that someone on St. John was killing people. A smart killer might target Neil because he was investigating the murders more competently than the police. Sabrina began to panic.

"He said to tell you he shouldn't be long," Grace said. She had an annoying way of being in her head, Sabrina thought.

"Where is he?" she asked, reluctant to acknowledge Grace might know more about Neil than she did.

"In with Detective Hodge, who insisted I come to the station this morning. I told him I wouldn't think of doing such a thing without my attorney," Grace said.

"And Neil is your attorney?" Sabrina asked, incredulous how intertwined her grandmother had become in her life in such a short time.

"Of course. I hear he's the best on the island, dear." Grace smiled over at Sabrina. She had an impish grin that wrinkles only flattered.

"Don't call me "dear." Sabrina had had it and stood up ready to leave. She'd call Neil and tell him to let her know when Hodge was ready to see her.

"I'm sorry. It slipped out. I met your friend Lyla last night.

She's lovely, and your dog is precious," Grace said. Sabrina saw she was trying to make amends for being presumptuous and sat down, although she wasn't ready to share her friends with Grace yet. And certainly not her dog.

"How are they?" Sabrina couldn't resist asking.

Grace described how she and David returned Henry to the Banks' home in a low whisper.

They sat in silence for a few minutes, both waiting for Neil for different reasons. Sabrina fidgeted in her chair.

"Why do you need an attorney? What do the police think you've done?" Sabrina finally asked. She could no longer contain herself. What was wrong with her family anyway? Her immature and selfish mother abandoned her as a toddler. Her grief-stricken Irish father took to the drink, leaving young Sabrina home alone and at risk. If Ruth hadn't rescued her from the pervert who'd been sitting at the local drinking hole and knew Hugh's presence meant Sabrina was alone, Sabrina would be just another DCF statistic.

Her paternal grandfather sounded like a nasty control freak. Her grandmother had capitulated to him, which had ensured Sabrina's destiny. Grace now sat next to Sabrina in a police station waiting to be interrogated by the police. Sabrina wanted to know about what. And she wanted to know what she ever did to deserve being born into such a dysfunctional family.

Sabrina had been determined to lead an uneventful life when she nearly lost her freedom after accidentally shooting her husband. Twice since coming to St. John, she had happened upon dead bodies, both who happened to be connected to Ten Villas clients. Sabrina could consider those "coincidences." But if her visit to Grace had triggered Heidi's death in any way, Sabrina was prepared to accept she was as abnormal as every other member in her family.

. . .

"Nothing that you need to be concerned about – eh, Sabrina. You've got enough on your plate," Grace said, looking down at her tiny hands folded on her lap. Sabrina knew Grace had caught herself before calling her "dear" again.

"Do you paint or write? What do you do to relax?" Grace asked her.

What did she do to relax, Sabrina asked herself. Did she even know how to relax, let go, and chill? Sabrina had always been so preoccupied with measuring up and beyond her peers. Making sure she was smart enough, well read, dressed well, fit, she never intentionally considered how relaxation might fit into her life. Trying to be normal was hard work.

"I'm not artistic or musical and have no creative talents. I swim with my dog every night to relax," she said, not really wanting to give even that much to Grace.

"Your mother was a painter. A gifted painter. She was able to look at the ocean and make it even more beautiful on canvass," Grace said, almost to herself. Sabrina felt her breath shorten. She had dreamed about talking to her grandmother about her mother, although not in a police station. She wanted to know everything. What was Elizabeth's blood type, did she hate lima beans like Sabrina did, what was her favorite color blue, did she love to swim in the ocean, what was her favorite book? Sabrina had a million questions she longed to know the answers to, and this woman probably knew them all. The larger question that loomed was for Sabrina. Could she overcome her pride and let Grace share the answers?

A door opened and Neil walked out, a manila folder under his arm bulging with papers. He looked as angry as Sabrina had ever seen. The desk officer looked up at him and then back down at his newspaper.

"Okay, let's go," he said.

"You want me to go in and talk to Hodge alone?" Sabrina asked. She knew he was furious at her for abandoning him on

Vinalhaven in Maine, but she couldn't believe he would really throw her into Hodge's den undefended.

"No, that can wait. Both of you come with me. And get on the phone and have Henry meet us. The three of you have some explaining to do."

Chapter 35

They rode in silence to Sabrina's cottage, the least likely place they would be disturbed and the closest to Henry's hideout. Grace wasn't sure how she became the default driver, other than Sabrina and Neil hadn't parked their vehicles near the police station. As uncomfortable as she was driving on the winding hills in the rain, Grace was grateful for the distraction from the silent fury within Evan's car.

She had doubted she'd ever be invited to Sabrina's home. Although this wasn't exactly a social occasion, Grace looked forward to seeing where her granddaughter lived. The cottage didn't disappoint. The stonewalls, though incomplete, and arched entrance into an immature but carefully designed tropical garden were charming.

"Oh, this is delightful, Sabrina. Even in the rain, it feels a tropical oasis. The pool and landscape are so naturally coordinated," Grace said. She could hear herself gushing, but this was the only form of self-expression she had seen from her granddaughter to date. Besides Grace had been a poolside, seaside gardener for half of her life. She felt a tiny bond of commonality with Sabrina.

"Right, well it doesn't belong to me and never will because

I'll never be able to afford it. I just haven't figured out how to return a pool," Sabrina said. She glared at Neil as she led them to the front door of the porch. "Where did all these dead bees come from?" Sabrina asked.

There had to be several hundred dead bees lying in front of the threshold of the door.

"It can happen before a major storm. David's been complaining about the number of drowned bees he's had to fish out of the pool," Grace said.

"Dead bees are the least of your worries," Neil said.

Sabrina led them into a screened porch with several wicker chairs, a rocker, and a loveseat.

Neil pointed to a chair where Grace should sit.

"The rocker's hers. So is the pool, but since your granddaughter seems unable to accept a gift given by a very grateful family who wanted to honor her, she's got a little problem," he said.

Neil plopped in the middle of the loveseat. Grace watched Sabrina place her hands on her hips and step in front of him.

"I never would have accepted the Keatings' gift if I'd been told about it," she said. Grace noticed how fiery Sabrina's green eyes grew and that her high cheekbones were pink with fury. She was reminded of Hugh's face during the conversation he had with Charlie the night he and Elizabeth came to tell them they had eloped.

"They wanted to surprise you. You saved two, if not three, members of their family's lives for god's sake. Why can't you accept anything from another human being unless it's on your own terms? What, were they supposed to come to you and say, 'Hey, Sabrina, we'd like to thank you for what you did. What's an appropriate way for us to do that?' Like I was supposed to be handed a script from you so I'd know when I should reveal my family history?"

Grace knew this was an argument she shouldn't be hearing.

"Maybe I should wait in the car until Henry joins us," she said. She rose from her chair.

"Relax, Grace, your granddaughter gives it as good as she gets."

"How dare you? I told you about every scintilla of my life, from my crappy childhood to my monstrous marriage. I spared you nothing. You know what happened to Ben and how I had to endure a murder trial, lost my television career and reputation, and was left pretty much penniless. What? You couldn't tell me you were taking me to not just any quaint island off the coast of Maine, but the one where you'd grown up, where you expected me to meet your family, the family I didn't know existed because I thought you were from frigging L.A.?" Sabrina was shouting now. She was using a booming television broadcaster voice Grace found phony on television but alarming in person.

"Am I interrupting something, kids? Who did in the bees?" Henry asked. He walked through the screen door as Sabrina and Neil fell silent.

"No. Sit down, Henry. Is your laptop here?" he asked Sabrina in what Grace thought was an intentionally calm tone.

"Yes, I'll get it."

She returned with her laptop, turned it on, and handed it to Neil. Grace was glad Henry had arrived before the argument had escalated any further. She wasn't sure who had given Sabrina a pool for saving lives or why she couldn't accept it, but Grace was certain it was all her fault. By not rescuing her granddaughter from her drunken father after Elizabeth took off, Grace set her up for a lifetime of not being able to deal with other human beings. It was Grace's fault Sabrina hadn't had a decent marriage and now she was about to lose a man whom Grace thought was a decent, if not perfect, human being. Grace had a lot of atoning to do and it seemed her granddaughter had a bit of growing up to do. Maybe there was still a chance for Grace to have an influence on Sabrina.

Neil pulled a thumb drive out of his pocket. It was in a

plastic zip lock snack bag. He stuck the drive into the side of Sabrina's laptop, hit a key, and placed the computer on the coffee table facing Grace, Henry, and Sabrina.

"It's show time, gang. Too bad none of you thought to tell your own lawyer you were movie stars. Take a look. Your names will be in lights, or on dockets, before you can say, 'Not guilty.'" Grace didn't know Neil well, but she could tell he was seething.

She watched the pebbly screen flicker and then could see the image of Sabrina coming down the walkway toward Heidi's room at the Westin. When she turned off the path, the image disappeared. There was no sound. Grace knew what was coming.

After a few more seconds of a blurred gray and black screen, Grace watched as her own image appeared on the walk until she, too, veered to the left toward Heidi's room. Shortly thereafter, Grace reappeared on the path and hurried toward the pool in the distance. Sabrina was never seen returning to the walkway.

After a brief interruption in the video a man in a Skinny Legs baseball cap appeared walking down the same path until he took a left off the walkway. In short time, the man, who also wore sunglasses, hurried back onto the path toward the pool and the camera.

The last image was of a tall thin woman with short blonde hair and a blue and white striped beach towel walking down the same path and taking a left. When she returned to the walkway, Grace observed her wearing large sunglasses. It appeared she was carrying something under the beach towel. She was clearly in a hurry.

"Shit," Henry said.

"Oh, dear," Grace followed.

"That last clip was Katie," Sabrina said. "I saw her there myself."

Chapter 36

"Unless one or more of you is going to confess to killing Heidi, I have to ask, what the hell were you thinking?" Neil asked. He couldn't see any of the people sitting before him with their mouths gaping open as murderers. None of them were stupid. Why had they gone to see Heidi?

They were silent obviously shocked they had been caught on camera.

"All right, let's go one by one. In order. Sabrina, tell me when you went to Heidi's room, what and who you saw, and when you left. Then explain why," Neil said. He noticed she gulped before answering. She only did that when she was scared.

"Um, I went before I came to see you at Bar None to tell you what Henry and I had learned from Katie. I was angry that Heidi had come to St. John. There was something off about her story to us when we met her in Beechwood. I went to confront her and find out why she was really here. The door was unlocked, so I went in. I could see someone in the bed. I thought Heidi had probably passed out, but I never had a chance to find out because I heard someone coming, " Sabrina said.

"So, what happened when your grandmother arrived?" Neil

asked. He really couldn't see Salty and Grace suffocating Heidi, no matter how angry either of them was. But then he didn't know how upset Grace might have been at Heidi. She had been furious that day in Beechwood.

"I didn't know it was her. When I heard someone coming, I stepped into the bathroom and shut the door. I actually locked it," Sabrina said. "I waited for about ten minutes after I heard the outer door close and then I ran out the door myself. I took off down the corridor behind the units onto the cement walkway that housekeeping and maintenance use."

Neil took a breath. He was relieved Sabrina seemed to be telling the truth. He had wondered why the video showed her going down the path toward Heidi's room, but not returning on it as had Grace, Henry, and Katie. He knew that distinction wouldn't be lost on the cops.

"What about you, Grace?" Neil hated to sound too tough with the old bird, but he needed to know the truth and each of his clients had at a minimum, committed sins of omission with him.

"I'd had it with that girl. She'd been pestering me since she arrived on island, threatening to come to Caneel to see me. That's why I was so desperate to find a place to live that was private. I knew if I stayed at the Westin, Heidi would find me. She was threatening to blackmail me. I decided I would set her straight for once," Grace said.

"Please don't say that to the police," Neil said. He shook his head. Grace was her granddaughter on speed.

"Tell me more, Grace."

"I got there. I saw dirty dishes on the floor from room service. I could see a lump under the sheets on the bed and was afraid I was interrupting an intimate moment, but it was so quiet. When I noticed a bottle of liquor and two glasses on the nightstand, I figured Heidi was not alone. Then I saw the bathroom door was closed and I panicked. I didn't know it was you in there, Sabrina," Grace said. She had recounted what happened so quickly, she was out of breath. Neil became concerned.

"Okay, Henry, your turn."

"I'm sorry. It was stupid. I hated sitting and waiting for you guys to dig up information so Hodge wouldn't arrest me. I kept thinking what it would be like to be in a cell. I went a little crazy. I guess thought I was Harry Bosch and I could talk to Heidi and learn more about Eric." Henry began choking up.

"Go on, Henry. You can tell us," Neil said.

"She was dead. She wasn't breathing, so there was nothing I could do but leave. I will never forget it. Her face looked like she was asleep, but she was dead. There was this awful smell," Henry said, heaving with sobs Neil guessed he had been trying to contain since he saw Heidi's body.

Sabrina sprang off her rocking chair toward Henry. Grace approached him from the other side.

"What a mess," Neil said, half to himself.

"We need to talk to Katie," Sabrina said, looking up at him.

"You're right. But first we need to ask your grandmother why Heidi was threatening to blackmail her? Grace?"

Neil looked at the tiny octogenarian. Of the three, only one so far seemed to have a motive to kill Heidi and that was Grace. Neil didn't want to consider that was a possibility. What would Salty do if it turned out her grandmother was a murderer? Her family tree couldn't get much weirder. Not that it was his concern any more.

Grace left Sabrina to comfort Henry and turned toward Neil.

"She had confidential information about my publishing career that she threatened to make public," Grace said without emotion.

Neil knew she was lying.

Chapter 37

Sabrina told Grace it would be easier if she drove them over to Katie's than giving her directions about how to get there. It wasn't true, but it felt kinder than saying none of them wanted to spend a half hour on a ride that should take ten minutes.

Henry insisted on accompanying them. Sabrina was too tired and bruised from her argument with Neil to fight back. Grace sat shotgun, while the men climbed into the back of Evan's Volvo. The rain had turned into a daylong affair and the wind had picked up. Sabrina loved nothing better than a long soaking rain, made even better by a little thunder and lightning, but only if she was on her porch rocker with a book in her lap and her dog at her feet. This didn't feel like that kind of a rain to her.

The ride toward Estate Pastory, the area off Centerline Road above Cruz Bay where Katie lived, took longer during a downpour. Sabrina wished once again she had the time to check the weather. Something was definitely brewing, and it wasn't the remnants from the storm that had just passed by. Tropical depressions formed daily during hurricane season. It was important to remain vigilant and not become complacent just because most of them amounted to nothing more than rain, wind, and a little surf. She hoped Lyla's family arrived before another storm prevented them from spending a few final moments with Evan.

"She lives in that?" Grace asked, breaking the silence.

Sabrina had pulled off the road onto a dirt driveway that sat at a 45-degree angle. She pulled the emergency brake tight.

"Yep. That's what a starter home looks like down here. It's not all HGTV," Sabrina said. She had to agree with Grace. It was hard to believe Katie had been struggling for ten years to pay for what essentially was a slab and cistern with two adjoining basement rooms. Above was a primitive unfinished wood-framed first floor with a great room that included a kitchen of sorts, a bath, and a bedroom. The interior studded walls were uncovered. Two large sliders ran along the front of the house displaying a view of Cruz Bay and St. Thomas beyond. The scene was a murky gray today, but Sabrina knew on a clear day the magnificent panorama was what inspired Katie to hang on.

They exited the car and headed up the steep driveway. Henry took Grace's arm, sparing Sabrina the awkwardness of offering to help her grandmother. They stepped around Katie's Suzuki and walked up a wooden ramp overgrown with vines toward the door. Sabrina could hear hammering.

Neil knocked at the door, then banged on it when it was clear they wouldn't be heard. Finally, he pushed open the door and bellowed, "Inside," repeatedly until the hammering stopped.

Katie appeared at the door, her hair wrapped in a bandana, with a hammer in her hand.

Sabrina stepped forward.

"Katie, we need to talk to you. You know Neil Perry, don't you? He owns Bar None and is, um, a lawyer. This is Grace Armstrong. And of course, you already know Henry."

Katie nodded as Sabrina mentioned their names until she heard Grace's

"You're Grace Armstrong?"

Grace seemed surprised that Katie recognized her name.

Sabrina thought Katie may have read Grace's books, but then remembered Grace wrote under the pen name, Eliza Higgins. Katie had mentioned Hodge had come to her home asking if she knew two women. One was named Grace.

"Yes. Have we met?" Grace asked.

"No, I - never mind. What's going on? I just got home from my Ten Villas job and have the night off at The Tap Room, which will probably close early with this weather. I'm kind of busy boarding up with the storm coming," Katie said. She held up the hammer as proof.

"What storm? I thought it went around us?" Henry asked. Sabrina wasn't sure how much more stress he could take.

"That one did. I can't remember its name. No, this is another. It's a hurricane. I heard it's a Category Five, but I don't have a television so don't go by me. But lots of people are heading for the airport hoping to get off-island before it hits, so I'm thinking they've heard something credible. That's why I'm battening down the hatches. You're lucky you live in a condo, Henry, and have someone to do your storm prep." Katie looked exhausted to Sabrina.

"Look, we don't want to keep you. It sounds like we should all be doing what you've been smart to dig into and get ready for the weather. Can we sit for just a minute, talk, and then we'll let you get back to it," Neil said.

Katie ushered them into an immaculate living room that was sparsely furnished yet managed to feel rich. The couch was covered in a colorful bird-of-paradise tapestry with warm red, gold, and mustard colors. Two chairs were similarly blanketed in tapestries. One was in indigo blue, the other in a vivid green batik. Sabrina knew the pieces beneath the covers were likely shabby finds from The Last Chance Center. Beyond the sitting area was a red Formica-topped table with four mismatched chairs. A bouquet of plumbago and Bougainvillea in a Mason jar sat on the table on top of a lace runner. Katie's artistic touch masked the shabbiness of her home.

Once seated, Neil took Sabrina's laptop out of the case.

"You know that a woman died at the Westin yesterday, don't you, Katie?"

Sabrina admired how Neil coupled a leading question with a gentle tone, enticing Katie to be forthright.

"I heard," Katie said. She sat on the arm of one of the chairs as if she might have to leave quickly.

"Did you know her?" Neil asked. Henry and Grace remained silent while Neil moved forward. None of them had anything to contribute to the inquiry. He was the professional. Sabrina no longer felt competitive, although she remained curious why Katie had gone to see Heidi.

"No, I didn't," Katie said, not meeting Neil's eyes, which were staring straight at her. Gentle voice, demanding eyes. Sabrina had been on the other side of those eyes.

"Maybe you can explain this then. I'm sure you'll have to do it for the police once they identify everyone who went into or near Heidi Montgomery's room yesterday." Neil hit a button and turned the laptop screen toward Heidi who looked at it for several seconds.

"Excuse me," she said, tearing out of the room

Sabrina's ears hurt from the sound of retching from the bathroom.

"I'm worried she may have an ulcer," Sabrina said to no one in particular.

"I'm more worried she may be pregnant," Henry said.

"What?" But Sabrina stopped when she saw Katie return to the room with a bottle of water in her hand. The thought that Katie's nausea was morning sickness had flitted across Sabrina's mind, but she had dismissed it. There just wasn't room in her head to accommodate one more complication.

"Sorry about that. I may have picked up something," Katie said.

Neil looked a little greener than Katie to Sabrina, but he pressed forward.

"Katie, do you know who killed Eric?" he asked.

"No. I only know that it's my fault. I asked him to borrow a machete so I could trim around the ramp into my house. This time of the year it gets so overgrown with all of the rain. I almost tripped on some vines a couple of times. How was I to know that someone would use it to kill Eric? It's so savage. It has to be someone psychotic or on drugs." Katie wept softly, but Neil persisted.

"If you didn't know Heidi, why did you go to her room, Katie? Sabrina, Henry, and Grace also went to visit her. They had good reasons. I'm sure you did, too. What was it?" Neil asked.

Katie's eyes flickered from left to right. She took a small swig of water. Then she sank into the chair and put her hands over her eyes.

"I thought I could talk to her as someone who had also loved and was now grieving Eric. I knew she still loved him, wanted him back. I was too late. She was dead. I thought she might have overdosed. I had hoped she might honor Eric's wishes." Katie heaved with sobs.

"Sweet Jesus," Henry murmured.

Sabrina knew she should never have dismissed the signs that Katie was pregnant. What had seemed like an irrelevant complication now explained Katie's connection with Eric. The baby had to be his, Sabrina realized. She had been lazy to assume Katie was hung over.

"What were Eric's wishes, Katie?" Neil asked. He leaned forward in the chair opposite her. Katie looked up at him and nodded.

"That we have the money to finish the house for our baby. Heidi owed him at least fifty grand from what he had saved in Massachusetts when they were planning to move to the islands. But she put it in a separate account instead of their joint savings. He would have gotten it back from Heidi during the divorce hearing in Massachusetts. I thought she might see his child needed it now because Eric won't be around to help support us," Katie said.

"Not a chance. Heidi was about as greedy and heartless as any human being I've met," Grace said, breaking her silence.

"That's what Eric said, but I thought maybe after losing him, she might want his baby to be taken care of," Katie said.

Sabrina wondered when Katie might catch a break. Geoff left her high and dry for the singer he'd done a duo with. He had refused to marry her even after being together for ten years. Then Eric got Katie pregnant, promised her he'd finish the house, and got murdered. Katie's rotten luck rivaled her own.

"Eric worked for me, Katie. I know his mother well. She's a lovely, generous woman. You'll like Margaret. You're not alone, dear," Grace said. She rose from the couch and went over to Katie, slipping on to the arm of the chair where Katie had first sat. Grace put her arm on Katie's shoulder.

Sabrina felt tears in her eyes. She watched Grace comfort Katie. Her grandmother was a kind, compassionate, and sensitive woman. Katie needed assurance she and her baby would be taken of and Grace had provided just that. The incongruity of how she had ignored Sabrina as a child felt like a slap in the face to Sabrina. If her grandmother were simply a heartless bitch to everyone, Sabrina wouldn't feel as singled out. It didn't make sense.

"I doubt Heidi would have been so generous. You'd have to have a solid legal claim to get her to share Eric's portion of the money," Neil finally said.

"But I do," Katie said. "I'm his wife."

Chapter 38

"That's why I was so angry when he didn't get the car home to me in time for me to get to work, Henry. Eric was my husband. He knew we needed the money and that I couldn't afford to lose my job. I panicked, thinking he was not as responsible as he'd let on. You may know, I have a little history with men letting me down," Katie said. She tried to laugh but ended up gasping a sob.

"I'm sorry, but I'm still confused. How can you be Eric's wife if he was still married to Heidi?" Henry asked. The room darkened as the clouds grew nearer. St. Thomas was totally obscured by the blackened sky

"We got married. Colleen Mader, you know the local JOP, married us on the beach at Denis Bay. We asked her to keep it secret until Eric's divorce was official in Massachusetts," Katie said. She looked down at her empty ring finger. "He was going to get us a set of those nice wedding bands with the petroglyph design at R & I Patton when he got the money."

Sabrina wasn't sure how any of this would help Henry. Regardless of the legalities of Eric's marriages, Henry was still only a centimeter away from being jailed by Hodge if they didn't find out who really killed Eric.

"Official divorce?" Grace asked.

"I think she means Eric got a 'quickie divorce,' Grace. Did he go somewhere and do that?" Neil asked Katie softly.

Katie shook her head in the affirmative.

"When we found out we were pregnant, we were thrilled. I never thought much about the future beyond saving my house after Geoff left me. It never occurred to me that I might have a child. Eric thought he'd be living the life of an island playboy when he left Massachusetts. No more long-term relationships. But that all changed when he came here couch surfing. He was pretty much keeping to himself until one night, one of my other house mates decided to surprise me by climbing into my bed after I'd fallen asleep. Eric took care of that situation, and well, we got to know each other. We started making dinner together, went snorkeling and hiking. We talked and talked, sometimes until sunrise. We became friends first, true friends," Katie said. She took another swig of the water.

"Where did he get the divorce?" Neil asked. Sabrina warmed at how earnest he sounded. Neil was a kind man. He was just screwed up. Damaged goods, just like her. She wondered how long it would take for her to stop loving him.

"The Dominican Republic. I had enough savings to pay for the lawyer. Austen lent him the money for the airfare," Katie said.

"I still don't understand," Henry said.

"You can get a divorce in the Dominican Republic within twenty-four hours of your arrival. The decree supposedly ends the marriage, but it can't deal with issues like support and property division unless the parties agree. The Virgin Islands and Massachusetts courts are likely to recognize that the divorce in the Dominican Republic terminated the marriage. The other issues would be reserved for the court in Massachusetts, which still has jurisdiction. Eric's divorce would be considered 'bifurcated,'" Neil said.

"Eric didn't want to wait to get married until the divorce was over in Massachusetts. He said our kid could be in kindergarten by then the way things go in the states. Eric was eager to have a family. He wanted to do right by us. We both thought we had finally found happiness," Katie said, tears running down her reddened cheeks.

"Did Heidi know that Eric had gone to the Dominican Republic for a quickie divorce?" Grace asked.

The hairs on Sabrina's arms stood on end thinking of the scene Heidi had created that day in Beechwood. The Heidi Grace had later described to them wouldn't have reacted well to the news her husband had secretly divorced her in a Caribbean nation. Sabrina considered her grandmother might not have shared the worst of Heidi with them. She couldn't imagine what Katie would have encountered if she'd found Heidi alive.

"No, Eric didn't think that it `was smart to let her know that. He knew he had a better chance of getting his share of the money if she didn't know about us. From what he said, Heidi was a bit of a nut. He called her "fanatically possessive." She was sure they would get back together. She'd been texting him obsessively after he stopped taking her calls. When she showed up in St. John, Eric knew there would be trouble," Katie said.

"So why go and talk to her at the Westin?" Sabrina pressed.

"Because, by then, what did I have to lose? I did get my keys back. I found Eric's man bag in her room. I'm sorry I lied to you," Katie said.

"What else was in it?" Grace asked. Sabrina was confused by the urgency to her question.

"Nothing. Not our marriage certificate or the divorce papers Eric considered too important to leave in the house. It's not exactly secure, as you can see." Katie pointed toward the cracks between the studs in the walls around them where rain was beginning to seep in.

"Look, I need to run to St. John Hardware for some supplies. I ran out of boards to cover the bedroom window. I need you guys to get your car out of the driveway," Katie said, rising from the chair. She turned toward Neil.

"Will I be in trouble for taking Eric's bag out of Heidi's room?" she asked.

"I wouldn't worry about that, Katie. You've got more important things to be concerned about," Neil said. He picked up the laptop and headed for the door.

Chapter 39

"Today is just one long cluster-," Neil said as Sabrina backed the car down the driveway. She assumed he aborted the final syllable when he remembered Grace was in the car.

"No kidding and it's getting worse. Mara just texted me. Her flight home has been canceled because of Irma. Who's Irma?" Henry asked.

"That must be the name of the new hurricane Katie was talking about," Sabrina said.

"Mara says to use her house during the storm. To get Evan over there into her hurricane room before it's too late. I didn't know she had a hurricane room, did you?" Henry asked Sabrina.

"It's the wine cellar she built for that jerk of an ex-husband. It's down in the lower level in the center of the house with no windows. The whole place is a fortress, but that room is impenetrable." Sabrina remembered Mara's story about building a stronghold to keep her stepchildren safe. The irony was it turned out they had been endangered by their own father.

"I'm calling Lyla," Henry said.

When there was no answer, they agreed it was best to get out to the Banks' home in Fish Bay without delay.

"Do you want me to drop you at David's on the way? We go right by," Sabrina asked Grace. There were too many crises to deal with. Having Grace tag along was too much baggage.

"You're forgetting. You're driving my car, Sabrina. At least it's my car for now," Grace said.

"What about the bar, Neil? Do you need to get back to Bar None to do storm prep?" Henry asked.

"I already texted Mitch and told him to do our usual routine when he closes. It's just a matter of bringing the bottles in from the bar to the back room and putting down the storm shutters. Bar None is basically outside, in case you guys hadn't noticed." Neil's chuckle sounded a little nervous to Sabrina.

"What about the *Knot Guilty?*" she asked.

"What about her? She'll either ride it out or she won't. I packed up my important papers and locked them in my truck before we went to New England. It's all just stuff," Neil said. Sabrina remembered the conversations she and Neil had about how island living transforms you into a minimalist whether you want to be one or not. There was no Wal-Mart on St. John.

"What about you? We can head to your cottage if you want," Henry said to Sabrina.

"No, I feel like Evan is the priority right now. Poor Lyla, the last thing she needs is a hurricane. I hope Girlfriend isn't getting spooked by the storm." While Girlfriend was normally a mellow lab, she took to howling when a bad storm was approaching. Sabrina had joked that she was the perfect dog for a meteorologist. Sometimes Girlfriend's predictions were more accurate than her own.

"How are you doing, Grace?" Neil asked. Sabrina looked over at her grandmother who was wringing her hands on her lap.

"I'm okay. I've gotten through enough Nor'easters to have a healthy respect for Mother Nature, but I know how to ride out a storm, Neil. I'd just like to secure my laptop after we're done at the Banks. I'm about 35,000 words into a new novel that's due next month. I usually email my drafts to myself as added protection, but David's internet is sporadic."

Sabrina was surprised to see both Austen and Tyler's trucks parked outside of the Banks' villa.

"I texted them and asked them if they could come help us move Evan. I figured the more hands, the less painful it would be for him," Henry said.

Sabrina remembered why Henry was her best friend. Henry didn't just love you. He loved you in small details. Sure, she cared deeply for Lyla and Evan, but Henry took it a step further. He understood that moving a dying man from one house to another in wind driven rain would be one more unbearable insult to him and how it would take many hands to make it gentler.

The four men and Sabrina carried Evan into the back of the Volvo wagon smoothly and swiftly, while Grace waited in Austen's truck. Sabrina drove with Lyla at her side across the road down Mara's driveway into the garage under the stone house where the men waited for them. Within twenty minutes, Evan was settled onto a foldaway bed under fresh linens in the wine cellar with Lyla at his side.

"I'll ride it out with them, honey. We'll be fine with all that wine. Well, probably not Evan-" Henry feigned a lightness Sabrina knew he wasn't feeling. "You be safe, sweetie. Don't let your pride stand in the way." Henry pecked Sabrina on the cheek. She felt like bawling.

Sabrina dashed around the Banks' home closing storm shutters with Neil, Austen, and Tyler, while Grace continued to wait in Austen's truck, which was rocking with the strong winds. She had to talk her grandmother out of helping them. It was becoming increasingly difficult not to admire the woman she had been determined to hate.

Chapter 40

"What will you do? Where will you go during the storm?" Sabrina had asked her when Grace dropped Sabrina off at her car at Mongoose Junction where it had been parked since breakfast.

"I'll do what I always do. I'll buy milk and bread at the grocery store and batteries for my flashlight at the hardware store. I might stock up on bourbon, now that I think of it," Grace said.

"Buy water. Lots of it," Sabrina said.

Grace texted David to see if he needed anything.

"Just you back here. This is a serious storm, Grace."

The normally sleepy streets of Cruz Bay were abuzz with news of the oncoming "monster" storm as it was being called. The two murders that had occurred on island seemed to have been erased from the island's collective memory. Grace noticed shopkeepers placing boards over windows. Restaurants had moved outdoor tables and chairs inside or fastened them to whatever was nearby and stable. Starfish Market was nearly wiped out which reminded Grace of the Stop and Shop in Beechwood before a blizzard. She snagged six gallons of water, three cans of soup, and a bottle of bourbon even though she had just bought one the night before. She remembered toilet paper and paper towels were often in short supply after a storm and threw some into her cart. When her cart was full, Grace felt storm ready.

Until she heard a voice behind her.

"Here, let me help you out to the car with that stuff," Austen said. Grace had met him only once, just an hour before at the Banks' home when she sat in his truck while he and the others moved Evan into a stone home across the way. The truck held the stench of stale beer and damp towels. The wind and rain were blowing ferociously so opening the windows wasn't an option. Grace hadn't eaten since breakfast and grew queasy. She spotted the outline of a bottle in a backpack sitting on the console between the driver's and passengers' seats. She reached in and pulled out a bottle of water wet with condensation with a plastic sandwich bag stuck against it. When she saw what was in the plastic bag, she had placed it in her purse and returned the water to the backpack. She would need to talk to Sabrina and Neil about it, but knew it would have to wait.

Austen sounded like a sincere young man offering an elderly woman assistance, but Grace wasn't buying it. She didn't know how he came into possession of Eric and Katie's marriage certificate and a batch of other papers she assumed were the divorce documents from the Dominic Republic, only that it hadn't been legitimately.

"I'm fine, but thank you," Grace said. She forged out of the store before he could reply and raced to the car. She threw her items into the back of the Volvo wagon where Evan had lain not an hour before. The toilet paper nearly blew out of her arms.

Grace took a right out of the lower level of the parking lot and headed to the upper level of The Marketplace. St. John Hardware was more crowded than the grocery store had been. Dozens of frenzied shoppers filled the aisles grabbing items from the depleted shelves.

Grace ran into Katie in the aisle that stocked duct tape.

Grace knew it could be placed across windows to prevent glass from shattering so she picked up two rolls.

"I'm duct taping and boarding up. I spent more money on those sliding glass doors than I make in six months," Katie said.

"You're not staying in your house during the storm, are you?" Grace was dismayed to think of a newly grieving pregnant woman stranded in such a fragile structure during the storm.

"Sure am," Katie said.

"Not alone, I hope," Grace said.

"Yep. Because that's what I am. Alone. I'll be fine. I'm not meant to be in a relationship. Except with that house." Katie attempted to laugh.

"Come stay with me," Grace said. She wasn't sure how much safer Katie would be, but at least she could offer her company. Grace was disturbed by the loose ends in the Heidi/Eric saga and what she had found in Austen's truck. She needed time to consider the implications, to see if she could weave together the parts she had learned into a cohesive story. Right now, the pieces didn't fit, and this wasn't the time to figure it out.

"I can't. I've been trying to save that house from the day I bought it. Leaving it alone to face Irma would be like giving up on myself, Mrs. Armstrong."

"Grace, please call me Grace."

"He talked about you, Grace. Eric did. That's why I knew your name. I'd like to tell you about it. Maybe after the storm passes?" Katie backed away down the aisle nearly colliding with two men with serious faces.

"After the storm, dear. And I have something to share with you then," Grace said. She let the two men pass her and found what was left of the batteries.

"Category Five," the man in front of her at the cash register was saying.

"Don't believe it. They're just making hype to sell TV ads. I bet it will poof out," said the man in front of him.

Grace walked out of the store into the gale winds raging in

the parking lot. She clung to her purse and purchases tightly. When she found Austen's truck parked next to the Volvo, Grace felt cornered. She opened the hatch hoping to pull away before Austen returned to his truck.

"We meet again. Are you sure you don't need some help getting home? I don't mind. I was just planning to stop by the ACC, that's the animal shelter, to see if they were all set before I headed to my apartment, but I can do that after. You are the boss's grandmother, you know," Austen said. Grace noticed how white his teeth were against his tan. Instead of looking handsome, he looked menacing like a wildcat ready to spring.

"I'm going right home. It's only up the road. You go help the shelter. They need you more than I do, I'm sure," Graced said, practically screaming over the sound of the wind, which had begun to roar. Austen shrugged and got into his truck.

Grace waited for him to exit before she left the parking lot. She had one more stop. She knew the island would likely lose power, which meant the gas pumps wouldn't work. The tank was only a quarter full. Grace took a left, in the opposite direction of David's house, toward the gas station.

She hadn't seen a line as long as the one at the E-C gas station since the seventies. Grace took it as a sign she should get gas since everyone else thought it was a good idea. She pulled into the line behind one of the women whom she recognized from the staff at Caneel. When she moved forward in the line, Grace glanced at the rear-view mirror. Austen's truck was directly behind her. Unnerved, she decided she had to tell someone about her suspicions about Austen. Grace wanted to tell Sabrina first, but Henry had refused to provide her mobile number. She had no way to contact Sabrina. She expected Austen to jump out of his truck and offer to pump her gas. She needed to contact someone else before he was in earshot.

Grace tried Henry's number next. When the call went straight to voicemail, she left an abbreviated message. "Henry, I don't have Sabrina's number, but I felt someone should know that it's very likely Austen, the young man who works for you, is involved with Eric's and maybe Heidi's death. He seems to be following me. He may know of my suspicions."

Grace hung up and dialed her new lawyer's number. Neil's voicemail greeted her, telling her to leave a message, so she repeated the same message she'd left for Henry. What more could she do?

When she pulled up to the pump, Austen knocked on her window. With two gas islands serving eight customers at once, Grace felt reasonably assured Austen would not abduct her.

"Here, let me pump your gas. I thought you were heading right home," he said. His windbreaker was plastered to him as the rain matted his wet ponytail against his neck. Grace handed him cash to pay for the gas and watched him fill the tank. When he was done, she thanked him and rushed toward David's house leaving Austen to fill his own tank. She wished she would hear from Henry or Neil. She wished she had Sabrina's number.

Grace clasped the steering wheel of the Volvo as the wind gusted. As wild as the gale was, she was less frightened by the wind than she had been the prospect of being alone with Austen. She held on tight at the pinwheel turn on Centerline Road where Sabrina had turned earlier in the opposite direction to take them to Katie's house. She remembered Charlie insisting she drive a Volvo wagon when Elizabeth was born. He wouldn't trust his family in another make vehicle he had insisted. Grace thought Evan Banks and Charlie would have liked each other.

Grace's shoulders dropped six inches below her ears where they had been clinging when she made the turn into David's driveway. She was home and safe.

Chapter 41

Sabrina walked down the aisle at Pine Peace Market that was usually well stocked with liquor. Her favorite Gray Goose vodka was nowhere to be found, but she scored a bottle of Tito's hiding at the back of the shelf. With the right crackers and cheese, a can of cashews, and a few lemons, Sabrina had all the provisions she needed to get through the storm.

She threw a box of Rosemary and Olive Oil Triscuits in her basket after she considered buying, Fig and Honey, a new variety. She fussed about whether she should go with her traditional favorite or be adventurous and try something new, realizing the dilemma was a way of not thinking about the impending hurricane. Sabrina grabbed the second box and tossed it in with the other. She figured she might need both to sustain her if the storm was as bad as people were saying. She hated how panic was spreading throughout the island faster than a hot rumor. It was easier to worry about which variety of crackers to buy than about the "monster" storm.

Sabrina snagged three lemons and a chunk of Cracker Barrel sharp cheddar. She headed toward the cash register where the line extended back into the aisle opposite it when her phone rang. Neil Perry's name appeared on the screen of her cell phone.

When she called him, she knew her name came up on his screen as "Salty." She'd have to reprogram his name to read "Cornelius."

Sabrina resented the flash of involuntary excitement his call triggered. She answered the phone and hoped he wasn't bearing more bad news. He didn't bother greeting her.

"I just had a message from your grandmother. She says she doesn't have your number. She may be in trouble," Neil said.

Sabrina wanted to scream, "So what? I was in trouble for forty years and she didn't care," but she didn't want the people in line with her to hear her outrage.

"Why do you think that?" she asked him, feigning a calmness she didn't feel.

Neil told her about Grace's message and that she hadn't picked up her phone when he called her back.

"This isn't good. Austen has a criminal record. He spent five years in prison," she said in a whisper.

"You hired someone who did time? Seriously?" Neil's disbelief was loud enough to be heard through Sabrina's phone causing people to look at her.

"I didn't know it at the time. He's following her? Shit. I guess I'd better call David," Sabrina said.

"I already did. My call went to voicemail," Neil said. Sabrina could hear the concern in his voice.

"I'd better head up there now. I'm checking out at the register at Pine Peace. It's crazy everywhere. I tried to pick my mail at Connections, but the traffic near the dock was so jammed with people catching the ferry to head to the airport, I couldn't get close." Sabrina said. She had advanced to the front of the line and remembered to pay with a credit card to preserve what cash she had on hand in case there was a power outage and the ATMs were shut down.

"Let me go with you," Neil said. He hadn't phrased it as a question, but Sabrina knew that's what it was.

"No need. I can handle Grace," she said.

"Yes, but can you handle Austen? He may be responsible for

two murders. Don't be stubborn, Salty. Your grandmother's life may be in danger."

It hit her like a punch to her belly. Her grandmother's life may be threatened because she hired casual labor without checking references or credentials. Grace could die before Sabrina ever had a chance to get information rooted in her grandmother's heart. Before she could decide if she could find a place in her own for her grandmother.

And he had called her Salty.

She picked Neil up under the portico at Ronnie's Pizza, which seemed to be doing a bang-up business regardless of the weather.

Neil slid into the passenger seat of the Ten Villa's van.

"Thank you," she said to Neil.

"It's okay. You know, it's what we do here on St. John for each other," he said without looking at her. "Let's start at David's. Maybe she's pounding away on her keyboard writing an island tell-all. I hope to hell she isn't writing about me."

Chapter 42

Grace's relief was short lived. The sight of David's house and her cottage boarded up drove home the reality that a hurricane was headed their way. She was surprised to see David's vehicle gone and the second pick-up truck she recalled from being at the Banks home earlier parked in its place.

She placed her wrists through the handles of the plastic bags holding the smaller items from her shopping trip so they wouldn't blow out of her hands on her way into the house. The car door was almost impossible to open against the thrust of the wind. The door to the kitchen wasn't boarded up, so she headed toward it. She wondered why the second young man who had come to help move Evan was at David's and where the hell David had gone since it was clear the storm was escalating.

"Here, let me help you," he said, opening the screen door while keeping a firm hold on it.

"No, I'm all set," Grace said. She stepped into the kitchen and shook off the rain from her soaking hair. "Where's David? I'm sorry, I don't remember your name."

"Tyler. David's gone to check his plane. They're saying this is a monster storm."

"I thought he'd already done that," Grace said. She noticed that David had moved her laptop from the cottage into the house where he had placed it on the kitchen table, plugged into the surge protector he had urged her to buy in St. Thomas. David was methodical, organized, and planned ahead, which was why he had already secured his seaplane when there had only been a hurricane watch.

"Do you have more stuff in the car?" Tyler asked.

"Just some jugs of water," Grace said. Tyler seemed jumpy to Grace, which she supposed was natural given the sound of the wind outside. "They can wait."

"No, let me get them. Can I have your car keys so I can lock it afterward?" Tyler asked.

Grace handed him the keys, thinking locking the car was an odd way to prepare for the hurricane. She took the supplies she purchased out of the wet bags and placed them on David's kitchen counter. She decided she could keep busy by using some of the duct tape to protect the pane in kitchen door. Grace remembered seeing a desk in David's living room where she hoped she might find scissors. She walked into the room, which was gloomy without natural light and the overhead lights flickering. She clicked on her flashlight and pulled open the drawer to the mahogany desk and found the scissors right next to the tape as she had expected. When she closed it, she saw a backpack that had been placed under the kneehole of the desk. Not David's backpack. Not Austen's as she had mistaken it to be when she sat in Austen's truck. It was Tyler's backpack from which she had removed the documents that chronicled Eric's divorce and remarriage. Grace slipped the shears she held into her rain jacket pocket.

Tyler slammed the kitchen door shut after placing the water jugs on the floor. He folded his hands across his chest and rested against the door like a sentry.

"I think it's time for us to have a talk, Mrs. Armstrong. I'm pretty sure I have some stuff of yours."

Chapter 43

"They're saying it's going to be a category five. Ever been through one of those?" Neil asked her as she clung to the steering wheel to keep on Centerline Road. The wind suggested the forecast was accurate. Sabrina had never experienced such force before.

"No. They're not that common. There's only been thirty or so category fives since the 30's." The van veered toward the left as a blast of wind seemed to push it aside.

"Hey, do you want me to drive?" Neil asked. Sabrina considered.

"Maybe. We're almost at David's. I hope they're both sitting in his living room playing Scrabble," Sabrina said. Did her grandmother even play Scrabble? Probably. She was a writer. There was so much Sabrina didn't know.

She pulled onto the dirt road that led to David's driveway. It was filled with large puddles surrounded by slippery mud. She navigated around them and onto the stone driveway where Sabrina was relieved to see the Banks's Volvo. There was no sign of David's Jeep.

"He's got this place in pretty good shape," Neil said. Sabrina agreed, thinking about her tiny stone cottage with its new pool sitting naked waiting for a hurricane to come and swallow it.

"Head for the back door in the kitchen," Neil said. He opened the van door letting a gust of air press against Sabrina. She followed suit, barely able to shut the door to the van. She slid in her flip-flops, which were soon covered in water, over the driveway onto the patio next to the pool that divided Grace's cottage from the main house.

Neil tugged the door open with one hand while he grabbed Sabrina by her arm. He pulled her through the door after him and leaned against the door.

"Jesus," he said.

"No kidding," Sabrina said. She looked around the empty kitchen while Neil wandered into the living room.

"David?" Neil called. "Grace? Anyone home?"

"Where would they go?" Sabrina asked. Her heartbeat raced. Why would they leave?

"Maybe he felt there was somewhere safer for them to ride the storm out," Neil said. Sabrina might ordinarily be irritated that he seemed to be reading her mind. Today she was grateful she didn't have to explain her fears, which would only magnify them.

"Let me try calling him," Neil said. He pulled out his cell phone. Sabrina flicked on the switch to the overhead light. Nothing.

"No power here. Already. Not a good sign." The darkness in the kitchen coupled with the howling wind cast a sense of dread within Sabrina. Life on St. John was rapidly spiraling out of control.

"It went straight to voicemail," Neil said. "I still have two bars. He must be somewhere without reception."

"What do we do?" Sabrina asked just as Neil's phone rang.

Neil picked up immediately. He put his phone on speaker.

"Where are you, man? We're at your place," Neil said.

"I'm stuck down by Maho. I came to get Grace," David said.

"What's she doing at Maho?" Neil asked.

"Good question. Someone called and said her phone battery was dead and that she'd gotten a flat tire going over some rubble on the way out to my place. Why she'd come to my place the long scenic route via North Shore Road with a hurricane on the way, I don't know. Any way I haven't found her and now I'm going to have to turn around and go the long way back because there's a tree down across the road running along the beach," David said, shouting into the phone over the sound of the wind.

Sabrina looked out the window of the back door to be certain the car she had seen in the driveway was Evan Bank's.

"That's crazy. Her car's here, but there's no sign of her. Just a lot of supplies you have out on the table and a laptop," Neil said.

"Supplies? She texted me that she was buying stuff and then coming home. Then I got the call she had car trouble. I didn't leave any supplies on the table." Sabrina could hear the concern in David's voice.

"The car she borrowed, the Volvo, it's in your driveway. She must have been here after buying the supplies," Neil said.

"Something's not right. I gotta go, Neil. Another branch just came down. This is getting really ugly."

Chapter 44

Sabrina jumped at the sound of another object crashing onto David's roof.

"Where do you think she is?" she asked Neil. She knew he had no better idea than she did. Why had she let Grace out of her sight when she knew a huge hurricane headed their way? It had been cruel, beyond what any human being deserved. Sabrina recoiled at the notion she may have unconsciously wanted harm to come to her grandmother.

"We'd better check out Austen. Do you know where he lives?" Neil asked.

"We just drove by his apartment on the way up here. It's one of those huge cement houses divided into apartments. I dropped him off there a few times after work," Sabrina said. She hadn't detected anything creepy about Austen during those times alone with him in the Ten Villas van. She wouldn't have taken him for a stalker, but she also hadn't known he had gone to jail and he had come to her cottage late at night to ask for money. What might have happened if she hadn't offered him a loan?

"Well, he seems to be the last person Grace was with, so let's give it a go. Maybe she felt she would be safer there with him after all. Concrete structure in a storm, you know."

Sabrina did know. Neil was trying to make her feel better, but neither of them believed Grace would be comfortable riding out the storm with Austen after the messages she had left.

They dashed to the van holding onto one another against the ferocious gusts. Debris had begun flying through the air. Sabrina caught a glance of several of David's lawn chairs tied together, lying on their sides.

Neil whisked her into the passenger seat. Sabrina watched him go over to the Volvo and walked around it twice, holding on to the door handles as the wind threatened to blow him away. Once he was in the driver's seat, he turned to her.

"Look, I know it's your van and that you're a badass, but I weigh a helluva lot more than you do and can probably steer this sucker against the wind a little better," he said. Sabrina said nothing. There was nothing to say. Fighting about who got to drive was inconsequential.

"I looked inside the Volvo but didn't see anything that might help us to know where Grace is," Neil said. Sabrina knew what he didn't say, which was that her grandmother wasn't in the car, something she'd been worrying about. Austen might have harmed Grace in the car if she had confronted him.

Neil maneuvered the van down through the muddy lane onto Centerline Road for a short distance where Sabrina directed him to take a left. He pulled into a driveway right behind Austen's island beater truck.

"Let me check and see if he's actually here," Neil said, but Sabrina leaped out of the van into the driven rain before he could get out. She headed for the side door of the lower floor where she had dropped off Austen before with Neil in tow.

None of the doors or windows to the house had been boarded up. Only a few of the windows seemed to have shutters, which were rattling against the house. The combination of the sound of the wind and the clattering hurt her ears.

Neil grabbed her by the arm and stepped between her and the door. He pushed the door open and pulled her in after him.

"Hello, anyone home?" he called out.

Sabrina could only see shapes in the outer hall where they were standing. There was a damp unpleasant smell. She reached into her pocket for her flashlight and pulled it out. The tiny beam revealed two inner doors, one of which had a pair of flip-flops outside on a mat. She walked over to it and banged on the door.

She reached into her belly to find the old broadcaster voice she used as a meteorologist on television. She tried to sound authoritative without being adversarial. She had established a rapport with Austen that she might need if her grandmother was with him.

"Austen, are you in there? I see your truck outside. Come on, open up. It's me, Sabrina."

She practically fell onto Austen when he yanked open the door.

"Hey, what are you guys doing out? We're having a hurricane, haven't you heard?" He backed away from the door to let Sabrina and Neil into a studio apartment with a futon, refrigerator, and a microwave set on a table next to a sink. In front of the futon sat a crate with several meowing kittens. On top of the crate, Sabrina spotted an open bottle of Carib next to a flashlight. Next to the crate on the floor were a case of Carib and a can of peanuts. Austen was definitely ready for the hurricane.

"Where's my grandmother, Austen?"

"Your grandmother?" he repeated.

"Yes, her grandmother. Grace Armstrong. You were one of the last people to see her and now she's missing," Neil said.

Austen fell back onto the futon.

"Whoa. I only just met her out at the Banks. And then I ran into her at Starfish and the gas station. I actually offered to help her home, but she said she was fine. She seemed skittish. Maybe with the storm on its way, you know," he said, shrugging.

Sabrina and Neil exchanged glances.

"Who else is here?" Neil asked looking above him at the ceiling.

"Just me and the cats. I took them home from the shelter. It's wooden and probably going to get nailed. My roomies are all already off-island for the summer or headed for the ferry when they heard how bad the forecast was. Even my landlord left. I don't have anywhere else to go. You don't think I'd do something to hurt an old woman, do you?"

Sabrina sunk onto the futon next to him.

"No, I'm just worried about her and you seemed to have seen her last. Hey, are you going to be okay here?" she asked. She realized Austen was in as much danger from the storm as everyone else.

"I think so. This island home has been standing for decades and went through a number of hurricanes, including Marilyn."

"How about Tyler? Where is he staying?" Sabrina asked. She realized everyone on island was in danger. She could hear banging outside like someone was ramming steel bars against the house. The wind had begun to screech.

"Tyler? Oh, he should be fine. He's got that basement unit in the fancy villa where he stays in for free. He watches it for the owners who only come on island for the holidays and vacations. Lucky bastard fell into that one, especially after what happened with Katie," Austen said. He took a sip of his beer.

"You guys want one? It's still cold," Austen said.

Sabrina shook her head.

"What happened with Katie?" she asked. Neil opened a bottle of Carib and gulped.

"He tried to put the moves on her when he rented a room at her house. I mean, it was pretty bad. He tried to, well you know. He said he thought she wanted him to- it's a good thing Eric was there. After that, Tyler had trouble finding a place to stay until he landed the villa gig. I was surprised Eric could work with him after that, although he barely spoke to him."

"Where's that villa? Does it have a name?" Sabrina asked.

"Sure, you know it. "Villa Write Off." It's right across the street from the Last Chance Center."

"Neil-" Sabrina began, springing from the futon.

"I know. Let's go, Salty."

Chapter 45

"What does it mean?" Sabrina asked as they exited the house into raging rain and wind.

"Shit," Neil said. He pointed to a large bough that had fallen on the van. The rain poured down on Sabrina's head saturating her hair through the hood of her rain jacket. She and Neil each grabbed a section of the branch and pulled it off the roof onto the driveway.

"Get in, we don't have much time," Neil said. He lifted her into the driver's side of the van. "Push over." Sabrina wiggled over the console onto the passenger side. Neil hopped in after her and slammed the door.

"Do you think Grace may be with Tyler?" she asked.

"There's only one way to find out," Neil said. He backed onto Centerline Road, which was empty of vehicles but where debris was beginning to accumulate and swirl through the air. Branches, sand, trash. It was hard to identify objects in the rain and wind, but Sabrina spotted a workman's boot go flying past the passenger window. She was reminded of the opening scene from the Wizard of Oz she watched as a kid with Ruth.

The visibility was so limited, Neil had to drive at a pace slower than they could have walked, but walking was not an option. They passed the turn off to where David lived and continued around a sharp curve. The contents of a public dumpster on the side of the road were being sucked out by the wind into the air. Branches flew around the van. Sabrina sighed with relief when they reached Gifft Hill Road. To the left she could barely make out the shape of the containers where the Last Chance Center was located. She wondered where the wild pigs that frequently roamed the area had gone. Where were the birds hiding? Where had the goats fled?

"That's it. Over on the right. The one with the metal fence," Sabrina told Neil. He turned onto the driveway and drove through an arched gateway. The metal gate had become unlatched and was swinging frantically in the wind. Neil rammed the van through it and over the debris piling up on the cement circular drive. There were no lights or signs that any one was in the house. Tyler's truck was nowhere to be seen.

"Did we come here for nothing?" Sabrina asked.

"Let me check out the apartment below," Neil said.

"I'm coming with you. It must be in the back, down that walkway to the left." Sabrina recognized what was a fairly common layout to the villas built in St. John. Many had a circular driveway facing the street and the main entrance of the villa opened into a large great room. The opposite side typically faced a panoramic view of the water and other islands. Below the main unit, owners often built studio apartments where spillover guests could stay, or caretakers live.

They leaned together, moving as a single unit toward the side of the house against the force of the wind. Neil stepped in front of Sabrina.

"Put your arms around me and your face into my back," he screamed. She didn't argue with him. The back of his wet hoodie felt cool against her face. Sabrina closed her eyes and let Neil guide them down a decline and then toward the right. When they were under what Sabrina figured was the deck above, Neil released her and pulled her toward a sliding glass door, she was sure would be locked. When Neil slid it open, she nearly cried with relief, grateful Tyler was like most St. Johnians who didn't lock doors.

"Hey Tyler," Neil called out several times, but the only sound Sabrina could hear was the howl of the wind beating on the house. She pulled out her flashlight. Tyler's apartment was a stark contrast to Austen's even in the dim light. A black leather sectional lined the right wall of the basement studio. A large flat screen television and chair matching the couch were against the rear wall, forming living space in a right angle. The opposite end of the room housed a queen-size bed against the left wall that had been neatly made and topped with a cotton spread. In between the two areas, there was a long picnic table with benches painted white situated in front of a small kitchen unit. The kitchenette was complete with stainless steel apartment sized refrigerator and stove, and a sink with a small faux marble counter. There was a door in the center of the rear wall.

Sabrina spotted a Coleman lantern sitting on the picnic table. She flicked it on. Tyler was well prepared for the storm. He had laid out an assortment of batteries, candles, matches, and bug spray. Smart, Sabrina thought. He knows the bugs come in droves after a storm. Where was he then if he had planned so well to sit out the storm in his snug little lair? With more light, Sabrina could see a desk with a hutch top next to the bed. The shelves were jammed with books and notepads neatly arranged.

"What do you make of it?" Neil asked coming back through the door next to the kitchen counter where he had tucked into.

"I don't know. I haven't known him for long. But I wouldn't have expected these," she said pointing toward the overflowing bookshelves. Instead of being lined with popular thrillers written by Lee Child, Michael Connelly, and Harlan Coben, Tyler's shelves were filled with classics and modern literary works by Zadie Smith, Jeffrey Eugenides, and Ian McEwan, along with several volumes of poetry.

"Maybe they go with the house," Neil said.

"Maybe. I know he talked about poetry." Sabrina shouted over the wind, which now sounded like a train was roaring through the house above them. Would someone who read poetry and books like these hurt an older person like her grandmother? Her head hurt more from the incongruity than from the growing sense of pressure she felt in her ears. She knew that meant the storm was growing close.

"But listen, he's not here, and more importantly, neither is Grace. I don't think we can keep looking for her. It's getting too dangerous outside. We have to hope she found shelter and is safe," Neil said.

"Okay, let's go," Sabrina said. She had asked more from Neil than she deserved. They were no longer a couple for reasons that seem to pale in comparison to the danger Grace might be in and the disaster that was set to hit St. John. She had no right to ask him to endanger himself further.

"I don't think we can," he said. A large rumble from above underscored his statement. "I think that was the roof, Salty."

September 6, 2017

Hurricane Irma Category 5

Latitude 18.1N
Longitude -63.3.6W

94 miles from St. John

Chapter 46

They were stuck in Tyler's apartment where the sliding glass door was beginning to bow. Water seeped beneath the bottom of it while rain pelted the glass sideways. A steady flow of water dripped down on them through the ceiling.

Sabrina and Neil sat at the table.

"She's probably fine," he said.

"It was unthinkable of me to turn her away in a storm like this. Regardless of who she is and what she may have done to me, she's a human being. An old human being." Sabrina stood up. She despised feeling confined, helpless.

"She's a tough old bird, Salty. You saw that. Give yourself a break for a change."

Sabrina began to shiver, even though the temperature was uncomfortably warm.

"Let me see if Tyler's got a dry tee shirt or two. Are you hungry?" Neil asked.

"I have cheese and crackers and vodka in the van," she said. The wind blasted against the sliders, making the bow even more pronounced.

"We may have to save those for later. I think we'd better push the table against the window," he said. He picked up the lantern and handed it to her. Sabrina walked over to the desk and placed it next to some papers and a notebook that looked familiar. She picked it up and admired the smooth buttery navy blue leather with the gold fleur-de-lis design. It was Grace's. She had been writing in it when Sabrina joined her at the police department. A loud crash outside the villa interrupted her thoughts.

"We may need to retreat into that combination laundry room/ bathroom off the kitchen, soon" Neil called over to her. He had pushed the table on its side against the slider and then shoved the couch against the table. Sabrina saw that water on the floor by the door was rising.

She held up the journal. "This belongs to my grandmother, I think."

"Did you look inside to see?" Neil asked. He had moved the chair and the table that had previously held the television against the other furniture. With each gust, the pile of furniture pulsated as the window bowed. The sound of glass shattering from above served as previews of coming attractions.

"Take the journal and anything else you want to read. We're moving in there," Neil said. He pointed to the door he had come out of earlier.

Sabrina grabbed the notebook and all the papers she saw off the top of the desk. She noticed they were dotted with tiny drops. She scanned the drawers of the desk, taking a few folders and notebooks.

Neil had opened the refrigerator and grabbed a gallon jug of water and a bottle of wine. He ushered her into the laundry room just as the sliders began to give way.

"Here, take these," he said, handing her the bottles.

"Where are you going?" Sabrina asked, watching in horror as Neil closed the door behind him. She could hear the sound of breaking glass behind the door. Then a knock. She pulled the door open.

"Quick," he said. Neil slid the mattress that had been

covering the bed into the laundry room and then reached behind him for the lantern. Finally, Sabrina heard the door to the laundry room slam. Neil propped the mattress against the door, the coverlet still clinging to it.

"There."

"Now what?" Sabrina asked.

"You sit on the washer. I'll sit on the dryer. We'll read until the storm passes," Neil said. He patted the washer and grinned at her. Sabrina saw a tiny cut on his forehead.

"Come on. You love a good story." He sat on the dryer. She slid up onto the washer next to him and opened the journal. A piece of paper fell from inside. Sabrina grabbed it before it fell onto the damp floor.

It was a canceled check dated November 19, 1977, drawn on the Beechwood Savings Bank payable to Elizabeth A. Salter in the amount of twenty-five thousand dollars. Sabrina flipped it over. It had been endorsed by her mother and written by her grandmother.

Sabrina had never seen her mother's signature. The sight of it felt personal, like touching a lock of her mother's hair that had been saved. It wasn't a graceful signature, but more a combination of printing and longhand. She quickly calculated that she had been two years old when her mother had endorsed the check, the same age Sabrina had been when her mother had abandoned her and her father. Grace had financed her mother's escape.

Sabrina handed the check to Neil. He knew enough about her miserable childhood she wouldn't have to shout to explain over the shrill of the constant high pitch of wind that felt like it was inside her ears. He looked down at the check and then turned it over. His expression left no doubt that he got it. The garish glow the lantern cast on his face accentuated his concern.

The sound of metal flying through the air was unmistakable. It wasn't enough that the house had lost its roof. Sabrina imagined plates of corrugated metal now flying outside like UFO's in a sci-fi film. The washer began to shake beneath her.

"Oh my God, that must have been the hurricane panels flying off," Sabrina said.

"Grab that stuff and get in the shower," Neil said. He pulled the plastic shower curtain liner off and took the journal and other papers from Sabrina and wrapped them in it.

She slipped into the shower stall that had a slotted wooden bench against one wall. She swooped the shampoo and soap off it and sat down, huddled in the corner. Neil slid next to her and put his arm around her, pulling her to him. The fiberglass walls began bending. The endless pitch reminded Sabrina of the stories her father would tell her about screams of the banshees in Ireland. Female spirits who heralded death.

"Are we going to die?" she asked Neil.

She felt him inhale.

"I don't know, Salty. All I know right now is that I love you and that I'm sorry I didn't show it better," he said tugging her into him. Water was dripping down the sides of the shower from above at an increasing rate.

"I didn't make it easy. I love you, too," she said, pressing against him. Sabrina closed her eyes, wishing she could shut her ears to the horrific sounds around them.

"I was eight," he said speaking into her ear. "She walked my sister and me to school, like she did every morning. She had packed our lunch boxes. Mine had a peanut butter and Fluff sandwich with an apple and cold milk in a thermos. When we got out of school that afternoon, my Aunt Karen was waiting for us. That had never happened before. She looked like she'd been crying. She said my mother wasn't well and that we'd be going to her house. That night, my father came over to tell Chrissy and me, our mother had died."

Sabrina listened as Neil continued to talk into her ear, blocking out the sounds of the hurricane with a story she never would have imagined. That night he overheard the adults talking, after quite a bit of whiskey, that his mother had walked into the ocean fully clothed with a down jacket and boots. Lobstermen found her body before school was dismissed.

"I never knew why she did it, only that it must have had something to do with me. I wasn't enough for her to hang on for and that everyone on Vinalhaven must have known it, although they were kind enough not to tell me to my face. It's such a tiny place. We spent holidays with the aunts and uncles and cousins who were always kind, but it was never the same as having your own family. My father was never the same. He just sort of shut down and went through the motions.

Sabrina listened to his words, which dulled the sounds of the storm. She knew what it was like to have a father so wounded by a woman he became impervious to the child she had left behind. She leaned into Neil while he continued.

"I did the best I could in school so I could go far away when it was time for college. I was determined to be successful and to live somewhere where everyone didn't know your name. I'd flown my father out to L.A. a few times over the years. The last time I went back to the island was for my father's funeral. Well, until you and I went together. I figured I could face going back if you were with me. I just didn't know how to clue you in. I didn't mean for there to have to be a Category 5 hurricane to tell you all of this," he said.

Sabrina found his hands and put them in hers, curling her fingers around his as tight as she could. He had been so charming, so witty, so good at insulating himself from human drama, she had never suspected he had demons of his own.

"Neil, I'm sorry. I guess I thought I had an exclusive on tragic childhoods. I should have known you'd taken me there for a reason. I should have given you a chance to tell me why. I was so sure you weren't being honest with me, I snapped," she said.

They sat entwined until Sabrina woke up and realized she

had fallen asleep and that it was quiet. Neil stirred and started to move.

"Is it over?" he asked.

"I think the eye is passing over us. We should sit tight a little longer. Let me see that journal. Maybe I'll learn why Grace paid my mother to go away."

Chapter 47

Sabrina stepped out of the shower, sloshing through several inches of rainwater on the floor. She slid back onto the washer and opened the journal, while Neil tried to peek through the door into the studio, but the wood was too swollen to open.

Sabrina unwrapped the journal and other papers she had taken from the desk. The first thing that drew her attention was a zip lock plastic bag with photos in it. She tugged open the bag and slid out the photos. They were all pictures of Katie. Many were taken while she bartended at The Tap Room. She had a smile in most and seemed to be perpetually busy. Sabrina came to several shots of Katie in her home when she wasn't posing and seemed unaware she was being photographed. One was when she was naked in her bedroom and appeared to be sitting on a yoga mat with her eyes closed. Sabrina guessed she was meditating.

The photos felt invasive and made Sabrina uncomfortable. They had what Sabrina called "The Ick Factor," which she used to describe when something felt not right, close to perverse, in an undefined way. She'd had enough of the photos and handed them to Neil.

She opened the cover to the journal and saw that Grace

wrote the dates of the first and last entries on the first page along with her name. The penmanship was classic cursive, something Sabrina had never mastered. It had been considered passé when she was in school, although her private school insisted students attempt it.

The journal began after her mother had eloped but before Sabrina had been born. Grace agonized about her daughter having a baby without having her own mother nearby to help. She ruminated over her husband's steadfast insistence that they have nothing to do with Elizabeth or her husband. The prospect of a grandchild didn't soften him, Grace reported with regret. She pondered whether Charlie's physical health was affecting him mentally. He had grown obstinate and unkind and seemed threatened by his wife's desire to reconcile with their daughter or meet their grandchild. Grace was left in an untenable position. She either had to choose her husband or the daughter he said had betrayed her. She wrote endlessly about whether Elizabeth had betrayed them or whether she was simply immature. She wondered how her grandchild was doing living in a household without loving grandparents to dote on her.

Sabrina read on and came to an entry where Grace reported receiving a frantic telephone call from Elizabeth, telling her she couldn't face another winter like the last. Grace was unable to press Elizabeth for details but was left with the impression that she was desperate. Grace feared for her safety and that of her grandchild. She agreed to pay her money, but it had to be a secret from Charles.

Several weeks later, Grace was shocked to learn that Elizabeth had left Hugh, but not with Sabrina. She had been certain Elizabeth intended to take the child. Charlie's "I told you so" response to Elizabeth's flight was as mean as Elizabeth's second betrayal, this one unmistakable.

Grace was shattered. The following pages fluctuated between sorrow, anger, and despair. Sabrina shut the journal and handed it to Neil.

"Go ahead. I'd like you to read it," Sabrina said. She handed him the pile of papers.

The horrible noise returned to their chamber, sounding like a jet had landed in the next room. Like a thousand motorcycles during the Laconia rally. It wasn't over yet.

"Hey, this is interesting," Neil said. He held up a white envelope and pulled a smaller red envelope out of it. He handed the smaller one to Sabrina who reached inside and pulled out a small key. She looked at the envelope. On the outside was the logo of Allerton Savings and Loan, where Sabrina had opened her first bank account, and the names Eric Hershey and Heidi Montgomery Hershey were printed.

"You think Heidi or Eric got their hands on these when they worked for Grace?" Neil asked. He held up the journal and canceled check.

"Well, you said Heidi had accused Eric of wiping out their safe deposit box when he came down here. My guess is these were in it," Sabrina said. Her head hurt from the noise. Her head hurt from the confusion.

"Blackmail. Someone was blackmailing your grandmother. But where does Tyler fit in?" Neil asked. A loud boom from above stopped him short. "Back to the shower, kid. These questions will have to wait."

A sudden shift in pressure propelled her to the shower stall. She slid onto the bench. Neil followed her. This time Sabrina didn't hesitate. She leaned into him and put her arms around his shoulders. She wondered what her grandmother was holding on to.

Chapter 48

Sabrina could see light through a crack in the ceiling above. It had been quiet for what she judged to be an hour. Both of their cell phones were dead. The light from the Coleman lamp had dimmed and would soon go out. Whatever their fate was to be, she knew it was time to find out.

Neil tugged on the door leading from the laundry room into the studio finally pulling it open. Sabrina stepped through the threshold into the apartment and wondered if a bomb had gone off. The sliding glass doors had blown in. All the furniture was gone except the refrigerator, which lay on its side, doors open. The books that Sabrina had previously admired were strewn everywhere, pages soaking, ink running. She could see the sun was shining. How dare it, she thought.

Neil put his hands on her shoulders. "We need to be careful, Salty. I'm sure there's structural damage. He eased her to the spot where the sliders had once been. The wooden deck was gone. Instead, there was a two-foot drop down to some rubble.

Sabrina squinted into the sun, looking out toward St. Thomas. She couldn't make out what she was seeing. Villa Write Off was set up high with an unobstructed vista, but there were many more modest homes built into the hillside and valley below. She could see some were partially blown away. Others were askew. Most were without roofs that had landed randomly atop and between the trees that were still standing. Sabrina thought she might be sick.

Neil stepped down to the ground from where they stood and held out his hand. She dropped next to him.

"Come on, let's see if the van's still there," he said. They maneuvered along the walk where they had passed earlier during the storm. Broken dishes, cushions, and pans from the house lay strewn along the way. The upper portion of the house was gone. A toilet was the only thing left inside.

The van was close to where Neil had parked it, except it was upside down. Wheels facing the sky like the paws on a puppy waiting to have his tummy scratched. In the distance, Sabrina thought she could hear the sound of a chain saw.

"Damn," he said, looking down into the van.

Sabrina went to the rear and tried to open the doors, but the dents made it impossible.

"I just need to get my sneakers out of there," she said. Wearing flip-flops had been dangerous during the storm. Climbing over debris and fallen trees would be worse.

Neil walked over and yanked on the rear doors, tugging and tugging, until he pulled one door open and off. He fell backwards onto a metal sheet that had once been a roof and down into a pit beneath it. The swimming pool, which had been emptied of water and was filled with everything but.

"Oh my God, are you all right?" she asked, stumbling toward him. He groaned.

She knelt down and gave him her hand as he kicked free of the tangled mess he had landed in. She hoisted him up. When he couldn't stand, she looked at his ankle and saw it did not match the other.

"I think you twisted your ankle," she said, trying to sound optimistic.

She helped him over to the step in in front of where the main entrance door had been and sat him down on a concrete step.

"Shit," he said. "You're going to have to get to your grandmother on your own. I'll just slow you down. I think I know where Tyler went. He probably took her with him."

"I know. To Katie's," Sabrina said. She had come to the same conclusion. It made as much sense as any of the events during the past several days had.

She reached into the rear of the van and found her tote bag. It was sopping wet. She unzipped it and felt carefully for broken glass. A major miracle. The Titos that she had wrapped in her beach towel was intact. And her sneakers were right next to it with two water bottles.

She brought the towel over to Neil to cover him from the searing sun. She handed him the vodka and the water and then laced up her sneakers.

"I'll head to the clinic first and get someone to come down to help you," she said. She pointed to the vodka. "That's just for medicinal purposes. Remember, add water."

He laughed. "Hey where's the crackers and cheese you promised?"

She kissed him on the forehead and headed up the driveway.

Chapter 49

Sabrina's wet sneakers squeaked with each step she took up the driveway. She squinted against the hot tropical sun beating on her back through her tee shirt. She couldn't believe what she was seeing, or more accurately what she wasn't seeing.

The tropical bushes she knew screened Villa Write Off from the road were bare. Not a single blossom remained on the fiery orange Poinciana tree that had fronted the property. Totally bare, it looked lifeless, no longer worthy of its nickname, "Flamboyant." The purple, pink, orange, and red bougainvillea that bloomed generously all year long were stripped clean and looked as sad as Sabrina felt. She searched the yard for a single blossom of any tropical flower but found none. Not even her faithful blue plumbago had survived the storm.

She climbed over boards and branches, beach chairs and bed linens, until she reached the top of the driveway where it met Gifft Hill Road, which ran along a ridge. Henry's condo was far down the road to her left, beyond her vista. Across the road to her right and up the hill a short distance stood the containers for The Last Chance Center. They were intact. Not much else was.

From where she stood, Sabrina viewed the ruins of houses

with roofs and windows blown away. Wreckage from the insides of the homes was strewn without any regard for property lines. Without the lush landscape to screen homes, she could see that many were simply gone. A platform or deck was the only sign that people had lived and loved in them. There were wires everywhere. Poles down. It looked like footage from a war zone.

She thought about the people who had come to St. John with hopes and dreams, just as she had. In a few hours, the hurricane had wiped out years, even decades, of their lives laboring to fulfill their dreams. Gone.

Sabrina looked beyond the string of houses at the badly damaged lower campus of the Gifft Hill School that had grown courageously and flourished against all odds. It felt like a blow to the St. John community gut.

When asked to describe St. John to people who had never been there, Sabrina told prospective visitors to Ten Villas that they should picture the lush rolling green mountains of Vermont and imagine someone had picked them up and plucked them down into the middle of the Caribbean. It had been the verdant green against the cornflower blue skies and the turquoise sea that finally gave Sabrina the peace she so desperately needed after Nantucket.

The view of heavily forested Bordeaux Mountain normally lush and green now looked as if the trees had been replaced with dry shredded wheat. Sabrina stared at the bare broken trees looking like a bizarre display of the letter "L" inverted. Tree after tree with tops snapped at a forty-five-degree angle. She leaned over and wept for the suffering of the rain forest. This had been no ordinary hurricane. The winds that had terrified her and Neil while huddled in the shower stall had been tornadoes. She prayed no lives had been lost.

She remembered Neil was in pain and her grandmother was missing. Henry was with Lyla and poor Evan. Who had survived, she wondered, and what were they left with?

The short walk up the hill to the Myrah Keating Smith

Health Center took much longer with the road covered with branches and dangerous wires. A few people were wandering around the homes along the sides of the road. Some waved, but many just circled their houses with dazed expressions on their faces.

Sabrina nearly forgot that there had been a murder at The Last Chance Center when she passed it. It had fared much better than many of the homes surrounding it. It didn't seem fair. Her spirits were buoyed when she came to Centerline Road and saw that a local favorite food truck, Tony's Kitchen, had survived and was intact, albeit standing a bit askew.

She crossed Centerline Road and climbed the hill up to the clinic. When she caught sight of the building, she realized she had been expecting it to look as it had before Irma. The crumpled roof reminded her that nothing was the same. No one had been spared. This was the new St. John.

A man in dark a blue St. John Rescue tee shirt approached Sabrina. She could see others gathered near the building.

"Are you okay?" he asked.

She explained what had happened to Neil and told him where he was.

"Oh, sure. I know Neil from Bar None. Okay, we'll dispatch someone there as soon as possible. It's kind of crazy right now." He offered her a bottle of water, which she gulped down in several swigs.

"Will you be going back and staying with Neil?" he asked.

"No, I have to find my grandmother. I need to know if she's safe," Sabrina said.

The man explained that they were starting a list where people could check in to report they were safe. Sabrina gave him her full name and Neil's to put on the list of people who were safe.

"There's no cell service anywhere on island at the moment and we have no idea when we'll have it again." He wished her well.

Sabrina raced down the hill onto Centerline Road. She could hear a helicopter hovering above the clinic, which was the only place on island with a helipad, other than the one over at Dittlief Point that Sean Keating had built. The realization that St. John was in survival mode made the need to find her grandmother more urgent. Before she had been worried Tyler might harm Grace. Now Sabrina was concerned Irma may have beat him to it.

She hesitated at the juncture where David's lane met Centerline Road. She debated whether she should check back at his house once more, but her gut told her to move on. She felt confident Tyler had been determined to be with Katie during the storm. Somehow, her grandmother was part of whatever plan he had. A woman in a Honda civic with a pleated hood and a smashed windshield interrupted her thoughts.

"Hey, are you okay? Need a lift?" she called over.

Sabrina dashed to the passenger side of the front of car to get in.

"You'll have to climb in the back seat. That door won't open. I'm lucky it started," the woman said.

Sabrina got out when they had to stop for several men who were chopping a limb that lay across the road. She could walk faster than ride at this point and her sense of urgency was growing. Tyler was at best a creep. At worst, who knew?

Katie's hilly neighborhood in Estate Pastory had been badly flooded. Sabrina was grateful to no longer be in flip-flops, even though she could feel her feet blistering in her wet sneakers. She looked up the hillside for Katie's house but couldn't spot it, so she continued along the muddy road. She stepped over clothing, broken planters, lamps, and pillows. Trivial losses felt personal and tragic to Sabrina. She worried she might be on the verge of hysteria.

When she arrived at the foot of Katie's driveway, Sabrina gasped. The house Katie has spent the last decade of her life trying to save was gone. The entire upper floor had blown away.

Sabrina spotted a batik tapestry that had covered a chair hanging from a tree. The kitchen table could be seen below inside a neighbor's pool. Water cascaded down the hillside from above causing Sabrina to worry about a landslide.

The lower concrete level of Katie's house where she rented rooms and the adjacent cistern seemed intact. There were two doors and four windows that Sabrina could see had blown in. She didn't see Katie's or Tyler's vehicles, but she knew if Irma was capable of obliterating a house, a car would be an easy target. She glanced around to see if either vehicle were visible from where she stood but didn't see them. There was so much stuff strewn about it looked like there had been a massive explosion.

Sabrina pressed on up the muddy driveway, remembering to place her feet at an angle so she wouldn't slide backwards. When she reached the ramp to the house where Heidi had asked Eric to trim the Catch 'n Keep, she paused. If there was anyone present, it had to be below. There was no sound from the lower unit, which either meant no one was there or something awful had happened. Sabrina wasn't sure she was ready to find out, yet she knew she had no choice.

She clung to the cinderblock foundation as she edged down the steep hillside someone had been foolish enough to consider a building lot. When she reached the first empty doorway, she looked in. All she saw was a mattress tossed up against a wall and a closet with the remnants of some wire shelves hanging.

Sabrina moved to the next door. Inside she found wet sheets and a broken chair. Water was pouring down the rear wall onto the floor. To the rear of the room, she could see another door which was closed but in one piece. Sabrina guessed there was a bathroom/laundry room on the lower level just as there had been at Villa Write Off.

She walked over to the door and listened for sound of any kind but heard nothing. The silence was more frightening than she could bear. She reached for the knob and pulled hard. The door opened much easier than she had expected.

Tyler greeted her by tugging her forearm and pulling her toward him. He closed the door behind her. Sabrina had only a few seconds to make out the wildness in his eyes and the gun in his hand before the room fell into darkness.

Chapter 50

"Sabrina, is that you, dear?"

Sabrina didn't correct Grace for calling her "dear" this time.

"Grace are you all right?" she asked.

"I am. Katie's a little peaked, though." Sabrina thought Grace sounded tired, but strong.

The small room went from black to sepia toned. Tyler placed the flashlight on the trash barrel next to him so that it was pointing toward Grace and Katie who each were seated low on two sand chairs where the water on the floor almost reached their bottoms. Tyler was perched on a stepstool.

"I'm afraid we've run out of seats, boss," Tyler said laughing nervously. He looked down at the small handgun he held as if he didn't know where it had come from. Sabrina wondered exactly the same thing and if he knew how to use it. She would have to assume he did.

"I can stand," she said.

"Well, it would be better if you could sit and help us with this little conundrum Tyler has," Grace said.

Sabrina spotted an empty five-gallon container with a lid on it.

"How about I pull that over?" she asked Tyler, who nodded. She sat down and decided she should go along with Grace.

"You mentioned a conundrum," Sabrina said. Her eyes had adjusted to the light. Katie looked frantic. Her eyes had black circles beneath them and danced from Tyler's gun to his face and then to Grace.

"Shall I explain, Tyler, or do you want to?" Grace asked. Sabrina worried her grandmother had gone over the edge. Grace sounded as if they were at a restaurant deciding what wine to order.

"Go ahead, Gracie. You and now your granddaughter have the most at stake and you are the woman who makes millions from words," Tyler said. Sabrina thought he sounded daffier than her grandmother.

"Well, not quite millions, Tyler. But okay, it's like this. Don't get the wrong idea, Sabrina. Tyler's not a bad person. You must know that since he worked for you, right?"

Sabrina nodded, not want to engage in the lunacy of this conversation if she could avoid it.

"Well, he's gotten himself into a bit of a pickle. The day Eric was killed, Tyler returned home from work early. He had been scheduled to paint inside because it was raining. Apparently, Eric failed to deliver the paint for reasons we all understand now. Anyway, Tyler lives across the street from The Last Chance Center. Did you know that?"

"Yes," Sabrina said. She did now, but she hadn't known before where Tyler lived and she wasn't about to tell him he wouldn't be living there anymore. She felt like she was back outside dodging the loose electrical wires she had to climb over to get to what was left of Katie's house.

"Tyler noticed Katie's car was parked across the street in the Last Chance Center lot. He thought she might have car trouble. She drives an island-beater and it breaks down a lot," Grace said looking over at Katie.

"It's a piece of crap," Katie said.

"Well Tyler went over to see if he could lend a hand. It turned out someone was having a very loud argument in one of the containers, but it wasn't Katie," Grace said.

"It was Eric and..." Sabrina wished her grandmother would just give her the Cliff Notes version and not tell this awful story in novel length. But she did appreciate what Grace was trying to do. She was buying time. How long had she been cajoling Tyler? Grace had to have been doing this for hours and during the horror of the hurricane. Sabrina could no longer deny her admiration for Grace. She might have sucked as a mother and grandmother, but she was one hell of a woman.

"My dear assistant, Heidi." Sabrina looked at Grace in surprise.

"Heidi met with Eric, just before he was murdered?" Sabrina asked.

"Before she killed him, you mean. I overheard the whole thing but I never expected her to grab the machete and go at him," Tyler said.

Katie let out a sob.

"You're better off without him, honey," Tyler said tenderly.

"Someone explain to me, why would Heidi kill Eric when she was crazy about him and how could she if she was over on the other side of the island stuck in Coral Bay without a car? That sounds crazy," Sabrina said, her voice rising in excitement. She knew Heidi had been angry with Eric for splitting and clearing out their small savings account and worse for freezing her account where she had deposited the money she had skimmed from him. Sabrina still couldn't believe she would kill him.

"You got the crazy part right. Heidi was crazy. Eric told me she had a psychiatric diagnosis he didn't learn about until after they were married. She was okay as long as she stayed on her meds, but once she stopped taking them, she would start to drink and get out of control," Katie said.

"Heidi talked Eric into meeting her. She wouldn't stop

texting him and threatened to find out where he lived. So, Eric agreed," Grace said.

"I didn't know. He was determined to keep her away from me and our home," Katie said.

"Heidi got some old geezer to drive her over from Coral Bay when Eric agreed to meet her. I suppose Eric felt the Last Chance Center was a safe location where they could meet. It was after hours when no one would be around, and he still had the key from when he first arrived on island. You know about that don't you?" Grace asked Sabrina, who was still marveling that Grace would dub an older man an old geezer. Sabrina said that she knew about the key and how Eric had come into its possession.

"Heidi wasn't just crazy. She was evil," Tyler said. Sabrina could see how Grace had tried to shift the dynamic in the room away from Tyler as their captor to Tyler as another victim of Heidi. It was a stretch, but it was all they had.

"Maybe you want to explain to Sabrina what you heard, Tyler," Grace said. Sabrina wished someone would.

"I heard it all. At first, Heidi was confident. She told Eric that Grace had been wrong to call the police and make a big deal out of a little spat. She claimed Grace was losing it and that Heidi had to finish her last novel for her. She told them they belonged together, and she wanted him back. She said she forgave him for running out on her and taking her money. She wanted him to drop the divorce. She told him she had something in the works that would provide them with regular income for a long time and that they could live the good life in the Caribbean like they'd always dreamed about. She was quite a talker. I have to say, I wondered if Eric was going to agree. I didn't know about him and Katie at the time," Tyler said looking down at the gun he held, but not long enough for Sabrina to grab it.

"Did Heidi get into specifics about her plan?" Sabrina asked.

"She had two. Her short-term plan was to give him back the $50,000.00 she had slipped out of their joint account, which was apparently his, if he would return the contents of the safe deposit box to her." Tyler sounded tired recounting the conversation he'd heard before he witnessed a murder. Sabrina wondered if he might forget he had a gun in his hand so she could lunge for it.

"What about the long-term plan?" Sabrina asked.

"Eric said he knew about her long term plan and that he wanted nothing to do with blackmailing Grace Armstrong. But he couldn't tell Heidi how to live her life. She could pay him the $50k, agree to an immediate uncontested Massachusetts divorce, and when it was over, he'd give her the contents to the safe deposit box," Tyler said. He was sweating heavily, Sabrina noticed. The room was hot and stuffy and smelled of body odor. Why Grace still had on her rain jacket, Sabrina could only guess. Old people were always cold.

"You can imagine how Heidi reacted," Grace said.

"Yeah, she went crazy. She screamed that she would never divorce him and that he'd suffer if he didn't give her back the stuff he'd taken. By then I was worried so I stepped next to the door and watched, but neither of them noticed me," Tyler said.

"Oh God, did he tell her was already divorced?" Sabrina asked. She could only imagine Heidi's rage.

"Worse, he pulled the divorce papers and a marriage certificate that showed he had already remarried out of that stupid man bag. Then he told her about the baby," Tyler said, suddenly alert and charged by the memory of the drama.

"That was when she grabbed the machete Eric had put on the floor next to his backpack and swung it like a tennis racket right against his neck. I could see the blood spurting everywhere. I ducked back around the corner of the trailer. I didn't dare go back home because I was afraid she'd see me and go after me. She was nuts." Tyler no longer seemed exhausted. The memory of what happened ignited him.

"You must have been terrified. Why would Eric bring the machete inside the trailer with him?" Sabrina wondered aloud.

She knew Tyler was no innocent, but still she sympathized with him. Witnessing a murder and thinking you might be next had to be horrifying.

"He must have brought it in with his man bag and his backpack. Eric would never leave stuff in my car. The locks don't work. He was probably just making sure no one took the machete that he'd borrowed from Henry," Katie said.

"Or maybe he thought he'd need to defend himself against that horrid woman," Grace said.

"What happened next, Tyler?" Sabrina asked. That was the question Neil always asked when he wanted someone to focus on a subject and not wander off like Tyler seemed to be doing. He was looking back and forth at the gun and then at the three women who sat opposite him.

"Heidi held the machete out in the rain so the blood would drip off. I couldn't believe how calm and methodical she had become in such a short time. She wiped it with the bottom of her dress. Then she grabbed Eric's man bag and backpack. She slammed the door to the trailer and put the padlock on while she held it with her dress. She took off up toward the clinic. I hid until she was out of sight and then I went home," Tyler said.

Sabrina felt a wave of relief envelope her. Tyler might feel guilty for not interceding, but it was hardly criminal. He was overreacting. The hurricane had everyone's nerves charged. No one was thinking clearly.

"Tyler, I understand how bad you must feel about what happened, but it's not a crime to witness a murder. I'm sure Neil can explain that better than I can," Sabrina said. After sitting through the storm for hours and discovering the devastation St. John had suffered, she was exhausted. With Eric's death behind them, all their energy could be focused on recovery where it belonged.

"I don't think you fully understand, Sabrina. Tyler's problem isn't that he witnessed Eric's murder. It's that he killed Heidi," Grace said.

Chapter 51

Sabrina had been so giddy thinking she'd solved Tyler's problem so he could put down the gun and let them all go home to whatever home they had left, that she'd almost forgotten Heidi's murder. It was Henry's vindication that was paramount to her.

"But why?" Sabrina asked.

"Well, it seems Tyler has been deeply in love with Katie for quite a while, right?" Grace looked over at Tyler who smiled.

"Madly," he said. Sabrina looked at Grace who was patting the right-hand pocket of her rain jacket. They were both mad, she decided.

"I overheard you and Henry talk about Heidi going into shock when she learned her husband had been murdered and that she was staying at the Westin. I knew she couldn't be shocked. I also knew she was evil," Tyler said, now looking down at the gun as if it were a microphone recording his confession.

"He wanted to do right by Katie. They'd had a little misunderstanding when he was her tenant and Tyler felt he could set the record straight by going to Heidi and getting her to pay Katie the fifty-thousand dollars so she could support the baby," Grace said.

"I never asked you to do that," Katie said. Her anger surprised Sabrina.

"You didn't have to, Katie. There isn't anything I wouldn't do for you. You'll see. Once we're out of here."

"The bottom line is that Heidi had been drinking heavily when Tyler went to her room after he got out of work mid-afternoon. He knew to walk up from the beach rather than by the pool to avoid the security cameras," Grace said. Sabrina understood she was explaining why he didn't show up on Detective Detree's hotel video. It irked her that Tyler had been cleverer than the rest of them who had visited Heidi.

"She laughed at me. She told me Eric deserved to die and that his bastard kid should grow up as poor as she had. She told me she was about to be paid a chunk of money and that she'd be one of the richest women on the island. I already knew she was planning on blackmailing Grace from her conversation with Eric before she killed him. He had something Grace would pay big bucks to keep quiet. Whatever it was, I figured he must have kept it in his man bag with all his other important papers. He never let that thing out of sight. The bag was lying next to Heidi on the bed in the hotel room. I knew I had to get it away from her. I told her to give it to me or I'd tell the cops I saw her kill Eric," Tyler said.

"You told her that after you saw what she did to Eric? Weren't you afraid she'd get crazy and go after you like she did him?" Sabrina asked.

"I didn't really think about it. She just laughed at me again. She poured us each a glass of whiskey and told me no one would believe my story about what she'd done. Then she tried to pull me into bed with her. Man, the last thing I wanted was to - well, whatever. I talked her into having another drink and before long she was snoring. I grabbed the papers out of the bag, went through them and quickly realized I could support Katie and the baby and buy her a nice new house on the money Grace would pay me to keep quiet. It was a perfect solution for everyone. Except-"

"Except for Heidi," Sabrina said. She realized Tyler didn't kill Heidi in a moment of passion out of fury or jealousy like Heidi had killed Eric. Tyler contemplated eliminating Heidi in cold deliberation. He was far more dangerous than she had given him credit for.

"I took a pillow and put Heidi out of misery and walked out with the contents of the man bag in my pockets. Except for Katie's keys. I wouldn't take those."

As awful as it sounded, Sabrina understood why Tyler thought it a "perfect solution." She also realized Tyler must have taken the missing key ring out of Eric's man bag. For a moment, she felt a wave of relief until she remembered the keys were for doors Irma had blown away.

"I feel like it isn't fair. I was supposed to be blackmailing you," Tyler said to Grace.

"I know. It just didn't work out," Grace said in a soothing voice.

"What are you talking about?" Sabrina asked her.

"Now, the three of you know what I did and can put me in jail for the rest of my life. That's why I'm going to have to kill you," Tyler said pointing the gun at them.

"You would kill Katie?" Sabrina asked. "After all you've done to protect her?" She was playing him, but it was clear time was running out. The only hope she had was that the house-to-house search she knew would be conducted to find survivors from the hurricane would lead the authorities to them. Sabrina looked over at Grace who was subtly patting her pocket again.

"That's the conundrum. Tyler doesn't want to kill anyone else, but he also doesn't want to go to jail," Grace said.

"How did you get here?" Sabrina asked Grace. Grace pointed to Tyler.

"I brought her. I told her I had some stuff of hers. Old stuff that could ruin her life and make you hate her. I was sure she'd pay some big bucks. I mean, Heidi was banking on it. But instead, Grace says, 'I'm planning on telling Sabrina all of that just as soon as she's comfortable having a conversation with me.' I killed Heidi for that? Maybe I should just kill myself," Tyler said. He pointed the gun toward his face.

"No, don't do it," Katie screamed. "Please Tyler, no more dying."

Sabrina leaped up toward Tyler, her arm extended, hand open ready to grab the gun. Before she could reach for it, Grace slapped a pair of scissors she had pulled out of her jacket pocket into her hand like a nurse handing a surgeon a scalpel. Sabrina clutched the scissors with a tight fist and slammed them point down onto the veins in Tyler's other hand with all the force she could muster.

The gun sounded like a canon in the tiny room when it went off. Blood spewed everywhere. Sabrina heard the plop of the gun hitting the water on the concrete floor. She knew grabbing the gun was more important than checking to see if someone had been killed by it because more people might die if she didn't. She grabbed the flashlight and reached for the gun.

She looked over toward Grace praying that her grandmother was alive and that they would have the chance to get to know one another. Grace was holding Katie, who trembled in her arms.

Tyler lay on the floor holding his left ear lobe that was bleeding like a geyser. His conundrum was solved. He stood and ran out the door into the post-hurricane madness. Sabrina looked at the gun in her hand and put it down. She knew better than Tyler that Irma had made sure there was no place to go and no way to get there.

Chapter 52

Katie's reaction to the loss of her home surprised Sabrina.

"I'm relieved, if you want to know the truth. Now I can concentrate on what matters," she said patting her tummy. "Where do you think Tyler went?"

"Not far, I'm sure. No one will be able to get off the island for a few days," Sabrina said.

She walked between Grace and Katie down Centerline Road passing people who seemed as lost as they did. They reached the island home where Austen lived. It stood proud and largely unchanged other than the windows had blown out.

Sabrina found Austen at the rear of the house sitting in the shade with the kittens still in the crate next to him.

"How are you?" Sabrina asked, a question she soon realized hurricane victims took quite literally. Ten minutes later, after learning how Austen had fared in minute detail, Sabrina asked Austen if he had seen Tyler.

"Not since before the hurricane," Austen said. Sabrina filled him in about what had gone on.

"Oh my God, you guys are so lucky to be alive. I knew Tyler

wasn't operating on all cylinders, but I never imagined he would kill someone," Austen said.

And I never imagined that the guy who did time would end up being the employee of the week, Sabrina thought.

"If you don't mind, I'd like to crash here for a while, Austen. I'm exhausted and need to sleep," Katie said. Austen readily agreed and led her to his studio where he had managed to keep the futon reasonably dry under a tarp.

Sabrina and Grace resumed their walk toward Cruz Bay where they hoped to find news about the island and rescue efforts.

"I feel like I need to do something about Tyler. It doesn't seem right not to report what happened to the police, but I'm sure they have their hands full," Sabrina said. She realized she was asking Grace for advice.

"We can stop by the police station when we get to town. If there's still a police station," Grace said.

"Or a town," Sabrina said. She couldn't digest what her eyes were seeing. Houses gone, trees down blocking the road, debris and wires piled high. Mud everywhere.

"When you're ready to listen, I can tell you about why Tyler was trying to blackmail me. It probably won't make you fonder of me," Grace said.

"I already read the journal and saw the canceled check at Tyler's. Neil and I went looking for you when you weren't at David's. Your messages frightened us. When we went to see if you were at Austen's, he told us a few things about Tyler that concerned us. We raced to Tyler's house and got stuck there when the storm got so bad we couldn't leave," Sabrina said.

"So, you know? I won't defend myself, but I would like to fill in the details. Or would you prefer I head to town on my own?" Grace stopped near the turn off for the Moravian church and waited for Sabrina to answer.

"Are you kidding me? I'm not letting you out of my sight

again. But sometime, after we find out how Neil's ankle is, how Henry and Lyla fared, where David ended up, and whether any of us still have homes, I'd like to hear more. I want to know whether my mother meant to leave me behind or if she didn't have a choice," Sabrina said.

"Of course. It's the question I've been asking for years. but you're right, now is not the time."

Sabrina looked at Grace under the relentless sun that was shining like it was any other day at the beach on St. John. She had more wrinkles than Sabrina had noticed before and her short blonde hair do was more tousled, but her eyes were as blue as the water in the distance. She matched Sabrina on the walk down toward Cruz Bay step for step as they climbed over the remnants of people's lives. Sabrina couldn't deny the surge of pride she felt toward her grandmother, who had been resilient and clever and fearless.

"So tell me, where'd you get those scissors?" Sabrina asked. She listened as Grace described her own adventure with Tyler at David's house before the storm.

"I wonder where Tyler managed to get a gun," Sabrina said, more to herself than to Grace. She could feel the weight of the gun in the pocket of Grace's rain jacket she had offered to carry.

"I think he may have found it at David's house before I got there. I have the impression David's seaplane business may occasionally require a certain level of security," Grace.

They continued at a steady pace seeing more people as they moved down the hill. Lucy Detree stood in plain clothes at the center of the rotary with a few other officers and St. John Rescue members. She was giving orders and dispatching people to locations where people might be trapped. Sabrina wasn't sure if she should bother her.

"Go ahead. It will be one less thing for her to worry about," Grace said in a whisper when there was short break from people milling around Lucy.

Sabrina stepped up to her and was surprised to find Lucy

hugging her, telling her she was so glad Sabrina was okay. Sabrina filled her in quickly about how Heidi had killed Eric and another of her workers had killed Heidi.

"But don't worry, he's no longer armed. Although he is bleeding a bit from an ear and a hand, so he shouldn't be hard to miss," Sabrina said. She handed Lucy the gun she had taken from Tyler.

"We just took a guy bleeding from an ear down to the makeshift clinic we've set up. He's not going anywhere soon," Lucy said. "He'd have to swim to get off island and the islands around us are in as bad shape as we are."

Sabrina rejoined Grace who was looking at the windows at Dolphin Market, which had been boarded up. Sabrina could see a large group of people on a balcony above Ronnie's Pizza. They had their cell phones out. She realized there must be reception. Her phone was out of juice, but Grace's wasn't.

Sabrina tried the numbers for Henry, Neil, Lyla, and David, but all of her calls went straight to voicemail. She felt disheartened as she came down the steps where Grace was waiting across from the Sprauve School. The only island public grammar school was a mess. Windows were blown in. The roof had been torn away and crumpled. No child would be attending classes here soon. The realization of how long it would take St. John to recover was beginning to take hold.

She found Grace hugging David. He told them he'd tucked into a vacant house in the opulent Peter Bay neighborhood when he couldn't get past the roads any further after leaving Maho Beach. Grace told him she was certain it had been Tyler who had dispatched poor David on a fool's mission to rescue her.

"I am so sorry, David," she said.

"No worries. Once I got over the fact, I'd have to break in to one of those units to find shelter, I picked the grandest of them all. I mean, why not, if you're going to commit a crime. I'm glad I did because I was able to tuck the Jeep under a stone portico and so, other than a couple of dings, I still have wheels," David said.

The trio walked toward Bar None, where Sabrina hoped to find Neil. The open-air bar that had been covered with sailcloth had disappeared. The beach was littered with boats of all sizes and shapes, from dinghies, to sailboats, to cruisers. There was no sign of Neil.

They found him across the street in the Catholic Church with his foot elevated on a pew.

"A medic said she didn't think it was broken and taped it up as good as she could. She told me to get an X-ray when I could. I think that could be a while," Neil said, looking around at the other people gathered in the church, all in various states of disarray.

"I'd like to check on Henry," David said.

"So would I," Sabrina said. They helped Neil to his feet. He leaned on Sabrina and David as they made their way slowly to David's jeep. People passing by offered tidbits of information.

"Coral Bay is devastated. Sorry, Neil," one woman said.

"Bordeaux Mountain looks as if someone poured desiccant down on it," said another.

"You can't get out to Fish Bay," a man told them.

"Watch me," David said. Sabrina admired his determination. She was eager to reach Henry too. She wondered how Lyla and Evan were.

The foursome decided to do a brief reconnoiter of their respective homes as they proceeded toward Fish Bay. It took forever to reach David's lane. The thick mud was covered with brush, limbs, and downed power lines. David and Sabrina got out to clear a branch. When they reached David's home, he gasped.

Cassies's colorful cushions and curtains adorned the piles of rubble that had previously filled the home David had bought from her. The pink stucco house was badly damaged but standing. The tiny white cottage Grace had commandeered was gone.

David let out a sob.

"Good thing I use the cloud," Grace said. Sabrina knew she was referring to the novel she had been working on.

"I took your laptop out of there under my rain jacket. It may not be in any better shape, but it's in the van," Neil said. Sabrina hadn't seen him rescue it. He hadn't told her. He wasn't a man of many words except when they mattered. She would have to remember that.

They turned onto the driveway that led to Tyler's home. Sabrina jumped out of the jeep and went over to the van where she had opened the back panel to retrieve her sneakers. Sure enough, she spotted a MacBook on top of the contents of the van. It had a few dings on the cover, but it was there.

Buoyed by their small recovery, the foursome continued toward Henry's condo farther along Gifft Hill Road. The metal gates were contorted but still locked. They could see the complex still had a roof.

Encouraged, the troupe proceeded along the road down a steep s-shaped curve that provided a breathtaking vista of Chocolate Hole and beyond where the devastation continued to shock them. Scores of homes were without roofs. Bedding and clothing hung from the trees that still stood. Giant piles of knotted power lines were everywhere. Utility poles lay next to fallen trees. The silence in the van said more than words could.

The road out to Fish Bay confirmed what they had been told earlier. It took three hours and several stops where they had to assist people removing obstacles in the road for them to reach Sabrina's stone cottage. She braced herself for the worst, having seen many of her neighbors' homes hanging from hillsides.

Sabrina's roof had blown off. Her beloved wicker furniture floated in her new swimming pool covered with branches and other articles from the cottage. But the walls to her stone house were standing. She had a place to begin rebuilding. And yes, she would keep the pool that had been gifted to her.

Neil squeezed her hand when she returned to the back seat of the Jeep where he sat with his ankle elevated.

"We'll get a tarp over that in no time, Salty," he said. She knew he wasn't in shape to do that but was touched he wanted to.

A sense of dread filled the vehicle as it rose toward the top of Fish Bay Road. It was literally the end of the road where you could only continue beyond by sea or air. Sabrina caught sight of the Banks's house first and was filled with gratitude they had been evacuated to Maura's stronghold. Glass had blown in despite their efforts to board up the windows. Other than that, the main house had fared decently, but the glass-walled room that had been added on so Lyla and Evan could sit overlooking the water as if on the balcony of a cruise ship had been ripped off.

Across the street, Sabrina saw Henry walking on the lot where Villa Mascarpone had once stood. Only the stone pillars remained.

David stopped the Jeep and jumped out. He rushed over to Henry and pulled him into his arms lifting Henry off his feet. Sabrina's eyes filled as she joined them. She hugged Henry with all her might. Any reserve she had previously about hugging had been swept away with Irma.

Henry picked up a piece of wood that had just been painted a warm shade of apricot.

"It was a great color scheme," he said.

Grace walked slowly toward them, giving Neil a hand as he hobbled alongside of her.

"How are Lyla and Evan?" Grace asked Henry after kissing him on the check.

"We lost Evan early during the storm," he said. "Lyla said it was better he not be frightened by the noise." Henry's eyes watered and seemed to look somewhere distant.

"It's a sad way to end," David said.

Sabrina looked up at the brilliant sun shining down on them.

The puffy clouds filling the enormous sky were as fair as she'd ever seen. Her grandmother stood next to Neil, her arm around his waist so he could lean on her. David stood behind Henry, his hands placed firmly on Henry's shoulders.

"Maybe. But I prefer to think of today as a beginning."

THE END

ACKNOWLEDGMENTS

My gratitude to readers of the Sabrina Salter series for their patience and encouragement while waiting for Tropical Depression. Without you, I may have given up on Sabrina, and that would have been a shame because I like her so much and it would have meant giving up on myself.

I wasn't in St. John for Hurricane Irma or Hurricane Maria, which followed shortly after, so the accounts of what it was like to experience a category five hurricane I offer in the book are from the generous descriptions and narratives of people who did. Anna Tuttle, Gerry Londergan, and other UU Fellowship members graciously shared their stories with me. I appreciate their willingness to describe their experiences with me in minute detail. Leanne DeGiacomo, thank you for telling me about the bees.

To my fellow writers too many to name, thank you for your continued inspiration and support. My special thanks to author Sharon Ward, my daughter Julie Grant, my friend and assistant, Toni Beauregard, who offered special attention and assistance.

As always, my biggest fan and helper was my husband, Steve, who let me read aloud to him for hours.

I would be remiss not to mention that there has finally been a conviction in the murder of Jimmy Malfetti on St. John in 2014. How slow the wheels of justice turn.

ABOUT THE AUTHOR

C. Michele Dorsey, author of *No Virgin Island* and *Permanent Sunset*, is a lawyer, mediator, and adjunct law professor. When she's not visiting St. John, her favorite island in the Caribbean, she lives on Cape Cod. This is her third Sabrina Salter mystery.

Made in the USA
Monee, IL
11 January 2022

b1fb1344-f59f-4114-8bce-000f7694cacaR01